Praise for 'Life an

"Of particular interest to s
everywhere is this tale of egoti
luck. Serpico are just yet anoth
are better than they are, but when they write the best album
ever, life rapidly unspools. Witty, terrifically well written and
so true to life it hurts." – *The Fly*

"I tend not to read books about music, musicians and musos,
partly because I get enough of that from my boyfriend, but
mainly because I think it's very hard to do well. It's too easy
for writers to end up proving their own muso credentials,
name-checking favourite bands, wallowing in purple prose to
show they "get it", rather than delivering an interesting plot
and characters to care about. Luckily for me, Mayhew
manages both with real ability, and charm. He delivers a
sharp, warm and, in places, very funny story about two lads
beginning to make good in spite of themselves, with a pace
that keeps you turning the pages and a finale that, while not
unexpected, is extremely satisfying. An enjoyable muso
novel. Now, there's a thing!" – *The Talk*

"Writing successful novels about music or bands is a notoriously
difficult thing to do, and something that rarely succeeds. Step
forward Daniel Mayhew to prove the exception to the rule… At
its heart, this is book is a black comedy and a worthy
examination of male friendship… The highest praise that can be
paid to Mayhew is that it would have been easy to simply write a
book that would only satisfy music fans with its myriad of cool
references, and while it will certainly resonate with anybody
who's been in or close to a band, the humour and the well drawn
characters neatly help to side step any suggestion of musical
snobbery….Fast-paced, hilarious, a wild ride." – *thisisull.com*

"This novel is a romp through Bristol and the dreams that go with being in a rock band. But you don't need to have experienced either to relate to this hugely engaging comedy of manners; you just need a decent sense of humour. Mayhew peppers his story about Serpico, a band who are soon to be the next big thing, with highly amusing comic gems that are like the finely tuned material of a seasoned stand-up comic. But aside from the pitch-perfect glimpses of Bristol and caustic wit, the real heart of the book is a portrait of friendship. The two main characters feel so real because they are expertly brought into focus by the perceptions of each other. The finale will leave you guessing and genuinely questioning your own values about the meaning of success. Ultimately, Mayhew's book is about ambition, the creative process and the battle between pragmatism and idealism. It really deserves to be a big hit, despite the mantra of Serpico singer Reilly: 'Success on these terms is failure.'" – *The Bookseller*

IS IT, IS IT?

2007

Life and How to Live It

A Quick Brown Fox Publications Book

First published in Great Britain by Quick Brown Fox in 2007.
This is a second edition, published June 2007.

ISBN-10 0955480418 ISBN-13 9780955480416
Cover image © Jamie Steane 2007 inkerjowe.com.
Used with permission. Edited by Adam Kirkman.

Quick Brown Fox Publications is an independent literary agency
and publishers. Why not let them know what you thought of this
book? Or maybe you're interested in being published yourself?
Quick Brown Fox loves to hear from unpublished first-time
authors. Get in touch as they'd love to hear from you.
www.quickbrownfoxpublications.co.uk

Life and How to Live It

Daniel Mayhew

Published by Quick Brown Fox Publications, 2007.

For Sarah, Always

"8/25/96 - When all of this music
sounds like you know what
you want to say, then it
will have been of all worth, ever.
You will be something complete
unto yourself, present and unique. "

- Jeff Buckley, sleeve notes from *My Sweetheart the Drunk.*

England and a broken radio

Reilly was off on one. He was becoming loud. Becoming dangerous. Jacob had thought they were talking about the new Stereolab album, but really should have known the next rant was just around the corner.

"It used to mean something, *they* used to mean something, now every bastard's got 'em. Why does everything good get hijacked and watered down?"

Reilly's question wasn't the kind that wanted an answer, but Jacob felt compelled to fill in the gaps, to jump in front of the train.

"Come on mate, it doesn't matter, lighten up a bit. It's Friday night – a few lagers, a laugh. Come on, it's your round – mine's a Stella."

"No, don't try to put me off, I've got something to say, and you know I'm right."

Jacob didn't yet know the source of Reilly's disgust, but knew better than to ask. Having a chat over a pint had become a delicate operation. A walk through a minefield. Jacob now had an extensive list of subject matter to avoid. These included the National Lottery, Jimmy Carr, brand name charities, Craig Bellamy, TV licensing, the family off the BT ads, The Stereophonics, *Watchdog* and Lexus cars. Not easy. As a result,

Jacob had started to feel like an extra in the opening minutes of *Casualty*, going about his business while fifteen million viewers at home guessed what hideous accident he was heading for. "I bet he gets his hand stuck in that vice..." "No way, that combine harvester's going to malfunction and tear his legs off!" "You're both wrong – Reilly's going to piss someone off again and they'll both get glassed..."

He tried again – "Reilly, I said it's your round and I'll have a Stella." Reilly was not receiving. His eyes were fixed on the couple at the next table who were developing the uneasy look of the stared at. A look Jacob was now learning to recognise. Jacob stole a glance at Reilly's latest targets, and immediately noticed the bloke's hair. It was one of those haircuts, styled upwards into a ridge, as if acknowledging the existence of the mohican without actually going all the way. It looked like the roof on a shed, didn't sit right.

Reilly began to speak. In a bizarre sing-song voice, not what Jacob was expecting at all -

"Ooh Gary! Yes, Lisa? Let's do something crazy and zany today, like on *Friends*. Lets's take a walk on the wild side – let's buy matching combat trousers! Great idea, Lisa – let's go down Gap straight away – and why don't we get matching soulless black polo necks and wear them down the Flyer tonight." The sing-song in Reilly's voice gave way to a shout-scream, "and after the Flyer we'll head home and look at car brochures while listening to fucking Dido!"

Silence. The worst kind. Jacob broke it. What he wanted to do was turn to the Gap twins and say something brave, something decent. Something like, "Ignore this idiot, he's mental. Your cargo trousers and polo necks are actually really nice, really suit you, can I get you both a drink?" But Jacob wasn't feeling brave or decent, he was feeling embarrassed. He turned to Reilly –

"What's fucking wrong with you? Go and get your fucking round in!"

The Gap Twins had heard enough and without saying a word, shuffled off to the other end of the pub, as balanced right-thinking people tend to do in these situations.

Jacob exhaled. That was grim, but not nearly as bad as it could have been. A 4.4 on the Reilly scale. A city shaken but able to laugh about it afterwards – no casualties. But would there be an aftershock? Jacob pictured the Gap twins waiting outside at closing time, with a scrum of rugby-playing mates summoned by mobile, all too willing to deal out some sweet Friday night justice – "That's the bastard who slagged off my clothes – and his friend did nothing – get 'em both." Jacob tried to blank out these thoughts.

"Reilly. I need a pint. Now."

"Yeah yeah, but did you see how badly made those combats were? You remember those ones I had in '97? Now they were cool. The real thing."

"I want a pint. And I didn't know you in 1997! And I was wearing combats back in '95. And anyway shut up. Listen to yourself, you're going off about fucking trousers now?" Jacob said this with genuine concern. This was indeed a new level. He wondered at what point an alcohol-fuelled gob-shite became a card-carrying madman. He made a mental note to look it up on the internet Monday morning. Go to Google, type in 'Combat Pants Psychosis' – click 'I'm feeling lucky.' He smirked at the thought.

"What's so funny? I'm serious. It's because of people like them that I'm back in a jeans phase. They've left me with no other choice." Reilly was indeed back in a jeans phase. He'd also taken to getting T-shirts printed with his own slogans. Tonight's T-shirt read 'SITUATIONIST.'

"A pint. Of Stella. Please." Jacob had one final try.

Reilly stood up, held up his hands in a 'you win' gesture, and headed to the bar. Left Jacob alone at the window seat. He rolled a cigarette – Drum Ultra Mild, green Rizlas and a Swan filter. Bristol loped by outside. The usual line up of wide-eyed kids, cackling girl's nights outs and the like. A huge homeless guy (what was he, 6' 4 and 18 stone?) lurched in and out of the traffic, shouting as he went. Care in the Community. Jacob imagined the homeless guy knocking on doors up in leafy Redland, housewives welcoming him in with the words, "Hi! Come on in, cup of tea? I'll run a bath for you. You poor thing – all part of the service, care in the community."

Inside the Flyer, the jukebox was running through the usual mixture of the sublime and the banal. Lauryn Hill's *X-Factor* and Massive Attack's *Teardrop* had sandwiched Toploader's *Dancing in the Moonlight*. The jukebox was now playing something by Destiny's Child – soul music with no soul. The Child were boasting that not only did they have lots of material possessions, but none of these were paid for by men. Jacob wondered idly what Germaine Greer would make of this.

He scanned the pub as he dragged on his cigarette. By the door, a group of impossibly good-looking boys and girls were lobbing thin chat up lines at each other like grenades. Jacob presumed them to be freshers at UWE, bright-eyed and far too healthy looking, as he himself had once been. At the bar, middle aged divorcees staggered around, as the compulsory perma-pissed ex-army guy moved in, picking up on the ham-fisted make-up and smell of desperation. The Gap Twins marched past the bar and out of the door. Poor bastards. Jacob relaxed, slightly. Maybe that was Reilly's explosion out of the way for tonight. A mere pipe bomb to last weekend's atomic blast.

Jacob took a mouthful of Stella, stubbed out his cigarette and rolled another. He considered Reilly's behaviour. Was he really losing it? Or was it just the beer? He had been working very hard this week, perhaps overdoing it a bit, like a real workaholic. A workaholic who could perhaps offer Jacob a way out of this accelerating downward spiral. He knew they had a real shot at a recording contract, a fawning music press and a big fat goodbye to the battleground of an everyman existence.

Bye-bye, Bristol.

He'd grown up in Kidlington, a little pocket of nothing just outside Oxford, and Bristol had initially blown his mind. But in nine years, he'd done all the pubs, done all the clubs, done most of the drugs, and now had little left to do. The scene that had once seemed vibrant and full of possibilities now felt desperate, cancerous and worst of all, infectious. He needed a change, needed Reilly to keep it together long enough to dupe some A&R man into chucking them a huge advance.

Jacob finished the cigarette and stared at his empty glass. Where the fuck was Reilly? How long can it take to order a couple of Stellas?

A squad of fat-headed locals marched past the window and into the pub. Four, no five of them. Jacob instantly had them pegged. Happy-go-lucky salt of the earth types who liked a laugh, who liked too many pints of Fosters. Great guys who ineptly harassed women and would beat the shit out of Jacob for dressing like a fruit. He feared them and hated them for it.

Incredibly, but perhaps predictably, they dressed almost identically – brutal hair gel, cheap silky shirts in various colours, chinos and shiny shiny shoes – the towny uniform. There were small differences, perhaps signifying some kind of tribal hierarchy. The fattest and loudest of the five wore a thicker gold neck chain than the rest, and his sovereign ring dwarfed the others on display. They were now at the bar, and sure enough five pints of Fosters were ordered. King Fat Head was relating an anecdote that Jacob couldn't quite hear, although he caught a couple of snippets – the story involved "the fucking Mrs..." and "...*TV Times* in her gob." Jacob missed the punch line, but the other fat heads didn't, falling about with cruel laughter.

Jacob studied the demographic of the group. How old were they? Four of them had that Alan Shearer thing going on, looked mid-forties but was probably only 27 or 28 – no older than Jacob and Reilly. The fifth was a raw faced 16 or 17, King

Fat Head's younger brother perhaps, out on a summer evening for his first proper pub crawl? He had the uneasy, queasy look of someone who knows he has already had too much beer but is desperate to hide the fact. Jacob fully expected him to vomit Fosters at any moment, right there at the bar. Nonetheless, Raw Face was laughing when required and gazing up at his heroes with the right amount of reverence and awe. Despite himself, Jacob admired Raw Face's effort in the face of adversity, he was giving it his best. Good on you, trainee towny!

But as Jacob looked more closely, he lost his bearings. His stomach lurched. He noticed something was wrong with this picture, something was not complete - something in Raw Face's uniform. He had the gel, the shirt and chinos, but instead of shiny shoes he wore a scuffed old pair of Hi-Tecs.

This detail struck Jacob like a knife in the heart. In that moment he felt it was the saddest thing he'd ever seen. Was nothing attainable? Even that which was plainly not worth attaining? What did this mean? For Jacob. For his band. He cursed himself for once again noticing this kind of shit. He wanted to grow another skin – why couldn't he just hate everyone like fucking Reilly? He tried another tack, a positive slant. Maybe Raw Face was an individual, striking out on his own by refusing to conform – or, perhaps apprentice townies had to go through certain stages before the whole uniform could be awarded, like geishas – "Raw Face-san, it is with great honour, that the Filton okiya, bestows upon you, your shiny shiny shoes…"

Reilly returned with a couple of pints to break Jacob's train of thought. "Jesus, Reilly, how long can it take to purchase beer?"

"I went for a piss, if that's alright with you, Mum." Reilly handed Jacob his pint and sat down. "And anyway, there was some girl wearing an Arsenal shirt, so I had a word."

"What did you say?"

"Well just said that her choice of attire signalled a moral and intellectual shortcoming. So I'm ready for a bit of a debate, you know, a bit of an argument, but she asks if I want to go to some party after the pub. She thought I was chatting her up."

Jacob laughed. "Was she nice?"

"Jesus - did you listen to anything I just said Jacob? I said she was wearing a fucking Arsenal shirt!"

Stevie sauntered in, clocked Jacob and Reilly, mimed the pint to mouth movement and headed for the bar. Good old Stevie. They both liked him. Reilly respected anyone who could argue back. Jacob admired his fearlessness. He showed what life could offer someone who wasn't crippled by cynicism and self doubt. Plus, he anchored Reilly, kept him in check. Jacob was pleased to see him.

Stevie got a bottle of Becks and came over, all rude health and wealth, the Brummie plutocrat. Jacob noticed Stevie's new Schott jacket, what were they - four hundred quid or something? Not Jacob's thing, but fair play.

"The mighty Serpico – thought I'd find you two here, how's that difficult first song coming on?"

"Fuck off yuppie," said Reilly, "what's with the new jacket – dealing again, are you?"

"No mate – an honest day's work for an honest day's pay, you know me. Anyway, Jacob - I've got something for you." Stevie pulled out a CDR and handed it over. "It's a load of rare Radiohead stuff I downloaded, there's some weird shit on there – not my cup of tea really. But have you heard *Big Ideas*?"

"Yeah, what a song mate."

Reilly took over. "It's not called that – it's *Nude/Newt* or something. But anyway, it's god-like. And they couldn't even be arsed to put it on the album. Thom Yorke just pisses genius."

"Dear oh dear, Stevie," said Jacob, "what would Metallica say? You stealing music and depriving poor old EMI – how they going to pay for limos and cocaine now?"

"Actually, I was thinking a bit about that," said Stevie. "I'm mean I know Radiohead aren't going to starve because I download a couple of out-takes, but you wouldn't expect a plumber to work for nothing, would you?"

"That's not the point," replied Reilly, "why should music be for sale in the first place? If people only understand something in terms of a market value, it might as well be fucking shampoo. But it's too important for that. Don't forget the music industry has only been around for two minutes. And it can't last. All these fuckers at the majors know the game's up, they're just squeezing out all the drops while they can."

Jacob didn't like the sound of this. "Yeah, but that's what we want isn't it? A record deal. The chance to... well, have people hear the songs."

"If a record company wants to give us money then great, but that's not the end in itself. I want to write the most challenging, awe-inspiring, scary, and beautiful music in the world – I want to write the best fucking album ever made. I'm aiming for nothing more, nothing less." The opening bars of Bjork's *Batchelorette* rose from the juke box speakers. "Like this, Jacob. Couldn't you just die happy if you'd created something as articulate and complete as this?" Reilly leant back in his chair, raised his eyes to the ceiling, as if to drink in the music.

"Reilly?"

"Yes Stevie."

"You're a pretentious twat sometimes, you know that?"

Jacob doubled up, the joke's impact being amplified by the fact he had a mouthful of beer. Damn it, spilt a bit.

Reilly didn't take his eyes off the ceiling, calmly shooting back, "Call me what you want mate. Especially pretentious. I love it. Pretentious is a word used by people who listen to David Gray. It's the word people resort to when something is just too hard for them to understand."

This irked Stevie. "I tell you what I understand," he said, "a drummer, a bass player, a shit hot lead guitarist and a kick arse front man. Big tunes, energy – fucking rock 'n' roll."

Jacob knew what Stevie was really getting at. There was some history here. A few years ago, Stevie and Jacob had formed a band. Jacob played the guitar hero and Stevie the charismatic vocalist. This was back when Oasis ruled the world and Stevie was definitely Mad For It. It was Stevie's show. He roped in a couple of scousers, names long since forgotten, to play bass and drums. He insisted on the band name Mirage, developed a bizarre simian swagger and started writing songs with titles like *Hey come on now*, *Walk this world*, and *Don't bring me down, man*.

Jacob had liked the first Oasis album as much as anyone but didn't really want to sound like them. For him, this was a chance to jam a bit and maybe play some gigs. His heart was never really in it, and he still felt bad about it. Stevie had paid for weekend long sessions at the Drumbank rehearsal studios and bought a dazzling array of PA equipment, mikes, and digital effects processors. Jacob's interest began to wane when it became clear that these gizmos were solely for the use of the front man. Jacob and the scousers would manfully hold the songs together with cheap guitars and drums hooked up to 12 inch practice amps, while Stevie stood in front of an 8 foot PA stack booming out his nasal cod-mancunian vocals, eighty quid tambourine in hand.

Reilly had missed out on the Mirage experience first hand, but on hearing Jacob's stories begged for a copy of the demo tape. He still played it once a month or so and would cry with incredulous laughter every time. His favourite track was *Tomorrow people*. The chorus ran, "*Yeah, tomorrow people, in the sky now, come on now, tomorrow's just begun...*"

Mirage disbanded after about six weeks. Jacob knew it was time to go when he looked up during a song to see Stevie with his arms behind his back, head cocked up towards the mike in full Liam Gallagher pose, checking himself out in the full length mirror he'd started to bring to rehearsal. Jacob told Stevie that they had musical differences. Stevie took it quite well, acted the jilted lover for a while but seldom brought it up again.

"Jesus wept! Who put this shite on? I'm not listening to this."
Bjork had been replaced by Reef. Reilly slammed down his pint
and headed for the door. He stood outside, indignantly checking
his watch.

"There goes a man who really needs to chill out a bit," said
Stevie, "needs a girlfriend or something."

Jacob laughed. "Between you and me I think he's, er, having a
few problems with his brain. I mean he's always had
tendencies, but it's getting a bit much."

"He's not mental. Not violent or anything. He's just
eccentric."

"Well he's a fruitcake alright, but he's a great songwriter… er,
not that you're not."

Stevie ignored Jacob's faux pas. "I know he can sing, but I
thought he just sat around playing on the Playstation all the
time?"

Jacob had been planning to keep his cards close to his chest on
Reilly's new songs. He'd been messing around in nearly-there
bands for long enough to know never to shoot his mouth off. It
always came back to bite you. But what the hell.

"Not this week. I don't know what brought it on, but he's
been writing like a demon. He phoned in sick every day, locked
himself in the flat and went for it. Fifteen songs and I'm not
shitting you Stevie, they're the real thing. I mean, I was blown
away by these songs. He's really pushed himself."

"What's it sound like? Fucking clever-clever art school rock I
bet."

"No not at all – it's just acoustic guitar and vocals. Nirvana
Unplugged kind of sound. But there's this… I'll probably
sound like a wanker here, but there's this… purity to these
songs. That bit of magic you can't fake. There's this ache in the
vocals. It's bruised, beautiful, it's fucking transcendent." There,
he'd shot his mouth off. Shit. Stevie raised an eyebrow. Jacob
took this as a queue to add a disclaimer. "I mean, I might be
wrong, I've only heard the tape once. It's very raw. I'll need to

do a lot of work on the arrangements, get the drums programmed, we'll need to completely re-record it all."

A familiar voice approached, singing along to Reef. It was little Alex, sweeping the pub for empty glasses. He saw Jacob and Stevie. "Alright, lads?"

Jacob raised his glass.

"Alex! The son I never had," said Stevie.

Alex laughed nervously. "Having a good night?" he asked.

"Good mate," said Stevie, "but is there any chance of table service?"

Alex missed the joke, shooting Stevie a bemused look. "No mate, you order at the bar. Are these dead?" he said, pointing at the empties.

"Yeah," replied Jacob.

"Right, see you later. Take it easy."

The pub was full now, an hour until last orders. The queue at the bar was four deep. Stevie was out of Becks, "Jacob, do you fancy moving on somewhere else. Down the Hobgoblin?"

Jacob froze. "Oh, no. Don't fancy it. Here's fine. You want a beer, I'll get them."

Stevie persisted. "Come on, I told a mate of mine I might see her down there tonight. Let's get Reilly and go."

"No, not the Hobgoblin, Reilly and I are kind of, well, barred."

"Barred? Since when?"

"Last week."

Stevie laughed. "Let me guess, Reilly slapped someone for saying the Doors were better than the Velvets?"

"No, no. Nothing like that." Jacob was cringing as he recalled the details. He'd kind of been hoping to never mention it again, he hoped that silence would erase the humiliation somehow. Maybe it would help to tell Stevie.

"We went down there on Sunday lunchtime for a cheeky pint, but you know how it is, the beer tastes good, you get another and the next thing you know you're trolleyed and it's only three-thirty or something. Anyway, Reilly's being calm and pretty funny, not like tonight. It's all good. But then I mention that *Godzilla*'s on TV that night."

"What that fucking cartoon, with that little knob Godzooky and that?"

"No, the film. You must have seen it. Loads of special effects, Godzilla's running around Manhattan twatting skyscrapers and trashing everything."

"Oh yeah. I know it."

"So Reilly just turns. Like that," Jacob clicked his fingers for emphasis, "and starts ranting about US imperialism and stuff. He's saying that September 11th was just a Hollywood fantasy come true and he's getting really loud. There's all these people having a quiet pint, reading the Sunday papers or whatever, looking around at us and getting really freaked out."

"Fantastic!" Stevie was loving this.

"So he finishes his rant, goes to drink his pint, and I'm thinking – thank fuck he's shut up at last. But then he takes a swig of his beer, puts the pint down, climbs up on the table, and shouts…" Jacob's face screwed up into a ball of tight embarrassment as he remembered. Stevie was giggling in anticipation. He asked, "What? What did he shout?"

"He shouted, 'Ladies and gentlemen. Me and my friend Jacob here need your help. We are now going to march down to the American Embassy and burn the fucker down. Why? For the government's complicity in the events of September 11th, and for their subsequent empire-building in the name of peace. Who'll join me? Who'll join me?'"

Stevie let out a roar of laughter at this, his eyes moistening. "Jacob, stop. Tell me you're making this up. This is fucking brilliant."

"So anyway, of course he gets no response, then the landlord comes over, really calmly, and says, 'Sir, three things – firstly, get off my table before you break it. Secondly, you're in Bristol, there is no American embassy. And finally, get out of my pub, neither of you are welcome here again.'"

"Classic, I wish I'd been there! Why didn't you tell me?" asked Stevie, now clutching his stomach, as if in pain.

"Why do you think, it was humiliating."

"So I assume he didn't watch *Godzilla* when you got in."

"He watched it from start to fucking finish. Taped it too. Screaming obscenities all the way through he was. He's got a load of those blockbusters on tape. You should see him watching *Air Force One*, he's practically foaming at the mouth."

The Reef track finished, and Reilly was back at the table. Stevie stood up, bear-hugged him and informed him he was a gentleman, a loan crusader, an inspiration. Reilly looked confused, but took Stevie's words at face value, thanked him and took a seat. Stevie got the next round, more Stella with Rum and Coke chasers. Jacob's nerves eased, the alcohol and Stevie's presence soothing him.

What jail is like

This was the plan. This was Reilly's plan. He would take the week off, lock himself up in the flat with the acoustic and the four track. He would shut out the buzzing, broken world beyond the front door and just write. He would write as many songs as possible. Get it all down. He would push himself to the absolute limits of his ability. He would reach inside himself and pull out whatever he fucking found. He would be unafraid.

This week would change the course of modern music. In years to come in dark corners of pubs up and down the land, connoisseurs of the alternative arts would speak in hushed tones about this week. The week that Reilly wrote the first Serpico album. The greatest album ever made. That was the plan. That was Reilly's plan.

Monday was a good start. First things first, Reilly selected his 'KILL YOUR HEROES' T-shirt, pushed a cigarette filter up each nostril and headed for the phone.

"First Choice Recruitment, this is Mandy."

Speak the language, speak the language. "Hi Mandy, this is Jon Reilly, I work at Western Telecom, sixth floor. I'm in Sandra Adcock's team."

"Oh, hi, how are you?" Reilly knew that she didn't have a clue who he was. First Choice had over four hundred other muppets at Western Telecom, contracted to the agency, not their place of work, no rights, no stake and all very sackable. She also knew why he was calling. But of course he'd have to actually say it.

"Mandy, I'm a bit under the weather actually. I've got this nasty flu that's going around. Unfortunately I won't be in today." Flu was perfect. Could be offered as a one-or-two-dayer, then stretched out, gradually embellished as the week progressed. A migraine was the king of single day sick leave, but its lack of longevity made it unsuitable here.

"Yes, you do sound a bit bunged up. Will you be in tomorrow?" Was she being sarcastic?

"I hope so, I'll certainly try."

"OK, I'll let Sandra know. Thanks for calling Jon…" Click.

"Not at all. Thank you, you ridiculous freak," he replied to the dead tone.

Trained to within an inch of her life, Reilly wondered if Mandy had ever been a real person. At what point had *they* sucked out her brains and made her into another cog? He tried to humanize her. He pictured her at her eighteenth birthday party – "Thanks for coming, what a thoughtful gift. Have you lost weight? Yes, you do sound a bit bunged up. First Choice Recruitment, this is Mandy…" No good. What did she do outside work? Did she have fears, dreams and all that other human bullshit? Did she ever just say fuck it, get utterly bladdered and take a load of drugs, end up dribbling on some stranger's floor? Reilly wondered if a person like Mandy could ever live long enough to come to the same conclusion he had. That life – that is to say careers, money, mortgages, relationships and all that fluff – were so banal and empty as to be beneath contempt, beyond consideration as an ambition. He decided that twelve hundred years was a likely timescale.

First job out of the way, Reilly removed the filters and rolled a cigarette. He looked around the room as he smoked it. Jacob must have tidied up before he left this morning, god bless him. The flat was small, functional, certainly not on a par with

Stevie's pad, but nothing which Reilly was ashamed about. The centre-piece of the lounge was a huge battered old bookcase Jacob had picked up from some place on Gloucester Road. Stacked on its shelves were hundreds of CDs, five hundred Reilly reckoned. Not a bad haul. Some were Jacob's but the majority, more than three quarters, were Reilly's. This was no anal-retentive collection, however. The CDs were not alphabetised, sorted by genre or really in any kind of order at all. There were no shrink-wrapped limited editions, no deleted Nirvana twelve inches. The collection was pure functionality, no space was wasted. His interest in these five hundred plastic discs began and ended with what was digitally encoded on them, on what the laser of the CD player read, processed and dumped out through the speakers. In every jewel case was a disc containing music that was life giving, life affirming, life saving. The book case was not Reilly's stamp album, it was his medicine cabinet. He walked over to the bookcase and browsed for today's prescription.

He ran his finger over the spines of the CDs, savouring the words on them and waiting for the rush he would feel when he saw what he wanted. Tricky – *Maxinquaye*, Linoleum – *Dissent*, Slint – *Spiderland*, dEUS – *The ideal crash*, Pavement – *Crooked rain, crooked rain*, Underworld – *Second toughest in the infants*, Silver Jews – *The natural bridge*, Madder Rose – *Bring it Down*. Then he saw it. He pulled out Mazzy Star's *So tonight that I might see* and loaded up the hi-fi.

Reilly slumped back into the sofa and let the opening bars of *Fade into you* wash over him. There were various magazines and papers on the coffee table – The Guardian, Four Four Two, Q. He picked up last week's NME, this week's big thing staring up at him from the cover with dead eyes. Fucking hell, he remembered this lot. They'd supported someone good (Sebadoh, wasn't it?) at the Anson Rooms that time, and Reilly was proud to recall that he'd brutally heckled them throughout their set. The singer had even told him to shut the fuck up. Except he'd said, "Fuck the shut up." Priceless. What a great night.

The front of the NME screamed, "THE LAST GREAT BRITISH GUITAR BAND – INSIDE THE FIGHT WITH THE NU-BIRDS." The Nu-Birds, that was it. Reilly laughed out loud. It had to be the worst band name he'd ever heard. He quickly flicked through the pages to the feature. The headline was, "TO LIVE AND DIE IN L8." They were from Liverpool apparently, and wanted to take over the world or something stupid, but best of all they were touring. Reilly checked the dates – Yes! Bristol Fleece and Firkin, July 25th.

Fade in to you finished and Reilly got up, flicked off the stereo. He'd got his daily dose of country-tinged post-Velvets melancholy and felt energised. Felt confident. Now he had work to do. He headed to the kitchen, rolling another cigarette on the way. A warm summer morning was cranking up outside, the sun lighting up the kitchen. It was going to be a good day. He could feel it, it was coming. Reilly pulled out the dictaphone and pressed play.

His own voice came back at him, full of long forgotten notes and ideas – "...ahem ...right, here's the thing. You know the secret of good art – so don't forget it. Honesty, be honest. That's all there is. Everything flows from this simple truth. Forget what you've been told music should sound like, do what makes sense to you, do what your instinct tells you. It might be shit. But maybe, just maybe, it won't be. Sing with your own voice...sing with your own voice, and it will come..." Reilly looked at the dictaphone. He didn't remember saying that. Still, he thought it was good advice. He located and rinsed out a mug, opened a bottle of Valpolicella. Took a deep swig. Oh yeah.

This is how Reilly wrote. He would go for months, sometimes well over a year without writing a thing, without writing any lyrics or even picking up his acoustic. He never forgot though. During these in-between times he would be filled with ideas, half-formed symphonies, philosophies and insights too important not to be shared, too vivid not to be communicated. He would hear a new album, see a great film or overhear the conversation of strangers and the shape of a new song would crystallise before him. These flashes showed him what he could achieve, and better. Everything would seem possible, unshackled by the practicalities of actually writing and recording music.

But he would balk at sitting down, writing the words, working out a chord structure and dusting off the four track. He would balk at making his ideas real, making them flesh and creating targets that could be shot down.

Every so often Reilly would swallow the fear and jump in. He would load himself up with various chemicals and charge into a song or two, filling up ten minutes on the four track. The next day he'd run the tape back, over and over, a pulsing hangover providing the bass line. He'd listen to the point where he couldn't hear the songs anymore, and conclude that he was nothing more than a third rate pub singer and the lyrics were sixth-form pap.

Jacob of course, had no idea. Reilly would airily allude to some new material he was working on, deliberately cultivating an image of an indifferent genius - an artisan from whom music effortlessly flowed whenever he could be bothered to turn the Playstation off and get his guitar out. Jacob listened attentively to Reilly's sporadic demos, enthusing about their raw potential, pestering Reilly to get serious and write a whole album. Reilly would generally provide a flippant response and feed the genius myth. For Reilly, there was nothing more dangerous than sharing an insecurity. He believed that if he spoke of his demons, said it out loud, they would have permission to seek him out and eat him alive.

Earlier that year, one Saturday afternoon, Jacob and Reilly were watching *Football Focus*. Garth Crooks was interviewing a promising young midfielder, on the cusp of the England squad, making a name for himself. Reilly and Jacob were going through the usual routine of nursing hangovers and talking shite.

"Little twat," said Reilly. "He can do ten keepie-uppies and suddenly he's the new Gazza. Did you see him against Italy, all pretty little step-overs and then giving the ball away!"

Jacob disagreed - "I really rate him, we need players who can run at defenders, make something out of nothing."

"You'll believe anything, Jacob. It's The Emperor's New Clothes! He's a numpty."

Garth was asking the youngster about his recent form and the Italy game in particular. He replied in the usual way, predictable platitudes for his team mates and the gaffer, taking each game at a time and so on. And then he said, "You know Garth, I'm my own biggest critic." Reilly jolted at the phrase. He was appalled that a cliché of such staggering inanity could so succinctly sum up his own predicament. *I am my own biggest critic. I am my own biggest critic.*

In the days that followed, Reilly sunk into a crippling depression as his familiar anger at the world around him began to turn in on himself. He was disgusted at his impotence. He knew how to write great music, but had somehow talked himself out of actually doing so. It was around this time that he vowed that this year, this summer, he was going to do it. He was going to forget it all. He was going to write the greatest album of all time.

So here Reilly was, sat at the kitchen table with a notepad and a biro. Listening to his own drunken ramblings in an effort to find a spark, a starting place. He finished the mug of wine and poured another. He was feeling lighter already, he had a familiar buzz as the wine settled in his stomach, its warmth flowing into his bloodstream. He switched off the dictaphone and started to write. Just phrases, groups of words, nothing really. He'd had an idea pawing at him over the last couple of weeks, an issue to address. He resolved to write, jam with the words, see where it took him.

He had noticed something over the last few years, a sensation somewhere between dream and sleep. At first he couldn't explain it. Some mornings just before he woke, he would have a stream of words running through his mind. Scrolling like film credits. He could see them, taste them. And they were eloquent, moving, intoxicating. And full of meaning somehow. As he woke fully, the words were forgotten, but the feeling remained. What was that? His brain filing the rubbish of the previous day? Was it gibberish that only seemed profound because he was unconscious? Reilly thought not. He was sure he'd tapped into something other people didn't see. He felt sure this was a glimpse of what his subconscious could produce when unfettered by the rules and restraints of the everyday. To Reilly, these pre-waking dreams were the purest form of creativity, unchecked by structure, doubt and fear. And he wanted some of that. He wanted to capture it and seal it in a fucking jar.

And this is where the Valpolicella came in. It was a device, a tool, a song writing aid. As practical but ultimately peripheral as a plectrum or a mike stand. He found it easier to write and enjoyed better results when drunk, therefore he would drink. Logic itself. He'd experimented with other substances, marijuana was another useful aid. Acid could open a few doors. Ecstasy also worked to an extent. But alcohol was the best fit.

Reilly sat at the kitchen table and wrote. And drank. And it started to come, to flow. Time passed. He was focused, productive, aggressive. By ten-thirty he had an empty wine bottle and a page full of words, a song. Well a lyric in any case. Twenty-four lines. It was something. He read it back –

Heaven can wait,
It's just not me,
I can't accept,
What we'll never see,
I'll leave you dreams,
Broken toys,
In a letter,
Leave this noise.

Forgive these songs,
They're just misled,
Why even let them,
Leave my head,
So loveless and torn,
And underused,
So infantile,
So what?

I used to know,
But I strayed,
Misplaced the address,
Memory fade,
So I'll steal it back,
Let no one see,
Who is this for,
If not for me?

He read it again. He thought it was alright. It scanned well, he had a tune worked out already. It could work. And he had a title. It was called *Analogue Soul*. In fact, he'd had the title for weeks, now he had a lyric to go with it.

He wondered what Jacob would make of it, whether he could use it. He knew what he'd ask, what Jacob always asked – "what's it about?" *That fucking question.* A fair question really, but one which Reilly could never fully answer. He always felt that Jacob wanted to hear some kind of convoluted anecdote by way of explanation. Some kind of insight. A story.

"Well, Jacob, I was stranded at Tel Aviv bus station, it was 4.30am. I was supposed to be meeting Ishmael and the Russian. I was out of my mind – hadn't slept in four days. They were late and I had their money. I was ready to freak out big time. And then the most amazing thing happened - I looked up and saw these three kids, no older than five or six. They were huddled together and I thought they were crying, like they'd lost their parents or something. I wanted to help them. But then as I looked closer I could see that they were laughing, Jacob, they were laughing! They ran off into the distance and *I* began to cry. I cried for me, for them, and for all the things that had happened. And then the smallest kid turned round and shouted something to me. Do you know what he shouted, Jacob? He shouted 'Hey mister, we've got analogue soul!' I just wanted to capture that feeling in a song…"

But the real answer would be, "Fucking hell Jacob, I don't know. It's not *about* anything. It is what it is. Don't be so empirical." To which Jacob would reply something like, "Don't be so precious, I only asked."

That was the problem with a conventional education, as far as Reilly was concerned. It taught you to look at everything like it was a code to be cracked. As if understanding was just a matter of sifting through the right equations. Reilly remembered studying Sylvia Plath at school. He was told that the moon was Plath's mother, the yew tree her father. His text book became full of notes, basically word for word translations of the prose, as if it had been written in Spanish. Poor old mad Sylvia, writing her weird poetry while furtively eyeing up the gas knobs on the cooker. Carefully crafting a poem called *I have complicated feelings about my parents*, and then translating it into obscure metaphors for A-level students to pick over and decode in years to come.

It wasn't Jacob's fault, he didn't know any better. Reilly resolved to explain himself better next time *the question* was asked. No, fuck that, he wasn't going to explain himself to anybody. Reilly stood up from the table and located another bottle. He continued writing, and drinking.

By four-thirty Reilly was dry-retching over the bowl, a trail of watery blood red vomit tracing his steps across the linoleum, vivid as a car crash. He'd forgotten to eat. His throat was raw, burning. His stomach felt bruised. But he smiled to himself. It had been a good day. He now had five songs on the four track. A good start, all part of the plan. And he'd realised that he still loved this stuff, this music, this process, whatever the fuck it was. He flushed away the wasted wine and headed for his bed. He lay staring at the ceiling, one hand on the wall to stop the spins, and waited to pass out. A thought occurred. He wondered if Thom Yorke wrote his music this way.

Hotel lounge (be the death of me)

Jacob was on the way to Stevie's, walking off the hangover. Three miles he reckoned, Bishopston to Clifton Village, far enough to work up a bit of a sweat, and let the toxins evaporate in the warm breeze. He'd left Reilly sipping Lemon Lucozade, nibbling at a scotch egg and sitting through a *Brasseye* omnibus on video, the whole series in sequence. Jacob left during the Claire Raynor interview, Reilly bellowing with laughter as Chris Morris asked the poor old dear, "If I were to attack you now, would you beat me off?"

Once out of the flat, Jacob joined Gloucester Road and headed downhill towards Cotham. Friday night's pissheads and chancers were nowhere to be seen now, washed away and replaced by another species, insect-like. The pavements were now heavy with the Saturday morning knuckle-draggers, hungry eyes and twitching hands rifling through cheap houseplants, mops and buckets and other tack.

Jacob slalomed through the crowd, doing his best to notice nothing, make eye contact with no one, to save himself the sickly sadness of seeing too much of another's misery. A couple of years ago he'd witnessed a battered old couple arguing over whether one-pound-fifty was too much to pay for a new bin. He'd carried the scene around with him for weeks, like a stain.

Couldn't shake it off.

He walked on, past the Flyer, and down opposite the Hobgoblin with his head down. The café/wine bars along the promenade were already filling up with the latte and broadsheet crowd, a half-arsed attempt at euro-cool amid the muck and dilapidation. Jacob did a double take at a well-dressed couple tucking into croque monsieurs outside one café, it took him a second to place them – the Gap Twins from last night. Shit. He quickened his pace and hoped they wouldn't spot him. He took a backwards glance as soon as he was a safe distance away. Had they seen him? Inconclusive. They weren't looking his way now, but this didn't make him feel safe. He took a hold of himself, told himself to be rational. He was an adult, they were adults, surely they wouldn't hold a grudge. But he couldn't be sure. He cursed Reilly, the fucking idiot, gradually building up a list of enemies for them both. Jacob just wanted to walk down the street without fear. Not much to ask, he thought.

He headed down the hill. Under the arches, then a right up Cotham Brow, willing himself away from Gloucester Road. He felt better with each step up the hill, it was good to be on the move. Jacob fumbled in his pocket for his walkman, pressed play and pulled out the headphones. This was the real reason for leaving the car at home and walking: Reilly's tape. His first listen last night before the pub had knocked him sideways, now it was time for the second. He wanted this listen to confirm what he had thought, that these songs were something special, that they had that x-factor that could lift them above all the other indie plodders out there. He prickled with anticipation as the first track started up, filling his ears and blocking out the world around him.

He was listening to *Swoon*, a slow building, lilting paean to something or other. Jacob couldn't make out many of the words, but the chorus ran, *"And I've been waiting, the longest time, for a little luck, and I would die for it, I would swoon."* He was relieved. It was very good. Jacob had never been in any doubt that Reilly had a great voice, a kind of hybrid of Jeff Buckley and the guy out of Wilco, but now he had his own voice, he sounded born to it, he had *soul*. This was great.

Jacob took a look around as he digested the song. Cotham Brow stretched on in front of him, the cold grey of the Georgian houses lining the steep climb ahead. He felt a warm flush of familiarity at the scene – willows, rhododendrons in full summer bloom, he could almost hear the lawnmowers buzzing from the back streets. He was still fond of this place despite everything that told him not to be. He passed a grand old house and realised he knew it, he'd been inside. He'd crashed a student party there years ago, must have been back in '94 or '95. He smiled at the memory. He'd sneaked in with a couple of uni mates on the off chance that they wouldn't be chucked out. And they weren't, it was great. The house had been cleared of furniture and a DJ was getting everyone going with a mix of hip hop, acid jazz and happy house. Jacob remembered launching himself into this group of strangers without fear. And he'd been witty and funny and everyone was his friend. He'd hit it off with a pretty young art student and they'd sloped back to her place at dawn. Was that really him? He was more confident then.

The next track on the tape brought him back to the present. It was *Analogue Soul*, and Jacob loved it. It was much more direct than the first track, he had it earmarked as the first single. There was no catchy chorus, Reilly didn't do pop songs as such, but there was an affecting tilt to the chord progression. The lyrics were clearer than *Swoon*, but Jacob was fucked if he knew what it was about. He guessed that it was in A minor, and was already planning what he would add to the track - drums, samples, and effects. He could taste it, it was a symphony in waiting. "The most immediate song Reilly has written to date," is how Jacob would describe it to the music press. "Imagine Six by Seven covering David Bowie's *Quicksand*, remixed by DJ Shadow," he'd tell them. They'd love that.

How could Reilly have sat on this undoubted talent for so

long? It was so effortless for him. It was a tap he could turn on and off whenever he wanted. Jacob knew his own limits, his place in the grand scheme of Serpico. He was no songwriter. He was a producer, a craftsman, a brickie to Reilly's architect. Reilly had no interest in, or indeed aptitude for the technicalities of recording and arrangement, therefore he would pass the uncut gems to Jacob to bang into shape. Symbiosis. But what Jacob would give for an ounce of Reilly's ability, just to create a song like this, say "this is mine, I wrote this," but the lazy bastard had always been too busy sneering at the world to take it on, until now. The change in Reilly, his sudden work ethic, had alarmed Jacob at first. When Reilly handed him the tape last night, saying, "there's about fifteen songs here. They belong to you now," he'd felt a queasy mixture of gratitude and apprehension. As if he'd got in from work to find Reilly cooking a meal for them both, or cleaning the flat. It was unexpected to the point of being creepy.

Track three arrived as Jacob reached the guitar shops at the top of Cotham. Habit took over, and he paused to take in the window display at the first shop. In amongst the reproduction Telecasters, Stratocasters and Les Pauls, was a neat SG copy, a real piece of class. Just the thing. He wanted a closer look but didn't really want to go inside. Reilly's distaste for guitar shops had rubbed off on him of late. There always seemed to be some self-regarding muso behind the counter, spouting jargon in an effort to intimidate and impress. Jacob knew his stuff when it came to music equipment, but had learned that it was better to act dumb. Reilly was always scathing about the shop staff, and musos in general, appalled by their complete lack of creativity. He called them "guitar plumbers." Jacob kind of agreed, but that SG deserved a closer look. He pushed open the door and squeezed inside, looked up to see Jimmy Reckon surrounded by his bandmates, playing a gold Stratocaster through a wah-wah pedal...*Wacker-Wacker-Wacker*.... Jacob was not in the mood for Mr Reckon and his disciples today, but it was too late. Jimmy saw him and stopped playing – "Jacob you spanner! How you doing?"

"Alright, Jimmy?"

"Check this axe out – makes me feel horny, know what I mean?"

I have no idea what you mean, please shut up. "Yeah Jimmy. It's nice. Shopping, are you?"

"Yeah man – looks like we're going to have a little windfall soon, if you know what I mean." He flicked his hair out of his face and tapped the side of his nose.

"Listen Jimmy, I'm in a rush. We'll catch up soon." He bolted for the door.

He walked on. It was getting hot, Jacob's forehead glistened with sweat, the salty liquid settling in his eyebrows. He swore he could smell alcohol in it, last night's rum back to taunt him, wagging a disapproving finger in his face. He thought about his liver, pictured it straining away like an overworked sewerage plant, ready to burst open at any minute, delivering a toxic spill. His jeans were now getting seriously uncomfortable in the heat, like he knew they would. Should have worn those shorts...but he didn't look good in shorts, in fact no-one did. He was fucking dying here, but was soothed as he caught his reflection in a shop window. He cut an impressive figure, the flares swishing rhythmically over his Converse One Stars: he looked like a rock star. Just as well.

He took a back street through Redland towards Whiteladies Road. He was now up to the fifth track on Reilly's tape, another cracker, this one called *Satellite Town*. It was a piece of simple beauty, just two notes plucked rhythmically from the top string. The lyrics ran, *"I think I feel like letting go, walk into the ocean, let the waves decide which way I go...I can change my name, or address, but those old ghosts still walk around, and break my bones, sit on my chest..."*

Jacob was floored all over again. Where had this come from? This was heavy stuff. The vocals were plaintive, instinctive in their delivery. And it hit him right there. That fucking nut he shared a flat with was a genius. He had no doubt now. He didn't need to hear any more. He'd heard enough to know that exciting times lay ahead, and he couldn't wait. He ejected the tape, stashing it carefully in his back pocket, and put in a compilation that he'd made, Portishead's *Half day closing* providing the soundtrack as he reached Whiteladies.

Jacob ducked into a newsagents for a bottle of coke and tobacco. He stepped back out into the sunshine and took a satisfying swig. Caffeine and sugar, just the ticket. He rolled a cigarette. Whiteladies Road flowed down the hill from his right and onto towards town. He'd always thought of Whiteladies as Gloucester Road's posh, university-educated cousin. Not university as in Oxford or Cambridge, but university as in, say, Hatfield Polytechnic. It was cleaner and brighter than Gloucester Road, with The Futon Shop and Italian Lighting Store rather than Sound as a Pound and Cash Converters. The NatWest staff here would cash a cheque without looking you up and down and scrutinising your account first.

Jacob and Reilly had drunk away the previous new year's eve on Whiteladies, and during a memorably poisonous tirade, Reilly had told Jacob a little about the history of the area. Years ago, the rich families of Bristol would walk up Whiteladies Road, right up to the top at Black Boy Hill to purchase freshly landed slaves, taking their pick from the human cattle market. Reilly had self-righteously, and to no one in particular, labelled the slave trade, "the secret history of this concrete-covered, cousin-fucking, spastic town." Jacob had to concede that Bristol's role in the slave trade had been rather swept under the carpet, Massive Attack seemed to be the only people who wanted to talk about it. But things move on. The cattle markets were now the various theme pubs up and down the road. Bohemia, Bar Oz, the Rat and Parrot, the Varsity, Finnegan's Wake. A crass magic mile of alcopops, Ben Shermans and random acts of violence.

Jacob finished his coke and headed down the hill, past the BBC and right up St Paul's Road, past the hotels. Up to the Anson Rooms, almost there now, Primal Scream's *Shoot/Speed, Kill/Light* pumping from the headphones.

He took a short cut through the cemetery and on, closer to Stevie's. The air felt different up here, cleaner, more exotic, expensive. A Porsche Boxster swished past him, cutting the air with that new car noise, some ruddy-cheeked ex-public schoolboy at the wheel. This was Clifton Village. An oasis of old money and old values. Jacob always found the contrast shocking, couldn't quite fathom how the inner city filth of St Paul's Road was just a ten minute drive away. But he'd noticed this in other cities as well; Birmingham, Leeds, Manchester, Glasgow. The rich closeting themselves away, shutting out the plebs and their funny accents, dubious morality and ingrained criminal tendencies. He told himself that the residents of Clifton Village were just a scared little clique, living in a moneyed ghetto. That's what he told himself.

Stevie's was the garden flat of a converted Victorian terrace, open plan, polished oak floors and minimalist furnishing. A bit on the wanky side for Jacob, but undeniably impressive. Stevie buzzed him in.

"Alright mate! Good to see you. Leave the pub philosopher at home did you?" Stevie was dressed for the weather, Hackett polo shirt and khaki shorts. He had an empty bottle of Sol in his hand. He didn't do hangovers.

"Yeah Stevie, He's got a busy schedule of TV planned. You know how it is."

"Bless him. What T-shirt was he wearing today then?" asked Stevie.

"Bit of a weird one actually – PLEASE DO NOT FEED THE WAIFS."

"Eh?"

"I know. I was trying to work out if it was some kind of attack on thin women. You know, all that heroin chic, or whether it was more like don't feed the waifs, they're fine as they are."

"Doesn't WAIF stand for something? Yeah - Why Am I Famous? All those Tara Lara types?"

"Fucked if I know mate, didn't want to ask in any case, I didn't have half an hour spare to listen to some lecture."

Stevie laughed and lead Jacob through to the lounge. The Libertines were playing. Jacob sat on the futon as Stevie went to get them both a beer. What the hell, it was now after midday, perhaps a little hair of the dog would even things out a bit, pull his disparate senses into focus.

He looked around the well-appointed flat and felt a twinge of jealousy. Not at the expense of it all, fuck that. It was only *stuff* - a Dell laptop, Technics sound system with a new iPod resting on top, an array of recording equipment from the Mirage days, a huge plasma TV, various other gadgets and some poncey furniture - just stuff. He wasn't jealous of Stevie's money, it was drug money after all. He was jealous because it looked like a real person's home. It looked like the sort of place that any twenty eight year old should be living in. A twenty eight year old who was any kind of success at least. He pictured Reilly across town, chain smoking in front of *Brasseye*, Chris Morris describing, "the twisted brain wrong of a one off man mental..." Reilly would now be flicking ash into one of last night's cans of Kronenbourg, posters blue-tacked to the walls around him - *Leaving Las Vegas*, *Taxi Driver*, the lyrics to *Fitter Happier*. Compare and contrast.

"I took the liberty of sticking a piece of lime in your Sol, Jacob."

"Thanks mate, you're so sophisticated. Do you want to hear this tape then?"

"Yeah mate, stick it on."

They listened and drank into the afternoon. All fifteen songs, start to finish. And Stevie was transfixed, although he tried to hide it. He did his best to take the piss, point out similarities to Guns 'n' Roses songs in the chord structures and so on, but Jacob wasn't fooled. He knew Stevie was as floored as he was.

As the tape finished he finally gave himself away, turning to Jacob - "There's this weight there. You know what I mean. Jesus, every song sounds like the last thing he'll ever do, the last fucking breath he'll ever take." Stevie praising Reilly's music, there was a thing.

They headed across the road to the Avon Gorge Hotel, Jacob buzzing from the beer and expectation of what destiny had in store. As they sat out on the deck, the suspension bridge and gorge filling the skyline and the afternoon sun burning into his pale skin, Jacob allowed himself a little daydream. He told himself - it's this time next year, you've come back to Bristol for a drink with your old mate Stevie. Everyone here recognises you, they've all heard your album, they all saw your witty and self-depreciating acceptance speech at the Mercury Music Prize. The barman asked for your autograph as he served up the Guinness, a table of girls in the corner giggling and stealing glances. The record company weren't keen on you coming out without security, but you're a man of the people, haven't changed and everyone loves you for it. You and Stevie are shooting the breeze, you're telling him about the endless press engagements, the people you've met and about the progress of the second album. You've done it, you've made it.

You're happy.

Jacob looked over at Stevie, who was staring out into the gorge. Jacob assumed that Stevie was doing his own daydreaming. Probably thinking - these jokers are going to be famous. Jacob and Reilly are going to be on the front of the NME, on Top of the Pops, doing acoustic sets for the cameras at Glastonbury. My mates are going to be the Next Big Thing.

Jacob dipped in. "What's on your mind, Brummie boy?"

"Oh nothing really. Just can't get that tune out of my head, the second one…with that chord change…"

"*Analogue Soul.*"

"Yeah, that's it. Analogue soul. It's a beautiful tune, that."

Jacob nodded his agreement.

"What's the album called? What's he going to call it?"

"I don't know… I've no idea."

"Hey, let's give him a bell. I want to know." Stevie picked up his Nokia and dialled. "Reilly – it's Stevie."

"…"

"It's Stevie, you novice, listen…"

"…"

"No, listen. What's it called then. This album?"

"…"

"OK. Er, nice one mate. Laters."

Stevie hung up, put the phone back on the table. Picked up his pint.

"Well, what did he say?"

"Life and how to live it, apparently."

"Isn't that…?"

"Isn't it what?"

"Give me the phone." Jacob dialled.

"Hello?"

"Reilly, what was all that about - *Life and how to live it*?"

"Who is this?"

"Reilly!"

"Jacob?"

"Isn't that an REM song?"

"Yeah. It's just such a great title - and they tucked it away as an album track. Wasted it. I want to do it justice. That's all." There was a melancholy in his voice.

"Are you OK, Reilly?"

"Of course I'm not fucking *OK*, if you must use that vile Americanism." Jacob flinched at the volume increase and moved the phone away from his ear.

"What americ…?" Best to leave it. "Why, what's happened mate?"

"Jacob, you're so naïve. 'What's happened?' Nothing's *happened*, it's just… it's like, well this doesn't work, this thing I've been lumbered with and told to use, the state we're in."

"Sorry?" Was he talking about Serpico? Jacob felt a rush of panic.

"Life, Jacob. Life doesn't work. And I'll tell you why…" Here we go. Jacob could just see Reilly's index finger jabbing at him all the way from Bishopston, making the point. "The basis of life, the aim if you like, is to achieve something approximating happiness, right?"

"Er, I guess."

"Well, a psychologist will tell you that you've got to assimilate, be part of something bigger, be part of the community. You've got to have this innate belief in human goodness, kindness, like the spirit of the blitz or some shit. But when you look at people, the human race as a species I mean - well, they're neither good nor kind. They're incredibly destructive. All liars and cheats, just greed-driven cowards. Rudderless fuckwits who'd mortgage they're children's internal organs for the chance to drive a fucking Lexus. So where do you start? How do you even start?"

Jacob took a breath. Was he finished? And what was he on about? Had he been watching that Bill Hicks video again?

"Reilly, forget all that. Yeah, people are retards, fuck 'em, leave 'em to it. Who gives a shit? You've got bigger fish to fry now. You're going to be a star. A recording artist. Those demos mate… they could be everything…look, we really need to make some plans, work out what we do next. We're in the Avon Gorge, do you fancy meeting us for a pint?"

How I made my millions

"Return to the centre, thanks." Reilly handed over his one-pound-ten and walked down the bus, looking for a seat. He grabbed an empty two-seater and tried to look wide and fucked up. He didn't want to share, not today.

His week off had made the prospect of work even more hideous, but he faced a simple equation. Not going meant no money. And so, he told himself - *Play the game. Speak the language. Tell them what they want to hear. Get this day out of the way, and then back to real life.*

But viewed from this end of the day, eight hours of telemarketing seemed an unbearable prospect, hideously hard. He'd toyed with the idea of extending the Valpolicella experiment into the working week. A bit of self-anaesthetising made a lot of sense in terms of his enjoyment and, indeed, performance. But Reilly felt that this solution didn't really have legs. The team leaders at Western Telecom could spot inebriation a mile off and Reilly had witnessed an impressive average of one sacking a fortnight for the use of controlled substances during working hours. He didn't want to join the steady stream of gurning muppets being escorted from the premises.

Reilly looked around the bus. Jesus, look at these fuckers.

What did they look like? A crate of veal on the way to the abattoir? No, this lot were already dead - pasty-faced corpses, they all looked so fucking...*defeated*. At the front of the bus, a thin-lipped little man in a business suit sat reading *Awaken the Giant Within,* a desperation in his eyes.

Reilly felt dizzy. He couldn't make sense of the situation, what was he doing here? He started to panic.

Jacob gunned up the M32, pushing the old Saab towards the speed limit. Reilly's demo tape was on the stereo and Jacob listened closely. He was still trying to get a handle on the tunes, trying to find a jumping off point from which the album would evolve. He was getting close now, could feel it forming.

He peeled off the motorway and made his way through the industrial estate. He pulled up outside The Bristol Fashion Water Cooler Company and killed the engine. He quickly checked his tie in the rear view mirror, grabbed his suit jacket and headed inside.

Marion was already there, wearing her usual weathered expression and amateurish attempt at power dressing. She was engrossed in her latest book, an Oprah endorsed panacea, entitled *Making Life Work.*

"Morning Marion, how are you?"

"Hi, Jacob. Not too bad, you know..."

Why did she always say that? *Not too bad*. How bad then? Just bad enough? Jacob hated himself for feeling sorry for Marion, she was at least trying not to be a victim. She'd just had a hard time, that was all. What with the divorce, that car crash, the dodgy investment property and the Prozac. And the self-help culture she'd immersed herself in. For Jacob, Marion was the unwelcomingly depressive reminder that however anxious, helpless and lost he felt, things could always be worse.

"Oh Jacob, I went to my group last night, and that Claire I was telling you about was there, and she just acted like nothing had happened." Jacob scanned his memory as he made himself a coffee. Claire, Claire, Claire? No, nothing.

"So I confronted her at Check-in."

"Check in?"

"Check-in, Jacob. That's where we address any issues or difficulties we've had over the previous week."

"OK, so like dumping all your baggage?" Oops, that didn't come out right. Jacob took a face-obscuring, face-saving slug of coffee.

"Yeah, I suppose so. Anyway, I told her that I didn't have room in my life for a friend who wasn't committed. That's why Rob and I split up after all. I told her I'd left three messages on her machine and I deserved a call back. I'm a human being, Jacob."

Jacob continued nodding and tuned out completely. While Marion vented he considered ideas. He had an ethic, a sound, an atmosphere in his head. Acoustic guitar, heavy bass, a slow motion dub kind of sound. Yes - distorted walls of guitar, white noise, heavy, awesome dub. Underworld meets My Bloody Valentine. *Kid A*, but with tunes.

"...so I turned round and said I need you to acknowledge that you've hurt me, and to apologise. I'm a special and unique person, and I deserve respect..."

What about samples? Jacob had never considered using a sampled bass line or riff to build a song around, he'd always found it a bit clumsy in guitar music. And in any case, these songs didn't need anything like that to drive them. He thought of using a choir sample, like in *Lucky*, maybe. Perhaps some distorted foreign AM radio station in the background for atmosphere. That could work.

"...so she turned round and said that I shouldn't be so self-obsessed, that she'd only met me last week and she'd not phoned back because she was busy." Why did everyone 'turn round' and say things in Marion's world? Jacob pictured her and Claire having a conversation while pirouetting like spinning tops. He tried not to laugh, especially as she leant forward and whispered conspiratorially, "Between you and me, I think she's a bit unstable…Oh, hi Phil."

"Morning, troops." Phil stood beaming in the doorway. Cardboard cut-out Phil, Buzzword Phil. He was 25, stunningly upbeat, genuinely passionate about marketing water coolers, and an absolute fascination to Jacob. After working for him for four years, Jacob was still in awe of his energy, his confidence, and his utter lack of cynicism. His computer password was SUCCESS, his mobile ring tone was *Simply the Best.* He spoke like a regional Hot FM DJ, replacing his t's with d's - "We're jusd gedding bedder and bedder." What a guy.

Phil was of course fucked. Fucked in the head. It was plain to see, not even negotiable. But Jacob carried with him the terrible knowledge that life was designed for people like him. The industrial estates and offices of England were his playground, he could take whatever life had to offer.

"Jacob, Marion. Exciting news - we've got the guys from Ellis and Stead coming in this morning, and I want you two there. They're very keen to get the feedback of us marketing types - let's be sharp."

"Great!" said Jacob, and he sort of meant it.

Reilly looked around the meeting room at his colleagues, his co-workers, his team mates. He couldn't tell them apart. They didn't have eyes, just shadows covering empty sockets. Ghosts. Reilly was starting to feel sick again, burning up, and his knuckles were turning white as he gripped his chair. He told himself to ride it out, ordered whatever misfiring synapse was causing this to do as it was told. Connect. He took another look around, told himself to concentrate. Who are these people? That's Mary, isn't it? She's the one who's always going on about her crap covers band. And that's, er, Jez. He seems alright, he wore that Spiritualised T-shirt on non-uniform day. And that's Michael, he's…well, he's a snivelling little shit actually, into Travis.

He wished for something to get him out of there. A fire drill, a malfunctioning sprinkler system, a coronary among his team mates. Anything. He pictured a 747 ripping into the building a couple of storeys up - a splintering fuselage, aviation fuel, implosion; panic, fire, blood and dust.

Like everyone else in the world, Reilly had transposed the incident in New York onto his own workplace many times before. Imagined what it would be like, wondered what he'd find out about himself in such a situation. There was a part of Reilly that genuinely longed for this kind of catastrophe - something to live through, something to define him, something that could offer him ongoing immunity from all the injustices and indignities of the everyday.

Sandra was still banging on about some sales crap, false objections or something. But she was winding things up at last.

"Now I know I say this every day, but we must stick to the script. It's a compliance issue. I listened to some archived calls this morning and there was some real deviation. Jon, in particular, I need you to pay attention to this."

Speak the language, tell them what they want to hear. "Oh, no problem Sandra. Will do." Did she just call him a deviant?

"Good. Now lastly, just a reminder that we've got the Quarter 3 Launch Party today at the Thistle Hotel. The coaches will be here at 1.45."

Fucking brilliant, a couple of hours off the phones.

"Right, let's get started." Phil stood hand-on-hips at the head of the table, rotating his pelvis revoltingly. "Jacob, why don't you tell Christyn and Stefan about our current marketing activity."

"Oh, right. Sorry, I haven't prepared anything, I didn't realise…"

"No problem, Jacob, you know your stuff. Here's the ball - run with it." Phil mimed a pass.

Jacob looked up at Christyn and Stefan. They looked like the kind of business people you see on IBM adverts, generically quirky. Christyn wore a black trouser suit, retro-NHS glasses, her hair in post-modern schoolgirl bunches. Stefan had a spiky haircut, fat tie and two-day stubble – his unconventionality was pitch-perfect. They were wankers. But their self-assurance intimidated Jacob nonetheless. He was fifteen again, trying to cadge a fag from the cool sixth formers.

Here goes. "Well, our main activity so far this year has been the mailing campaign. We've been playing around with the format of the flyers. This comprises approximately sixty percent of new business. The cost is somewhat prohibitive, and so we've been dipping into fax broadcasting which has given mixed results. Our referral business is still strong. We also have the reps door-knocking in various places in the south-west, and of course we have outsourced telesales teams cold-calling as we speak."

Christyn and Stefan nodded sagely. Incredibly, they both looked like they were taking Jacob seriously.

"So, we have strong organic growth?" asked Stefan after a few seconds.

"Yes, that's correct."

"Good stuff. We've found that the other regional offices have reported similarly solid foundations. It certainly bodes well for the new brand."

Ah, yes. The new brand. The reason why these two glamorous young creatives had even set foot in this West Country backwater, this rotting industrial estate. And also the reason why Jacob still worked here. He couldn't wait to work for a company with a credible name, a proper logo, real business cards. A fucking website even.

Christyn stood up and went through some Powerpoints. She talked for a few minutes about brand values - she asked why people buy Heinz baked beans even though they're more expensive than home brand. She marvelled at the fact that the word Hoover - initially, a brand name - had become a noun, and what's more, a verb! The ultimate brand: will wonders never fucking cease. Phil pursed his lips and nodded, as if to say, "just imagine that if you can." Marion laughed out loud, genuinely astonished.

Christyn pressed on, describing the groundwork they'd been laying for the new brand. While she described focus groups and think tanks, Jacob checked out her shoes. They were trainers, those ones that look like racing driver's shoes, flat and pointy. And fair play, they looked pretty cool.

"...so you're probably asking - where are we now?" continued Christyn.

"Well, we've pencilled in the brand launch for August 20th."

Marion gasped, hand over mouth.

"Now people, we know that doesn't sound very far away. And we have a lot to do before then. We need to work together on this. We're not just creating a logo and a brand name here, we're creating a new culture. We plan to run workshops with every member of staff to lay the foundations for the new brand."

"Workshops?" asked Marion.

"Yes, we need to get everyone singing from the same hymn sheet before the launch. You see, our research so far has uncovered a great deal of apathy towards the industry from the average customer. What we need to do is get people talking about water coolers. We need to make water coolers aggressive, sassy and sexy. We want our brand to be 'street,' if you will. And to do this we need everyone within the company to be in this mindset. And I know we can do it."

"You bet we can," shouted Phil, prompting Marion to whoop and clap. Jacob clapped too, forcing a smile through his embarrassment.

"Hello, my name is Jon, and I'm calling from Western Telecom. I'd like to ask for two minutes of your time to tell you about our latest exciting product. Am I speaking with the bill payer?"

"Hello?"

"Am I speaking with Mr Groves?"

"Oh yes, that's me."

Read the script. "Firstly, I notice that you don't currently use our excellent call handling service, Western Call Butler."

"No, I don't really use the phone that much."

Features and benefits. "Let me tell you about Western Call Butler. It's a revolutionary all in one answering service. It takes messages when you're out or when you're on the phone, but not only that, it lets you know during a call when another call is waiting to come through." *Stick to the script.* "Pretty great, huh?" *Fucking hell. Take my soul.*

"Oh yeah, how big is it?"

"Erm, it's not an object." *Hide your disgust.* "It's a program located within the network, Mr Groves."

"OK. I don't think I'd use something like that. Sounds too complicated."

Create empathy, tell him a story. "To be honest with you, Mr Groves, I myself felt a little intimidated before I first tried Western Call Butler, but then I realised how easy it is to use and how useful Western Call Butler is. Now I don't know how I coped without it."

"You use it?"

"That's right. I have to say though, it's not for everyone. I don't know your situation, but it might not be suited to you."

"How do you mean?"

The hook. "Well. We've found that the kind of customer who appreciates this technology is generally very well educated, and, hmm, how can I say this? High up the socio-economic scale. These kind of people all have this product."

"Oh, right. How much is it?" *Buying signal.*

"It's just four pounds a month. And Mr Groves, we can have Western Call Butler on your line within twenty minutes."

"Can I have a think about it and call you back?"

Finish this. Offer an alternative close. "Mr Groves, would you like to pay for the year up front, or would you prefer a monthly charge on your phone bill?"

"Well, I suppose I'd rather pay monthly."

"Great. I'll put your order through right away."

"OK."

"Thanks very much for your time today, Mr Groves."

Another sale. That was Reilly's fifth of the day. He'd met his target already. He stood up and rang the bell. With a magic marker, drew another smiley face on the whiteboard. People clapped, whistled. Sandra shouted, "Well done, Jon. Keep going, you sales star." He wanted a bath and, in honesty, needed it.

He sat back down and dialled the next number.

"Hello, my name is Jon, and I'm calling from Western Telecom. I'd like to ask for two minutes of your time to tell you about our latest exciting product. Am I speaking with the bill payer?"

"Is this a cold call? I'm ex-directory. How did you get my number?"

"I'm calling from Western Telecom, we provide your phone line."

"Why don't you fucking leave people alone you fucking bastard!" Click.

A fair point, thought Reilly, and well made. He dialled the next number, using his left hand to grip his right, to prevent it from shaking.

Christyn's briefing was drawing to a close. "Right, that's it from me. Are there any questions?"

Jacob felt a strange impulse, an impulse to take a chance, to put something out there.

"Yeah. I'm sure this is something you've considered already, but there's a tactic I think might be really suited to what we're trying to do here."

Phil looked a bit taken aback by Jacob's confidence, but urged him on - "Out with it, Jacob, this is what we're all about. Brainstorm away."

"Well, I've been reading a bit about guerrilla marketing. Could work for us."

Marion piped up, "What do you mean? People in chimps suits? That's a bit cheap, isn't it?"

"No, Marion - guerrilla." He spelt it.

"How could this work for us?" asked Phil, "Give me an example - let's get this into the present. Let's get creative."

"OK – just an example. We get some sharp looking actors to go to a networking evening for business execs - have them posing as trendy young hip entrepreneurs, or something. And have them ask people where the water cooler is - and then have them say stuff like, 'oh no this brand of water cooler is *sooo* nineties, I only drink x-brand.' Have them make a scene that people will remember. Get the new name out there." Jacob looked up at blank faces. "What I mean is, the people that are marketed to, don't even know they've been marketed to." He cringed at the hole he'd dug. He looked up.

Stefan and Christyn were nodding, Marion looked like her head might explode with confusion. Phil was staring at his notes and tapping his pen on the conference table. Then he spoke – "Jacob. My friend. You are brilliant, brilliant, brilliant."

The bus ride over to the hotel was uneventful enough. Reilly sat next to the guy who was into Spiritualised. They exchanged a few words - "Nice to get some time off the phones." "Yeah." "That Call Butler's a good product. You seem to know how to sell it." "Yeah."

A couple of rows back, Mary was eliciting gasps by inflating the success of her crap band. "It's going really well," she was saying, "we were in NME last week." Reilly knew this to be true, but it was a statement that needed qualifying. He wanted to scream, "Yes you were in NME - in the fucking GIG GUIDE! Let's all be in the NME - simply fax them the date and venue for your shite band and hey presto - you're a pop star." He kept quiet. She could wait.

Western Telecom had hired the largest conference suite, it was huge. There were five hundred chairs set out in rows, facing a stage. As Reilly walked in, Moby was booming from the PA, one of those tasteful tunes off the car adverts. Reilly slinked away from his team mates and found himself a seat. He'd heard a bit about these launch parties although he'd never before seen one first hand. Apparently, they got some big cheese from head office to say a few things about the last quarter's results, hand out some awards and stuff. Reilly was getting used to this kind of thing, and he sat down, ready to soak up some corporate mind-control.

His eyes were drawn to the stage. There was a huge plasma screen, and in front of it some kind of pulpit.

The hall gradually filled up, and the lights came down. Through the darkness, Fatboy Slim's *Right Here, Right Now* started up, and people started clapping. After a few bars, the plasma screen burst into life, the company logo pulsing through a range of psychedelic colours, and finally exploding into a million pieces. The screen went black, the music stopped.

Then a voice from the darkness - "Are you ready Western Telecom Telemarketing Division?"

Reilly's colleagues, having done this before no doubt, screamed as one - "YES!" Reilly remained silent.

"I can't hear you! I said - are you ready?"

"YES!!"

"Are you really, really ready?"

"YES! YES!"

"Then please give it up for Spencer Drummond, Western Telecom's new Director of Acquisitions – Comin' Atcha!"

The crowd went wild. Just wild. Absolutely mental. The stage lights went up, revealing Spencer Drummond who was standing at the pulpit. His face filled the plasma screen. He was a plump, faintly idiotic-looking man in his late thirties, his hair closely shaved in an attempt to tackle his baldness.

He was sweating profusely and he looked like he'd rather be

anywhere else in the world.

"Colleagues. Big up massive respec' in da area," he said, in a stiff BBC accent.

There were more cheers, and a smattering of embarrassed laughter.

Spencer pushed on, slightly awkwardly. "Now I expect you're all wondering what a boring old stuffed shirt like me is doing using phrases like 'massive respec.'" He paused for laughter, which was forthcoming. It was very clear that he hadn't written this himself, his body language and jerky eyes screamed *Not My Idea*.

"Well," he said, "let me explain. As you all know, the theme for Quarter 2 was 'In The Army Now,' and I'll be handing out awards to the winners of the 'Most Enemy Kills' incentive. But more of that later.

"Now I know you'll be wondering what this quarter's theme will be…"

More cheers.

"Well I'm pleased to announce that Quarter 3's theme will be… 'Ring Ring, Bling Bling.'" Nelly's *Hot In Here* started playing in the background. "That's right, home boys and home girls, this quarter we're all going to be keeping it real, and taking care of business and making plenty of dead presidents. Or I'll damn well bust a cap in your asses."

Spencer, seemingly now resigned to his discomfort, pulled on a baseball cap, back to front, and slipped on some dark glasses. "Big shout out for the Western Telecom Telemarketing Division massive!" he said.

Reilly swung a look around the room, hoping for a face that mirrored his own – aghast. But none was forthcoming. His colleagues were loving it, shrieking and clapping like schoolchildren, apparently happy to accept without dismay what was being shovelled their way.

And now Spencer was gone, and the plasma screen was running through a sequence of photographs and moving images

- rap stars with Western Telecom logos poorly super-imposed on top - Missy Elliot, with a cheaply super-imposed telephone in her hand, a digitally altered Eminem forced into wearing a Western Telecom T-shirt. Interspersed were stills of Mercedes, tacky jewellery and other crass symbols of wealth.

Reilly slumped into his seat, open-mouthed, incredulous. Terrified.

Five o'clock already, and time for a look at the internet. A few of his regular favourites and onto then his email. Hey, three new. He scanned down the list, and his heart almost stopped. There was a mail from S. He opened it –

Hey Jacob – bet this is a surprise!

Sorry I've been crap at staying in touch. Anyway, I've had an eventful few weeks, and to cut a long story short, I'm back in the old country. Staying at my folks at the moment and hopefully have some work lined up in London Village – would love to catch up – are you still in Bristol?

S

He clicked on reply and positioned his hands over the keyboard. The words wouldn't come. He did want to see her, but didn't know how to reply. He did the mature thing: bottled it, logged off and headed for his car.

Reilly was watching *Pet Rescue* when Jacob got back. Some poor rabbit's teeth were out of control, the narrator was explaining that in the wild this would be a fatal problem.

"Jacob."

"Hello, Reilly."

"Good day, mate?"

"Yeah, bit freaked out though – got an email from S, she's

back in England, wants to catch up."

"Oh yeah. Nice one. I went to Nuremberg."

The rabbit was now in the vet's surgery, looking pensive. The vet was explaining what he would do. He was going to knock the fucker out and saw off his teeth. Reilly was appalled.

"Jesus, that's disgusting. What sort of sick bastard saws off rabbits' teeth for a living?"

Jacob didn't answer. The vet fired up his saw and was away, ripping through rabbit enamel.

"Jesus," repeated Reilly.

"Fucking hell," was all Jacob could muster.

"Jacob mate. Pub?"

"Pub. Yeah."

Brand new you're retro

The support band were on. The paying tour support. And they weren't very good. Reilly was off at the bar, fighting through the scrum, trying to top up on the Valpolicella he'd been stuck into before they left the flat. Jacob was confiding in Stevie, shouting over the band to make himself heard.

"…so she's coming down to stay next weekend," he said.

"Well, that's good, isn't it?"

"I guess so, yes."

"How do you know her again – you were an item, right?"

"Yeah, years ago. It was pretty serious, we moved in together. Things got messy and we fell out. She went travelling round Australia to get her head together and think things through. And she didn't come back, ended up marrying some Aussie."

"Shit Jacob, that's rough."

Jacob tried to sound nonchalant - "It was a long time ago now. I mean, if she'd got in contact any sooner I would have told her to fuck off, but, you know, it's all in the past. I assume that it didn't work out with the Aussie and that's why she's back."

"What's with her name – S?"

"Oh, she's called Sharon, but she hates it, everyone's always called her S."

"Fair enough, Sharon's a shocking name."

"Yeah."

The band were ploughing on gamely. They were a stodgy,

guitar-driven affair, weird rhythm changes and sparse vocals. Didn't really work. A few kids at the front were nodding along, trying to get into it, but it wasn't happening for them.

"So anyway, Jacob my friend, how you getting on with those demos? I could tell you were pretty excited about it last time I saw you."

"I'm just listening to the songs over and over, writing notes, getting a feel for them. I'm going to start getting some loops and samples together probably next week, start bulking them out a bit."

"Excellent. I tell you what, you two are better than this shite."

"Oh, they're doing their best. They're probably nervous, supporting the Nu-Birds at the Fleece. They're only young."

Stevie laughed. "So Jacob, what are you going to do with these songs, I mean what's the plan?"

"Well, once I've got these full demos done, I'm going to book some gigs, try to get a buzz going. Then I reckon I'll start contacting the record companies to see if there's any interest. Hopefully a label will then give us a deal and we can record an album."

"What does Reilly reckon?"

"I don't really know. He always changes the subject and starts ranting when I start talking about the practicalities. I guess that side of things is going to be up to me. He'll go along with it I'm sure."

Reilly came back from the bar, three plastic pints in his hands. He had a couple of girls in Nu-Birds T-shirts following him. Jacob and Stevie took their pints and waited for an introduction.

"Reilly?" asked Stevie, nodding at the girls.

"Oh, these two latched on to me at the bar," offered Reilly by way of explanation.

"Hi," beamed one of them, "are you guys in Reilly's band?" Americans. Great teeth.

"He is. *He* isn't." explained Reilly.

"Awesome, I'm Denise, this is Josie. We love your music

scene. You must be Jacob, your band sounds awesome. What was that funny thing you said back there Reilly?"

"I said, 'my band is so good you wouldn't be able to comprehend it. It would blow your tiny mind.'"

"That was it." Denise let out a raucous laugh.

Jacob instantly fancied her. And Josie too. It occurred to him that copping off with a well-groomed American college girl might be just the kind of ego massage he needed at the moment.

Josie spoke. "We love you British guys, your accents are so cute. Jacob, are you Reilly's guitarist?"

A bit of attention when the three of them were out was nothing new. It wasn't unusual for Reilly's rugged looks and fuck off attitude to prompt a certain kind of girl to ask if he was in a band. The T-shirt he was wearing tonight ('OVEREDUCATED AND UNDERWHELMED') wouldn't have deflected any attention either. Stevie's easy Brummie charm and winner's smile were always a hit, and Jacob himself – well, he dressed alright, wasn't short or fat or ugly. He had boyish features that some girls seemed to go for. He did alright.

"I play guitar among other things. Also play a bit of bass, my main thing is programming drum loops and..." Too much information, she was losing interest. He corrected himself - "yeah, I'm the guitarist."

Stevie jumped in - "Are you from New York?"

"Yeah! Well, Long Island. How did you know?"

"Your accent. I've been there a few times. Business."

"Awesome, what do you do?"

Stevie was so good at this stuff. He glanced over at Jacob, a cheeky glint in his eye.

"Actually, I'm a Veterinary Psychologist."

"Wow!" said Josie, her attention now fully turned to Stevie.

Jacob downed his weak Heineken as quick as he could, in an effort to buy an excuse out of this conversation. Reilly and Denise were also now deep in conversation. She was reacting to him with textbook hair-flicking and arm-touching. Meanwhile,

Stevie was now into his familiar bullshit spiel on manic depressive budgerigars and bulimic cats. Jacob was the spare part. He headed to the bar as the support band ended their set with a squall of feedback and a muffled "fank yooo brizzel."

Jacob joined the queue, and using the back of his arm, wiped away the sweat from his forehead. It was getting hot in here. A big crowd tonight, and a real buzz about the place. It was definitely happening for the Nu-Birds. There were the expected throngs of indie boys, long sleeve T-shirts and Docs. But a lot of girls too, always a sign that a band had broken out of the indie ghetto. Everyone seemed to be wearing a Nu-Birds T-shirt, and everyone seemed to be glancing at their watches and up at the stage, wondering when the latest saviours of rock would appear. The atmosphere reminded Jacob of seeing Oasis here back in '94. That gig had a sense of history about it, everyone there seemed to know they would be able to impress their friends in years to come, simply by having been there, in the tiny Fleece and Firkin, before the band went supernova.

Jacob had actually played here himself once. He'd stood on that very same wooden stage under the burning lights, wrestling with his heavy bass guitar. He'd been in a Nirvana-inspired band back in college called Zepher Man. A tight little three piece, all quiet/loud dynamics, catchy melodies delivered in a second-hand Seattle accent. And they really weren't that bad, *Venue* had written them up, concluding that "Bristol grunge has never sounded so fresh."

A local label offered to fund a single, and about fifty people had turned up for their show at the Fleece. It was all happening. A young Jacob had been totally bowled over by the experience, by the possibility of making a living doing what he loved. They were great days. Of course, it all fell apart. Ryan, the singer, decided he'd rather take his bar exams and become a legal eagle: and that was that.

Jacob finally got to the bar, and assumed the pose, his elbows in the sticky spilt alcohol and a tenner waving in his hand. He felt a tap on the shoulder. It was little Alex from the Flyer, bless him.

"Jacob, thought that was you - get us a pint of Strongbow, will you?" He handed him a fiver.

"No problem."

Jacob got served next. For himself, he got another Heineken and a double Bells, no ice. He took a swig of the beer and dumped in the whiskey in an effort to beef up the alcohol volume.

"Alex! Managed to get the night off then?"

"Oh yeah, wouldn't have missed this. They're a great band."

"I thought the single was alright, I haven't heard the album yet."

"I'll lend it you, it's fucking excellent. They're on Jools Holland on Friday. Oh and they're headlining Reading on the Sunday."

"Right." Jacob couldn't share Alex's greasy-haired indie kid enthusiasm.

"I saw Reilly when I came in, he's with some fit bird, lucky bastard. I thought he hated the Nu-Birds though."

"Oh believe me, he does," said Jacob, "he hates any band that has a tune on a car advert."

"It's a good advert that," offered Alex.

"I think he finds their stuff a bit derivative. And the lyrics *are* a little bit ropey."

"I reckon they're great. Definitely as good as the Stereophonics. They're going to be huge. A mate of mine knows the manager, told me that the US label signed them for one and a half million."

"How much?! Fuck me." Jacob almost fell right over. "That can't be right, isn't the music industry supposed to be in decline?"

"I suppose that's why they paid that much. Wanted to make sure they got them."

"Shit," said Jacob, shaking his head.

"Great venue this," said Alex.

"It is mate. Nice and intimate. I like the low stage myself, makes you feel part if it, don't you think?"

"Too right, are you up for a bit of a mosh later?"

Jacob laughed. "No way, I don't really do that anymore. Don't like exchanging sweat with strangers. I've got a feeling you might see Reilly down the front later though."

"Nice one."

Jacob looked up to see Stevie gratuitously snogging poor Josie. How did he do it? And Reilly was definitely in with Denise. Fair play to him, a bit of action might do him some good. He realised he was stuck here with Alex.

"So, what's the stuff on the album like then?"

Reilly was kind of enjoying himself. He was feeling good. He was properly pissed now and this American was actually quite a laugh. She was a lot brighter than he'd given her credit for. Turned out that her brother was a promoter in the States and she'd helped him out from time to time. She'd worked with Yo La Tengo, Sparklehorse and Elliot Smith. Reilly was a little disappointed that she hadn't dealt with the Afghan Whigs, but she knew all about them, even had an amusing anecdote to relay.

He was definitely attracted to her, but knew he wasn't going to do anything about it. Wasn't going to take her home. The thought of making a predatory move, a reptilian male advance, it repulsed him. That clumsy etiquette negotiating an exit by cab, the weary ritual of undressing and the tangling and untangling of unfamiliar limbs did not appeal. He could already taste the guilty embarrassment of the morning after, the things he'd say and not mean, the things he'd have taken that couldn't be given back. Years of sporadic promiscuity had left him jaded, ambivalent. He couldn't be bothered, couldn't remember the last time that he had.

He glanced over at Stevie and Josie, who were now snogging like teenagers. Denise also looked up at them, and then back to

Reilly. He decided that now was the time to fuck things up, to destroy this rapport that was developing. He asked her about September the 11th. Her face fell.

"Shit, well I saw the second plane hit. I thought it was a missile. I didn't know what the fuck was going on, it felt like the end of the world. You know, I've got friends who work down there. Not in the towers, but on that block."

"Who do you think did it?"

"What do you mean? What sort of question is that?"

"Let me tell you about a theory I have…"

The air was thick with the smell of alcohol, cigarettes and dry ice. The lights came down and the kids started pushing toward the stage. A chorus of "Nu-Birds! Nu-Birds!" started up, Alex joining in and setting Jacob's teeth on edge. It just wasn't the done thing. One by one, dark figures emerged onto the stage. Firstly, the drummer, locating his sticks and sitting down. The bassist and the guitarist followed, slipping on their instruments, heads down, cool as fuck.

Finally the front man emerged to huge applause, a clenched fist held high above his head.

"Hey hey, Bristol town! Let's go!" he screamed, and the band started up.

Alex was now jumping up and down, spilling cider over Jacob's leg. He was oblivious. He turned to Jacob - "This one's called *Give it Up*," he shouted, "fucking amazing tune, man!"

Reilly was struggling to make himself heard over the shite now coming out of the speakers. God, he hated this band.

"All I'm saying is, right - I don't find it inconceivable that a government that is bent on reducing civil liberties at home and expanding influence abroad would make a sacrifice in order to create a climate in which both were possible."

Denise was now addressing Reilly as a psychiatric nurse would a patient, the desire having drained from her eyes - "You're saying the US government flew the planes?"

"No, I'm saying it's possible they knew about it and allowed it to happen. I don't want to believe that it's possible, but I reckon the question needs to be asked - I mean, where were the air force?"

"It's been fun talking to you Reilly, but I've gotta go. Take care of yourself."

She patted his arm and retreated into the crowd, dragging a confused Josie with her.

Stevie burst out laughing and made his way over to Reilly. "What happened then? That pheromone spray not working for you?"

He ignored the question, replying instead with, "Can you believe how bad this band are? They're even worse than last time I saw them I reckon. And I think they need to know…"

Alex had downed his cider and surged for the mosh pit, leaving Jacob alone again. The bar wasn't busy anymore and Jacob propped himself against it.

He took a long pull on his cigarette and tried to get into this band. Despite the mania erupting around him, they left him cold. They were solid, efficient. That first song had a decent middle-eight, he noted, and the guitarist was good at what he did.

But he couldn't shake the feeling that he'd heard all this before - The La's, Cast, The Real People, Dodgy, The Bees, Ocean Colour Scene, blah blah blah.

What was he missing here? He looked around at his fellow bar-dwellers and saw them determinedly nodding along. He felt desperately out of touch, but he didn't feel wrong. The song finished.

"Thanks Bristol! We love ya! Keep music live, man," instructed the singer, "This one's called *Big Sky*."

Oh yeah, Jacob knew this one. This was the single that was all over the radio. It was catchy enough, a good summer pop song.

The band bounced along toward the chorus, and the Fleece sung as one -

"You've gotta let it in,
You've gotta let it out,
You've gotta big sky,
Makes me wanna shout."

Jacob rolled his eyes, took another drink. Stevie appeared from the crowd dripping with sweat, steam rising from his head. He spotted Jacob and mouthed "fucking hell," as he approached.

"Jakey! There you are. It's mental in here tonight, good band this lot. You want another pint?"

"Yeah, thanks. Where's Josie?"

"Don't know, mate. Easy come, easy go, ships that pass and all that. What you drinking?"

"Heineken."

"Nice. Hey, Reilly's headed down the front."

Big Sky came to a polite end and the crowd went wild. Jacob, his pint now finished and his hands free, clapped too. Stevie let out an ear-splitting "yeahhhh!" as he collected the drinks off the bar. On stage, the Nu-Birds were tuning up. A fat roadie handed the singer an acoustic guitar and plugged it in for him. Here comes *the ballad*, thought Jacob.

"Thank you Bristol people, it's great to be here. We love your trip-hop," said the singer. There were loud cheers.

"Now we're going to slow things down a bit - this is a song called *Some Day Soon.*" More cheers.

"It's about having to sell your records to pay your rent." More cheers, and some clapping too. And then an unmistakable voice from somewhere down the front -

"Like you'd fucking know, you logo-wearing whore!"

Stevie quickly looked at Jacob, a delighted grin on his face.

"Was that...?"

Jacob nodded. Stevie started to laugh.

Then the voice again: "Fuck off, you talentless vadge! And

what is this shit you're playing?"

Now Jacob was laughing too. He couldn't fault Reilly's opinion of this band, and his own safety wasn't threatened by this outburst. The singer spoke, "Hey man, whoever said that - I don't want to make you sad. Go someplace else. Peace." There were loud cheers of approval.

"And you're supposed to be saving our lives, you useless fucking knobs. You're a hobby band - hobby, hobby, hobby!"

Stevie was now crying with laughter, bent over and holding his stomach. The singer spoke again, he was riled now. "Security, get this guy out of here."

And with that the Nu-Birds launched into *Some Day Soon*, providing a jangly-rock background to Reilly's heavy-handed ejection from the premises. It was curiously epic, a cinematic soundtrack for his comic removal. From where he was standing, Jacob couldn't see Reilly, but he saw the faceless tornado of security sweep through the crowd to suck up the trouble-maker.

"You and me,
Will always be,
Shining bright,
Through the night," crooned the singer, as several cigarette lighters lit up the Fleece.

And then the big chorus –
"We're gonna fly,
so high,
Some day soon."

Stevie turned to Jacob - "Suppose we should go and find Reilly…"

"Yeah. I've heard enough of this lot anyway."

Jacob followed Stevie to the exit, his stride fortified by a new resolve. Serpico were so good, so much better than the Nu-Birds. Musically, lyrically, stylistically. It was time to stop thinking, making notes, procrastinating. He was heading straight home to get to work on those demos.

(She's a) Satellite

Jacob looked out over the platforms, and watched the dirty trains as they slid, one by one, into the station. Temple Meads was now heaving with travellers and transients, coming and going. There were trains heading into Bristol from all over - Exeter, Birmingham, Cardiff, and of course, London. To Jacob, the arrivals suggested an invasion. An influx of people with better lives than his own. People with careers, families, hobbies and futures. Their arrival threatened to dilute him, negate him. He tried to shake off this unwelcome feeling.

He glanced over to the list of departures. He read the destinations as escape routes. Realised he could hand over forty quid and be in Oxford by mid-afternoon. A short bus hop would take him home to the middle-class bubble of Kidlington. He could drop in on his folks, alleviating the guilt he felt at not having seen them since Christmas. He could ring round his school friends and be drinking in the Black Horse by 7.00pm. The compulsion briefly overwhelmed him, and he started walking to the ticket office. But he thought better of it, checked himself, and went back to his spot opposite the newsagents, where he'd agreed to meet S.

Jacob was all nerves. He blew his nose again, a fizzing shot of amphetamine scorching the membranes in his nostrils, bitter and dirty. S's train would be here in three minutes, and he knew he looked like shit. He hoped she would too. Hoped she would look older, fattened up, got rough around the edges. He hoped she'd picked up one of those repugnant cockney-aussie accents and had her hair cut short. He hoped she was down at his level.

It had been a mistake to have that wrap of speed after the pub. The wrap he'd had stashed inside a book since Reading last year, and had previously had neither the stomach nor the inclination to consume. He'd intended to stay up and get the rest of those demos done, have the whole album mapped out by morning.

The logic was unquestionable. Piecing together the drums, bass and effects was an arduous process, and concentration was key. Using the toy-like music software on the Playstation, he'd build up the drum loops one by one, brick by brick. A bass thud here, a cymbal crash there. There were various technical problems to surmount, the most difficult being pacing the drums along to Reilly's vocal and guitar demos. A BPM of between fifty and sixty usually did the trick, but it was a frustrating process, all detail. Last night, he'd got half way through a track called *Lower Maudlin Street,* realised it wasn't working, and had to scrap everything. Start again. The speed had a filthy punch to it and he'd spent the rest of the night watching TV, his mind racing through an assault course of hideous notions and hare-brained ideas, all now forgotten.

He'd crashed out at about eight o'clock, with an empty head and a gut full of regret. He had three and half hours of dirty, sweaty sleep before his alarm intervened. A couple of coffees and a careful drive across town and he was at the station, ready to meet S.

Jacob looked across the open platforms as S's train pulled in. A calmness came over him now that the moment was upon him. Too late to escape, he told himself, just go with it.

The Paddington passengers began emerging from the underpass in front of him. He scanned the faces as they rose the stairs, waiting for the hit of recognition. Strangers, all of them. Students, tourists, wasters. And then emerging into the light, S.

She saw him, cracked a warm smile and ran over. She dropped her rucksack at Jacob's feet and without speaking gave him a familiar hug. Jacob hugged her back. It felt great.

She let go - "It's good to see you, Jacob."

"And you. You look great, you haven't changed."

"Well you've had a haircut, and you look taller somehow. But judging by your eyes, I'd say you've still got an interest in pharmacology." She laughed. "Anyway, I'm starving. Let's go for a proper English pub lunch. I'm paying."

The summer rain lashed down as they drove through the city, the downpour giving Bristol a surreal underwater appearance. S pointed out new pubs, clubs and shops; pointed out old landmarks; and cooed or grimaced depending on the memory each location provoked.

"Has Bristol got more dirty, or is it me? I remember it being nicer than this."

"I think it's your standards that have changed, S."

As they drove toward Whiteladies Road, Jacob surreptitiously inserted the Serpico cassette and waited for a reaction. He felt a rush of pride as the beautiful noise rose from the speakers. His noise, his band.

Last night had been a wash out, but Jacob did have much to be proud about. Over the preceding evenings, he'd broken the back of the demos, and despite the successive set-backs, the album was falling into place. His programming had added a dimension to Reilly's songs, adding pace and space, atmosphere and movement. Jacob had a recurring thought, one which he tried to head off at the pass every time - something truly special was taking shape here.

"This tape's good," S said to Jacob's delight. "Who is it, Radiohead?"

"It sounds nothing like Radiohead," Jacob snapped back. "Well, bits of it do I suppose."

"No, I like it. He's got a great voice. Who is it?"

"This is my new band."

"No way. It's amazing. Last time I saw you, you were making that awful jungle music with that guy Giles."

"Drum 'n' bass, not jungle. And it wasn't awful."

"Hmmm. I beg to differ. Is Giles still about?"

"No, he moved to London. He's got a record deal now, does all this ambient stuff. One of his tunes is on a building society advert. He made a packet."

"Wow, a building society ad eh? Rock and roll. Are we there yet?"

"Yes S, this is it, you remember the Coach and Horses, don't you? Still does an excellent roast."

"Great."

Inside the pub, and out of the rain, Jacob was at home. The Coach and Horses was all old oak, warm laughter and Saturday newspapers. Jacob felt better, having got the initial meeting out of the way. He noted that S's presence hadn't dredged up the bitterness of their break up, but the everyday knockabout humour that they'd shared.

"Pubs smell different in the day time," he said, but S wasn't listening. She was already ordering the lunches.

Jacob found a table and rolled a cigarette. He now felt incredibly together considering his lack of sleep, but there was an intermittent twitch in his right eyelid, and his nose and throat were a little raw. But he could see the way out - an afternoon of drinking and catching up, watching the rain run down the pub's windows and talking about the old days.

S came over from the bar, a pint in each hand and a meal ticket stub in her teeth. The reassuring smell of pub lunch drifted from the kitchen, and the juke box was playing *Big Area*, a classic slice of over-blown FM rock.

"I love this song," said Jacob, "It's brilliantly, magnificently crap. You know what I mean?"

S laughed, "yeah I do. I remember the singer, prowling around the stage on Top of the Pops, swishing his pony tail around and miming along. Very earnest, he was. Can I nick one of your rollies Jacob?"

"Of course. Thanks for the pint, by the way. Just what I needed."

"Hair of the dog is it?"

"Sort of yeah, usual Saturday thing."

S lit her cigarette and took a swig of lager. Jacob looked her up and down, trying to work out if he still fancied her. She met his eye, catching him out.

"So anyway Jacob, what's going on with you?"

"What do you mean?"

"I mean your life - what are you up to?"

"Oh shit, right. Well, not a lot. Trying to get this band off the ground, really."

"Jacob, you're useless! Of course you're trying to get this band off the ground. You were always trying to get *a* band off the ground - I mean all the other stuff. Job, house, romantic attachments…"

"God, I don't know, nothing of note."

"OK." S sighed, and tried another tack. "What does it say about you on Friends Reunited?"

Jacob laughed "That creepy fucking website? I wrote something like - Living in Bristol, working in marketing, would love to hear from anyone who remembers me."

"OK - so you're using your degree then?"

"Yeah. It's not as good as it sounds, though - I work for this water cooler supplier, it's all business to business marketing. It's pretty dull. I mean, I can do the job, but I'm hoping I won't have to for too much longer.

"I know you'll take the piss, but this album we're doing, that stuff you heard in the car, it's well, it's in a different league to anything I've done before. If this doesn't get me a record deal then nothing will. If it doesn't work then that's it, I give up, it's euthanasia time."

S looked him in the eye, her expression somewhere between affection and pity.

"Well, good on you Jacob, go for it," she said finally.

The rain changed pace, a sudden acceleration and it was hammering the windows, making everyone in the pub stop and look out.

"You bring your snorkel with you, Bob?" shouted an old guy at the bar.

"No, looks like we're stuck here," Bob replied. The pub laughed as one. They were all stuck here.

"So, where are you living then?" asked S.

"I've got a flat over in Bishopston, just off Gloucester Road."

"Did you buy it?"

"Oh no, still renting. Bristol's really expensive now, I couldn't afford to buy anything. My mate Stevie's an estate agent and he's loving it. Raking in the commission, he is."

"So are you living… with a girl?"

Jacob laughed, "No. I live with this guy Reilly, the singer." He knew he hadn't answered her question, not really.

"So you and Reilly are best mates as well as colleagues?"

"Yeah. Well, no actually, now I think about it. Reilly's a bit unusual. Like, I've known him for three years or so, we've shared a flat most of the time, but I don't really know much about him, not really. I know he grew up in Newbury. I know he went to Glasgow University, studied Theology or Phrenology or something weird.

"He has strong opinions, he's a nightmare with a few drinks inside him, starts arguing with strangers and stuff."

"Sounds like a bit of a weirdo."

"He's not. Well, he is, yeah. He just thinks too much. He's actually a really decent person, that's where the anger comes from I reckon."

"He's got high standards to himself, and others. One of those."

"Yes, exactly. It's like he can't tolerate any sort of human fallibility, he sees it as an injustice. I don't know, you just have to take him as he is."

"Well, he can sing."

"You've got that right – he's the perfect front man really. Dysfunctional, pseudo-intellectual, good-looking, photogenic - the NME love all that shit, they'd make him into a god."

"Good looking eh? You should get him down here, I might like to meet this Reilly."

"Calm down S, he wouldn't be your type."

S laughed, and Jacob knew he had taken the bait. Fell into the trap. He rolled another cigarette as she did the same, a satisfied grin spread across her face.

Jacob lit his cigarette, excused himself and headed for the pay phone. He dialled Stevie's mobile.

"Hello?"

"Stevie my friend. Fancy a pint?"

"Do I ever, where are you?"

"Coach and Horses."

"Sweet. See you in a bit."

Then he called Reilly -

"Yes."

"Reilly, I'm in the Coach and Horses with S, do you want to join us?"

"Who is this?"

"Fuck's sake Reilly. You know who it is."

"Jacob?"

"Yes, it's Jacob."

"What the fuck are you doing on Whiteladies?"

"Come on Reilly, it's not so bad. This is a nice pub. Some of the new ones aren't so bad either."

"Jacob you fool. You can't polish a turd."

Click.

Reilly slammed the phone down. Why was Jacob drinking on Whiteladies? That was miles away, a cab ride. And he didn't like the sound of S either, Jacob had mentioned that she liked the newer Manics albums, but thought *The Holy Bible* was crap. How could he have a conversation with someone like that? But the lure of a cold pint was too strong. And he really needed to talk to Jacob about those demos.

He turned off the TV, and went to the bathroom to brush his teeth. The incessant rain had exposed the leak in the bathroom ceiling, highlighting Reilly's stark domestic circumstances. It was too much. He needed air, needed to get out. He spat out the toothpaste and met his reflection in the mirror. He stared himself out, trying to work out who this person was. Crow's feet, three-day stubble and red, red eyes. He looked away from the mirror and down at his clothes. His jeans looked stale, generic, he looked like *anybody*; today's t-shirt read "WRONG PLACE, WRONG TIME."

Reilly marched to the front door and out into the rain.

"So," stuttered Jacob, "I assume you're single at the moment, then."

"Yep. Divorced actually. Doesn't that sound weird? I'm a divorcee. I mean, I'm only twenty-six. That's life, I guess."

Now it was Jacob's turn to wear a satisfied grin. "So what happened? Did he chuck too many snags on the barbie or something? What was his name again? Bruce?"

"You cheeky git. You know full well his name wasn't Bruce. Isn't Bruce, I should say. He's called David. And enough of your stereotypes, he's a good man, but it just wasn't right."

"Yeah, I'm sorry. What really happened? Did he rack off with that sticky-beak Mrs Mangel to the Bungle Bungles?"

"Very funny Jacob, very funny."

"Sorry, I'm finished, I swear."

"Well, if you really want to know - we had a stupid argument and it all came to a head. He did this thing, he had this thing that he did, that just drove me insane. It kind of became the straw that broke the camel's back, so to speak."

"What was it?"

"I have to explain this - I was extremely bored, we'd both been aware for a long time that things weren't right. I was a photographer when I left England, you remember all that stuff I used to do. I told myself I could be happy by shooting the countryside in my spare time and doing weddings to make money. It was going fine, and I *was* making money. But it wasn't what I wanted to do when I started, it wasn't right."

"So…"

"Sorry, so the point is, David was just a full on Aussie - you know, likes a cold beer on a hot day, his idea of fashion is a polo shirt with a racing car on the front. All that stuff. And I probably only married him for the passport, in retrospect. That was really the reason, I guess, but you can't leave someone for that can you?"

"I don't know, sounds fair enough to me."

"Shut up. Well he was such a nice guy. But, he did do this one thing that just drove me insane."

"What was it?"

"It was such a small thing. It's sounds silly now. But you know I'm a bit particular with pronunciation?"

"Er, yeah."

"Well, he pronounced the word skeleton - skellington."

Jacob started laughing. "Go on."

"I noticed him saying it a couple of times, you know it's not a word you use a lot. But one time I just had to say something and he swore blind that he was right, that the word was skellington. I mean, he sounded retarded. Ridiculous."

Jacob was really laughing now.

"So it was all forgotten about until about three months ago and he said it again. There was some documentary on TV and the narrator was saying something like, 'This skeleton dates back to Roman times.'

"So I say to David, have you noticed how he pronounced the word? And he said, 'Yeah I heard him, he said skellington.' So I just flipped out, packed my bags, went to a friend's place for a few days."

"That's too funny S. You obviously haven't changed a bit. Poor Bruce."

"David, it's David."

"Whatever."

Jackals, false grails: the lonesome era

Stevie was first to arrive. He closed up his golf umbrella and hung up his Berghaus rain jacket by the door. Not a drop of water on him, despite the downpour outside. He walked over to the table, where Jacob and S were tucking into their roast beef.

"Heh heh! Jacob. And this must be the lovely S." He took her hand and kissed it. Jacob looked on. Smooth bastard.

"Are you Reilly?" S asked.

Stevie laughed. "No, no. I'm Stevie. I'm a veterinary…"

"Shut up, Stevie. And sit down."

"Anything you say, Jacob. But first I'm going to the bar. Can I get you anything, S?"

"Oh yeah, thanks. I'll have a pint of Stella."

"Jacob?"

"Same please. Thanks, Stevie."

"What about the car?" asked S.

"Oh, I'll get it tomorrow."

"Heh, that's the spirit," said Stevie, slapping Jacob's back extravagantly before heading for the bar, laughing.

"He's very charming," said S as she chucked salt over her chips, "did he say he was a vet?"

"Er, no. He's just being stupid. Stevie's an estate agent, would you believe it."

"But he was a vet?"

"No, he *was* a dealer. That's where all his money's from."

"Ah! That explains how you know him then!" S jabbed her fork in Jacob's direction to ram home the point.

"Shut up S, I don't really do drugs anymore. Really I don't. There's only so much you can take." He lowered his voice. "Beer's my only vice these days."

"And smoking."

"Yeah. And smoking."

"And hopeless daydreaming about pop stardom."

Jacob's cheeks reddened. She had him there. Nail on the head.

Stevie returned with the Stellas, and a Smirnoff Ice for himself. S turned to Stevie - "So, I hear you're a big time class A drug peddler."

"Aha, no. Not quite. You really shouldn't believe everything this plum tells you. He tends to exaggerate to make himself seem more interesting."

S laughed, "I know, I know."

"To be fair, he's telling the truth to an extent. I used to move small amounts of MDMA to make ends meet."

Jacob almost spat his food out - "Small amounts! Fucking hell. I don't know how you're not in prison, Stevie! Remember that boot load of pills you drove down to Glastonbury? And you bought your flat with cash for fuck's sake."

"Jacob, Jacob, be calm." Stevie looked at S and raised his eyebrows. "He's being a bit over-dramatic. I sold a few pills as a favour to a friend of a friend. Then I sold a few more. I realised it was a very good way to make money. It kind of escalated a bit, I did alright but then I got out of it."

He had S's full attention now. "Why did you get out? Did it get a bit heavy?"

"Not at all. All that stuff you hear about guns and knee-cappings…well, I'm sure it goes on, but I never saw any of that. Never sold to kids or anyone who looked like they might suffer. Never had to fight for my turf or any of that, never even raised my voice. It was a good time."

"So why did you stop?"

"I just kind of figured it was only a matter of time before someone tipped off some CID hero. Never liked the idea of prison."

"Fair enough."

Stevie took a swig and turned to Jacob - "Where's the front man then? Is he coming out?"

"He'll be here."

The three of them drank away the afternoon, S freaking out Jacob and Stevie with tales of deadly insects and deadlier snakes, of forty-degree heat without air conditioning, of back-packer serial killers.

They talked about their university days, Jacob telling Stevie the one about S's attempt to photograph the entire Bristol homeless population over a weekend. She gave up after being chased through Broadmead by a guy with a knife - "He kept shouting 'I'm going to gut you like a fish!' I really thought I was going to die."

S told Stevie about Jacob blowing his whole term's grant on a guitar only for burglars to relieve him of it two weeks later - "I had forgotten that. Those fuckers broke my heart. I hope they got a good price for it."

By 5.30 Jacob's hangover was a distant memory. He was now drunk. Daylight drinking always gave Jacob a feeling of warmth, of calm. Six pints of Stella and Jacob had his own protective shield, a huge, down-filled duvet insulating and reassuring him. And now when he spoke, his pronunciation was approximate, the hint of a slur.

Stevie was deep in conversation with S, relaying the glorious details of Vanessa Feltz's nervous breakdown. S was howling with laughter. Jacob tuned out, and honed into the conversation on the next table. A couple of spotty indie kids were talking about the Nu-Birds gig.

"I'm telling you Brett, they're the best band in the world. Genius. And they really rock."

"Fuck yeah!"

"Even better than Snow Patrol."

"Fucking right."

"I loved the way he dealt with that heckler, so cool. A lot of bands would have risen to it. But he's just like, 'hey man, peace.' So cool."

Jacob sniggered to himself and looked up at the bar. Reilly walked in. About time. "Stevie, Reilly's here."

Stevie spun around, spotted Reilly and burst out laughing. "Reilly! Over here! What the fuck are you wearing?"

"What does it fucking look like?" replied Reilly as he walked over, "it's a fucking suit. Do they not have suits in Dudley or wherever the fuck you're from?"

"Not like that they don't! Where did you get it?"

"Oxfam."

Stevie fell off his stool, and just sat on the floor laughing. Tears began to flow down his cheeks. He was trying to say something.

"What?" demanded Reilly.

"Moseley," said Stevie, through his tears.

"What?"

"Moseley. I'm from Moseley."

"So?"

"The Greenwich Village of England."

"Oh, for fuck's sake!" said Reilly, now quite agitated.

Jacob spoke up. "It's a nice suit Reilly. A bit tight maybe."

Stevie doubled up again, gulping air - "He's walking round in a dead man's suit. Fucking dead man's suit."

"What's up with him?" asked Reilly, "Is he drunk?"

"Yes. We all are. And I'm S by the way."

"Hello."

Stevie's hysterics had attracted the attention of the rest of the pub, and the landlord was looking over with concern. Time to go.

"Come on," said Jacob, "next pub."

The Roo Bar was getting busy by the time they got there. The queue at the bar was three deep. Jacob got the drinks in as Reilly sulked about the choice of venue.

"Stevie, what are we doing here?" he asked. "This isn't a pub - it's fucking Alton Towers."

"Poor Reilly," said S, "it's not that bad. It's funny. A nice bit of Australiana in the middle of Bristol. And anyway, you were outvoted, fair's fair. Hang on, there's a table, let's grab it."

Reilly looked at S. Bossy cow. But a good-looking one. She had a great figure, pretty face, and her tan gave her a healthy, exotic look. And she dressed well. What the hell had she seen in that anaemic little runt Jacob?

Reilly followed Stevie and S to the table. He sat down and scanned his surroundings. There were boomerangs hanging from the wall above the bar, a portrait of Paul Hogan on the wall opposite. In the far corner there was a cave set back into the wall, stencilled aboriginal drawings on the walls. The pub seemed to be full of rugby lads and fleece-wearing girls. Reilly felt incredibly self-conscious in his suit and trainers. He had never wanted a beer so much in his life.

He realised S was talking to him - "I heard some of your music in the car. I thought it was great, I really did. You've got a great voice."

Here we go, some false praise as a conversation starter. "Oh yeah, what did you like about it?"

"It sounded natural, not forced. Does that make sense?"

"Yes. Yes it does."

Jacob was back with the beers. He sat down and drunkenly pushed each pint across the table to its owner, a stupid grin on his face. What a pisshead, thought Reilly. Time to start catching up. He took a swig and turned back to S. He wanted to continue hearing her comments.

"My only aim, when I write music, is for it to be sincere. I don't care if it's crap. The worst insult I could get would be that I'm trying to sound like someone else," he said.

"But every band has influences, right?"

"Of course. But it's what you take from it. Like, Jeff Buckley was brilliant, right. And then he died. And now you have all these bands that sound just like him. They think if they amp up their guitars the same way and sing in a swooping falsetto they'll be as good as Jeff."

"But they're not."

"Exactly. These bands like Coldplay are listening to the wrong parts. They're taking the wrong things from his music."

"What do you mean?"

"Well when *Grace* came out, it was desperately unfashionable. American rock was all ugly grunge, Kurt Cobain had only been dead for a year, and Blur were doing their cockney knees-up *Parklife* stuff. And Jeff brings out this elegantly produced, soulful, sexy record. And he sings like Nina Simone, not Kurt Cobain. And no one bought the fucking thing. He was totally out of step, *but* he sung with his own voice - that's what fucking Coldplay should pay attention to, not the type of mixing desk he used."

S reflected on Reilly's words, took a swig of beer, and replied, "but I quite like Coldplay."

"Well, yeah they've got some good songs, there's no denying it. I *quite* like them too. But I don't trust them, do you know what I mean? I don't *trust* them."

Stevie was ear-wigging. "Reilly the righteous!" he said.

"What's that?" asked Jacob.

"Reilly here, he's my hero. You should have your own column in *The Sun* mate. Your angry face slapped on the top, putting the world to rights - bring back hanging! Save the Pound! Don't trust Coldplay!"

"Fuck off, Stevie. But I am right, that's the point."

Jacob jumped in, slurring - "You're both right."

"Coldplay are loads better than Jeff Buckley anyway."

"Oh for fuck's sake, Stevie! That's like saying Shakin' Stevens is better than Elvis."

"It's true. Jeff Buckley was crap. And he couldn't fucking swim!"

"Shut up."

"You shut up."

"Oh go and listen to *Tomorrow People*, Mirage boy."

"Fuck off."

S spoke up. "Why don't all of you shut up? You two are supposed to be a band. Aren't bands supposed to like each other or something? You're on the same side."

A fair point, and well made. The three of them took a drink simultaneously, a silent contract to let it lie.

Reilly considered the best way to raise the subject of the demos with Jacob. Maybe it was best to wait until they were alone, he didn't want Stevie and S chucking in their tuppence worth. Maybe he could get him outside for a bit.

A familiar voice broke his train of thought.

"Fucking Serpico! It's fucking Serpico, can I have your autographs?"

It was Jimmy Reckon, now standing over the table, a travesty of leather and facial fluff, his lank shoulder-length hair and plaid shirt giving away his grunge leanings.

Reilly didn't look up. Jacob replied, trying to summon some enthusiasm. "You sarky bastard Jimmy. How are you?"

"Bloody great actually. It's all taking off for us now, I'll tell you. Fending off the record companies until we get the deal we want. We're moving to London next week."

"Oh yeah. Nice one. Which record companies?" asked Stevie.

Jimmy looked stumped - "Er, I can't really say at this stage. You know, it's a legal thing."

Bollocks it is, thought Jacob. Jimmy had always had an elastic idea of the truth, hence the nickname. In the brief period that Jacob had been Cloudfunk's lead guitarist Jimmy had told him a string of outlandish tales, which Jacob, at first, had believed. One winter night Jimmy phoned him at 3.00am and with breathless excitement told him that he'd sent a CD to Pearl

Jam's management company and had just a received a call from Eddie Vedder himself. Eddie wanted to congratulate Jimmy on his excellent voice and asked if Cloudfunk would be available to do a support slot next time Pearl Jam came to London. It was preposterous. Jacob told him so and was sacked for his lack of ambition.

In the years since there had been maybe half a dozen of these awkward chance meetings between the two. Jimmy would lie, Jacob would pretend to believe him.

"So Jacob, we're off to London. Our manager's got us a house in Battersea. We're booked on the gig circuit there. It's all happening man. We did a showcase at the Barfly last month and blew them away. I had A&Rs queuing up afterwards offering me all kinds of stuff - coke, girls, whatever. Cool or what? I didn't see him myself, but apparently Bono was there and he loved us. We're funky monkeys, man."

Jacob and Stevie were nodding, S was looking impressed. Reilly was still staring at his pint.

"So our manager's told us we've got to push on with this buzz. Get on it. We're thinking we might record the album in LA, maybe NY…"

Reilly slowly stood up and turned to face Jimmy.

"Alright, Reilly? Woah, what are you wearing?"

Reilly didn't reply, he just stared back at Jimmy.

"Are you OK man? Hey, we're playing Ashton Court tomorrow, are you going?"

Reilly still didn't reply. He slowly pulled back his arm, and with an open palm slapped Jimmy right across the face. It was astonishingly loud, a real Hollywood slap.

"Shit!" Screamed Jimmy as the rest of the pub looked round. "What was that for you freak?"

"Shut up," said Reilly. "Just shut up. Listen to yourself. Fucking A&Rs and showcases. Jesus! Have you actually got any songs?"

"Chill out, man. What are you talking about?"

Reilly pulled back his arm and calmly delivered another slap. Jacob jumped up as Jimmy held his cheek. "Reilly, what are you doing? Sit down."

Reilly did as instructed and calmly rolled a cigarette. Jacob put an arm around Jimmy, who was stunned, and led him away, out of the danger zone.

Reilly lit up and sat back in his chair. S and Stevie were staring at him with concern.

"What?" he asked.

"Sorry Reilly, that was just a bit, well, unusual," said Stevie.

"No, it wasn't. You heard him. He's a bloody business man."

"He's just making music, like you are," said S.

"I have nothing in common with that fucker. Nothing. He's forgotten what it's all about. And he thinks Pearl Jam are the best band in the world for fuck's sake! Fucking Pearl Jam!"

"It's just taste at the end of the day," said Stevie. "You make it sound like being into Pearl Jam makes you a bad person."

Reilly considered this for a moment. "Well yeah, that's pretty much how I see it."

Stevie shook his head with dismay and downed the rest of his pint.

"I'm well pissed," he said. "S. Where next?"

"I fancy King Street. And then The Thekla."

"Good plan S. Let's get the Jakester."

Idioteque

Reilly saw his opportunity and collared Jacob as they left Renato's. The walk from King Street to the Thekla would give him a few minutes to discuss the demos, the rain having stopped for the time being. Stevie and S walked on, ahead.

"Jacob, what's on at the Thekla tonight?"

"No idea, mate. DJs I guess, maybe a band downstairs. Ask Stevie."

"Doesn't matter. Look, we need to have a talk."

Jacob stopped dead and turned to face Reilly. "This isn't going to be heavy, is it? I'm having a bit of trouble just walking."

"Me too, actually." They started walking again anyway. "I just wanted to talk about what you've done with my songs."

"*Your* songs? I thought they were my songs now. That's what you said."

"I didn't say that."

"Yes, you did."

"Fuck it, whatever. What I wanted to say is that, I think what you've done so far is... well, it's fucking crap."

Jacob stopped again, swaying on the spot. He tried to look Reilly in the eye, but had trouble locating his face. He eventually found it and stared Reilly out.

"You ungrateful twat, Reilly. Do you know how fucking difficult it's been trying to build songs around your crap musicianship? You can't even keep time!"

"If you were any good as a producer, it wouldn't matter would it?"

Jacob turned and stormed on towards the club. Reilly shouted after him - "Hey! Wait!" He caught up with him and laid a hand on his shoulder.

"Jacob, I'm... er. Look, it's just that the songs don't sound like I expected them to. They sound cheap, amateurish."

"They're fucking *demos*, you idiot. They're not finished. I'm using an ancient four-track, the fucking drums are off the Playstation. Shit, I just need some proper digital equipment – we need to get into a recording studio like real bands do. It sounds amateurish because we're amateurs."

"Alright, alright. You know your stuff. I just think we're on the verge of something here, I don't want to fuck it up. Do you know what I mean?"

Jacob breathed a sigh of relief at this. At last Reilly was showing some ambition.

"Reilly, I know *exactly* what you mean. I try to keep it out of my mind, but I kind of know it's going to happen for us. I can taste it. I can see us playing Glastonbury, the Saturday evening, the sun coming down. Fifty thousand people listening to every note we play. Singing along to every word, loving us. We'll never have to do a real job again."

"You're aiming too low Jacob."

"Eh? You reckon we could headline the Pyramid stage?"

"No, that's not what I mean. I don't care about people liking us or buying our records. People have no taste anyway, ninety nine percent of the population are complete fucking retards. I don't want their approval, thank you very much."

"That's just elitist crap."

"No, it's not. I wouldn't stop anyone buying the album, wouldn't put up any barriers. I just don't value other people's opinions. I know music."

"So what are you aiming for then?"

Reilly let out a weary sigh - "Well, how to explain? I'll expand on your adolescent Glastonbury fantasy, if you like."

"Go on."

"Well, no one knows us, we're on before some popular but soulless crap like David Gray, or Jamiroquai or something. The field is full of pissed up indie kids but only because they're waiting for the next band. Anyway, we start playing and one by one, the whole field falls silent. And they're speechless. They're in awe. And by the end of our set there's people crying, doubled over, lying in the mud. We go off stage and these people get up, silently pack up their tents and go back to their lives, changed forever. They become better people, we save them."

Jacob paused, taking it in.

"OK. I think I understand."

"Good."

"Do these people, the people in the field, do they go out and buy our album or what?"

Inside the Thekla, it was hot. A filthy, health-endangering heat. Jacob put his coat in the cloakroom and joined the others at the bar. A techno soundtrack was pounding from the speakers. The Thekla wasn't built for this kind of thing. It was a boat, now permanently moored in the Bristol docks, presumably designed for gentle pleasure cruises. A capacity crowd had it straining at the seams, creaking under the pressure. Jacob was sure that one day the hull would burst open, drowning them all in toxic river water. This notion just added to the appeal. It was uncomfortable, impractical, unhealthy and utterly fantastic.

Stevie passed Jacob a can of Red Stripe, and then a vodka and Coke in a plastic tumbler. Jacob's stomach turned at the smell of the spirit, and he downed it just to get it out of sight.

"Woah there!" said Stevie. "Slow down. You look absolutely fucked."

"Thanks," Jacob replied.

"I am too, actually. I thought this might happen, so I came prepared."

"Oh yeah?" said S.

Stevie tapped the breast pocket on his Berghaus and winked conspiratorially.

This got Reilly's attention - "You fool. What have you got there?"

"Finest Bolivian Marching Powder, Reilly my good man."

"You utter dick," said Reilly with disgust, "'Bolivian Marching Powder' my arse. Listen to yourself, you're from Birmingham for fuck's sake. 'Oh look at me everyone, I blew a hundred quid on drugs. Aren't I cool?' And Coke is such a wanker's drug anyway, turns you into an asshole."

Stevie laughed. "Reilly, mate. You are a one-off."

"I know." Replied Reilly as he downed his vodka, "Oh fuck it. Come on then, let's have a line."

Stevie followed Reilly to the toilets, leaving Jacob with S.

"How you doing?" she asked.

"Bladdered. Yourself?"

"Yeah."

"I'm definitely not having any of Stevie's stuff though. That's too much."

"I might. I haven't had coke in a long time. It's good to treat yourself once in a while, don't you think?"

"I think it would make my head explode. Shit, check this bloke out."

Jacob nodded towards a Robert Smith look-alike along the bar. He had the full get up - white trainers, make up and huge hair. He even had an authentic paunch under his baggy jumper.

"Wow," said S, "are The Cure still going?"

"I think so. Must be, I suppose. I hope Reilly doesn't spot him, poor guy."

"Poor Reilly, more like. He really needs to calm down. It must be exhausting thinking of a rant to reply to every opinion anyone offers."

Jacob laughed. "Yeah. Must be."

"How did you meet him? Was it one of your adverts in NME?

'Wanted: singer for great new band. Must be intelligent, but not as intelligent as he thinks he is.'" S laughed at her own joke.

"I met him at a cinema, actually. I went to see *Titanic*."

"*Titanic*? Wouldn't think you'd like that, Jacob."

"Oh, I didn't. It was utter bobbins. I was sort of seeing this girl for a while, and she wanted to see it, so…"

S's expression changed, just a little. She took an awkward drink from her can and carried on. "A girl, eh? What happened with her?"

"Nothing. I mean, it didn't work out. We had nothing in common."

S smiled. "Oh well. Never mind. Have there been many others?"

Jacob took a step back - "S! fucking hell. Mind your own business."

"I'll take that as a 'no' then."

"There's been plenty, thank you very much. Just none that have lasted. No one's lit me up since…" He trailed off.

"Since what?"

"I thought we were talking about Reilly."

"Right you are. So you went to the cinema with some floozy…"

"I'll ignore that. So yeah, Winslet and Di Caprio are doing their thing and I'm not really enjoying it, not my kind of thing. And then I hear this voice from the row behind, really quite loud - 'what is this shit?' and I turn round and there's this rough looking bloke with this look of utter disgust on his face."

"Reilly? Who was he with?"

"No one, he was just sat there by himself like a freak. He keeps muttering stuff to himself and this girl I'm with, Lauren her name was, is tutting because she's trying to watch the film. And I'm really trying not to laugh because he's reading my mind."

"Why would you go to see a film and slag it off?"

"I don't know. I have no idea. But it was bloody funny." Jacob considered what he'd said for a moment. "Well it does wear a bit thin after a while though, I have to admit. But anyway, we get to the bit where Leonardo and Kate finally cop off, and it is pretty bad, I mean I was cringing. And Reilly starts shouting - 'This is disgusting! Look at their fucking rotten teeth!' and all this stuff, and I couldn't hold it in any more, I started laughing my head off. Then Reilly stands up, shouts 'This is a fucking abortion!' or something, and storms out."

"What happened then?"

"Well, Lauren starts having a go at me for laughing, so I just got up and walked out as well. Reilly was in the foyer demanding to speak to the manager, wanting his money back. So I went over and on an impulse shook his hand, offered to buy him a pint. And we hit it off. Turned out we were both into the same kind of music, both support Spurs, both hated *Titanic*. And that was that."

"Well, what a beautiful story, Jacob."

"I thought so."

"Well, anyway, I need a wee. Stay here."

Jacob nodded and turned to prop himself against the bar. He was really suffering now, that vodka had triggered something inside, an alarm of some kind. A familiar dizziness was gently pawing at him, threatening to take over, drag him under. He knew he was close to passing out. He drew a deep breath and told himself to concentrate on the music. The nausea would pass.

The DJ was a talented guy. He was playing a slick variety of Detroit techno, all tight rhythms and clever samples. Jacob listened closely, trying to glean some kind of insight into how this kind of music worked. He tried to judge the beats per minute, wondered what computer program created the snare, and with the effort of concentration, his sickness began to lift. He started nodding along to the beat, really getting into it now.

Reilly snorted one line and then quickly changed nostrils to demolish the second. He stood back against the wall of the cubicle as Stevie took his turn. The hit was instant, like a light going on in his head. He could *feel* his own brain cells bursting, his heart now pounding through his rib cage - a messy ball of muscle, trying to escape. He could feel everything. Every sinew, every chemical message shooting back and forth in his head. Every firing and misfiring synapse. "I'm on fire," he heard himself say. Or it could have been Stevie. He opened the door and purposefully led the way.

They found S and Jacob, the latter shuffling like a dementia sufferer next to the bar. Stevie started smooth talking the girl behind the bar, asking if they had any champagne.

"What are you fucking doing, Jacob?" demanded Reilly.

"I'm dancing, this DJ's great."

"Fucking hell."

The music was too slow, and the clientele suddenly too unsophisticated for a man of Reilly's standing. An artist. A pioneer. A man out of time. Jacob was saying something. He was slurring and his speech was just too slow, too *fucking* slow.

"I've got this idea Reilly, for the album I mean. To bring it together, to make it a whole."

Reilly realised he was grinding his teeth. Where did he put his beer?

"Fucking hurry up then, tell me."

"Shit. Steady on. God, you're really sweating Reilly, are you OK?"

"For fuck's sake!"

"Oh I get it, the coke. Good is it?"

"Fucking hurry up!"

"Yeah well I'm going to do something with the BPM. I've been listening to this DJ right, and it's so clever what he does. I can't believe I didn't think of this sooner. He builds up the pace really slowly, takes the crowd along with him."

"What the fuck has that got to do with anything? He's just some overpaid prick - he's not an artist. I really don't have time for this. Where's my beer?"

"No, no, what we should do, right, is over the course of the album build up the pace track by track, have the drums really pounding by about the eighth track, and then wind it down towards the end. Have no breaks between the tracks, like a DJ set. The last track can be like the denouement, the come down."

"Fucking hell, Jacob." Reilly wiped his brow on his suit sleeve, thought for a second. "That's fucking brilliant. It really is. I can't believe it. Yeah. Fucking hell. I can see that. Shit."

Jacob was beaming - "It's going to really bring it all together, don't you reckon?"

"God yeah. Fuck me. You are mighty Jacob. We are. You and me, we're the future. You know what I mean. I want people to hear this album and just... just fucking fall over, dead, bleeding, fucked up. You know what I mean?"

Jacob looked baffled - "No mate. Not really."

"It's not enough to just *like* music anymore, that's no good to anyone. It's got to grab you by the balls, fuck with your head. Change the way you see the world. I don't want to please people, I want to injure them! Fucking kill them! Leave a trail of dead in our wake."

"Right," said Jacob, with a furrowed brow.

"Shit, look at him!" Reilly had spotted the Robert Smith-a-like. He started waving at him. "Oi, chunky! What fucking year is it?"

This mess we're in

Jacob opened his eyes. Looked over at his bedside table. The alarm clock read 11:31 - AM? Must be, there was a little leak of light from between the curtains. He slowly rolled onto his back, a fierce stab of pain hitting him behind the eyes. He was back where he had started on Saturday morning, with a raging hangover.

He thought back to last night. What had happened? He remembered the Coach and Horses, The Roo Bar. Reilly slapping Jimmy Reckon - fucking hell. Renato's and then the Thekla? The memories were vague, elastic. He'd try to pin one down and it would slip away. He felt sure he'd seen Reilly arguing with the lead singer of the Cure, but that couldn't be right. He tried to recall getting home, but drew a blank. Nothing.

I am never drinking again, he told himself. More from habit than from any real conviction.

He carefully rolled his head to the left, and realised he wasn't alone. S was also under the duvet. As a reflex, his hands darted under the covers to check his state of dress. He was relieved to find himself still wearing yesterday's clothes, and interestingly, still wearing his trainers. S had her back to him, and from what he could see, she was also fully clothed.

Panic set in. Had he disgraced himself? He had visions of

himself making a clumsy move on S, opening his heart and lunging for her. But no, she wouldn't be sleeping next to him if that were the case. Maybe something big had happened, they were back together and would live happily ever after. Yeah, right. He quickly discounted that particular possibility.

Jacob looked more closely. S was wearing one of his T-shirts. His *OK Computer* tour shirt, an excellent choice. He could smell her hair, expensive conditioner tainted with cigarette smoke - and she fairly reeked of alcohol, the aroma of a big night out. But it felt great to be close to her again. To have her warmth in his bed.

In an alternative reality somewhere, say the film version of Jacob's life, he would now make an assertive movement towards her. He would roll her over and kiss her firmly on her mouth. She would respond, and without opening her eyes, hold his head in her hands in an overblown gesture of complicity. They would then hungrily start to undress each other as the camera panned away, perhaps to the ringing telephone that would never be answered...

But this was real life. Jacob's real life, and such things just didn't happen. Couldn't happen. His morning breath precluded even breathing in S's direction - fags, booze and gastric acid that had crept up into his mouth while asleep. Rotten and unwell. He was just mightily relieved not to have wet the bed, as he had after his last big all-dayer.

He heard shouting and the crashing of furniture from the front of the flat and jolted upright. That pain again behind his eyes, and now a terrifying vertigo. What was going on?

He crept down the hall and peered into the lounge. Reilly and Stevie were squared up to each other and both shouting furiously. Jacob couldn't understand a word. "What's all this?" he weakly croaked.

"Ask this cheating brummie fucker!" said Reilly.

"Bollocks," retorted Stevie. "The ref's made his decision. Fucking calm down you cockney twat."

"Cockney? You cheeky bastard."

Jacob looked at the TV. They were playing football on the Playstation. And with the score at nil-nil, Birmingham City had a penalty in the eighty-eighth minute.

"How can I be cheating, Reilly? It's a fucking computer game, you can't take a dive."

"I've seen you pressing those keys, you made him dive. Typical Morrison that, diving when a shot was on."

"You do realise that's not *actually* Clinton Morrison don't you? That this is a game?"

Reilly thought for a second, and then muttered, "fuck off, Stevie."

They both sat back down on the sofa, and prepared for the penalty. They were both utterly wired; crazy, darting eyes and shaky movements. It was clear they hadn't been to bed, an almost empty wrap of cocaine on the coffee table giving them away.

"Does anybody want a cup of tea?" asked Jacob, concentrating hard to get the words out, holding his head at the temples.

"No thanks mate," said Stevie. "I'll have another beer though."

"Yeah, me too," said Reilly.

Jacob shuffled back down the hall to the kitchen and slowly and deliberately located the tea ingredients. While the kettle boiled he took two beers from the fridge and into the lounge. Stevie and Reilly were now on another game, tapping away on the controllers and grimly staring at the TV. Fucking nutters.

S was in the kitchen when he returned, making two cups of tea and looking disconcertingly fine.

"Are you not hung over, S?"

"No. I feel alright. I was kind of sick when we got back though, which always helps."

"I can't remember a thing. What happened?"

"Jacob, how could you say that?" she said. "It was such a beautiful night. We got back and you proposed to me. I said yes of course, and we're off to Las Vegas today."

Jacob stood opened mouthed as S handed him his tea, her hurt expression slowly changing to a grin as she gave herself away.

"That's not funny, S. You shouldn't play tricks on someone as hung over as me. It's cruel."

"Yeah. I'm sorry. You kind of fell over in the club, could hardly speak. You were a bit of a mess, so I slept in with you because I was a bit worried. Who's that shouting?"

"Reilly and Stevie are still up, drinking. They're both absolutely insane."

Stevie appeared at the kitchen door.

"Hey, you two - glad you're up. The taxi's coming in half an hour. You'd better get ready."

"Taxi?"

"We're off to Ashton Court. You remember? Jimmy Reckon's band's playing, what are they called again?"

"Cloudfunk."

Stevie laughed. "Yeah, that's it. Reilly wants to chuck stuff at them. Come on, get ready."

Jacob turned to S, who gave a 'what the hell' shrug of acquiescence. He turned back to Stevie and asked, "have you got any Nurofen?"

"It's your house, mate."

"Right."

Stevie instructed the taxi driver to drop them in Clifton Village, and for the sake of ritual, they walked over the Suspension Bridge, passing the Samaritans hotline while swapping urban myths of failed suicide attempts. The coke had rendered Stevie and Reilly deranged and chaotic. Reilly in particular had seemingly devolved into some kind of sub-human, staggering along the pavements and barking bizarre observations as he went - "Give me your head back!" "Don't point those fucking shoes at me!" He was still wearing *that* suit, but he'd managed to change his T-shirt, 'HELL IS OTHER PEOPLE' now printed across his chest.

The sky was gin clear, not a cloud in sight. A clean, fresh heat radiated down on the fields of Ashton Court, slowly drying up the mud created by yesterday's downpour. The field was already nearly half-full, swarms of Bristol people on a big day out. The first band were on now, and the crowd in front of the stage bobbed along politely. S and Jacob headed straight for a falafel stand in an effort to cure his hangover, while Reilly and Stevie made a bee-line for the beer tent, weaving through the crowd.

"I can't drink fucking Carling. Stevie, what else is there?"

"That's the only beer they've got. It's either that or Strongbow."

"Oh fuck. Is there any coke left?"

"'Fraid not mate."

Although he'd rather die than share it with Stevie, Reilly was suffering now. His cocaine invincibility shield was fast eroding, and he was shattered. Emotionally shattered. He'd hit the wall. The payment for a high was always a corresponding low, and suddenly he found himself with the self-assurance and poise of a spotty adolescent. He was sure Stevie would soon also be in turmoil but he didn't want to blink first. It was too late to bail out and head home for sleep. He couldn't let that brummie, that brummie estate agent for fuck's sake, win this particular race.

"Are you alright there, mate?" asked Stevie.

"Of course I'm alright. Why?"

"Oh nothing. Let's go down to the stage, have a listen to this lot. Cloudfunk are next I think."

Reilly walked down the hill mentally preparing himself to loathe and detest this bunch of amateurs with all his being, but something strange happened. They weren't shit. In fact, they were damn good. They were playing a slow-building country waltz, the bass and percussion were measured, the lead guitar assured. And the voice - what a voice. Female vocals delivered with grace and humility. This was soul music. This was for Reilly. He listened closely, clinging on to the sound as if it were a life jacket.

Stevie pointed to a dry-looking spot of grass and they sat down as the song drew to a close. Reilly clapped enthusiastically. Stevie looked at him with an expression somewhere between shock and bewilderment, as if Reilly had just given a hundred quid to a beggar.

"You like this lot?" he asked.

"They're fucking brilliant. That was a beautiful song. Just beautiful."

"I think your mind has snapped mate. It's just boring folk or something. It's really depressing."

"Depressing? What a fucking stupid comment." Reilly spat the words out. "You're an intellectual pygmy, Stevie."

"No, it is depressing. And the singer's a moose. It's just 'ooh look at me, I'm dead ugly and everyone hates me. Want to see my scars?'"

"She's fucking brilliant, you sexist idiot."

"Sexist?" Stevie dissolved into giggles. "I love you Reilly, you know that?"

Reilly did not reply. His eyes were fixed on the stage. The singer was speaking. "Thanks very much. This next one's called *An Unkindness of Ravens*." Four slow clicks from the drummer and they were into it, weaving their magic. Reilly was overwhelmed. Maybe it was the come down, the lack of sleep, but something about this band destroyed him. They were a little miracle.

The singer was telling a tale of love and loss -

"Am I out of touch?
Did I ask too much?
I know now,
That if you're not on my side,
And if what you felt has died,
Then so have I..."

He felt the tears building in his chest at first. A constriction slowly rising up his throat and a heat behind his eyes. He pulled his sunglasses out of his jacket pocket and slipped them on as he blinked the first tears away.

The falafels were a dry and expensive disappointment, and Jacob's suffering had not eased. He was dizzy and hot, and he had a thirst that could not be sated. They were sat at the top of the hill, half-listening to the band. Jacob caught S regarding him warily as he gulped from another can of Coke.

"Hangover," he said. "What can you do?"

"You know Jacob, feeling like this doesn't have to be just part of the weekly routine."

"What do you mean? It's just what I do. What else is there to look forward to?"

"There are other things to do with your spare time. I just worry that's all. I mean, it's not a healthy kind of life."

"You can talk! You were necking the pints yesterday."

"I know I was. But I don't do that every week anymore. I'm not saying you have a problem with drink exactly, but I think you might be in a rut." She paused for a moment, and then said, "You should move to London, there's loads to do there. We can hang out together."

"What are you saying? Is something happening here?"

There was an awkward pause.

"I don't know, Jacob. It's just been so good to see you, that's all."

"I know, it's been great. I'd love to move to London, I really would. When we get a deal, that's the first thing we'll do. It's compulsory if you want to be taken seriously."

She gave him that look again. Pity. And then said, "OK. If this band is what you say it is, then make it happen. Get yourself organised. I mean I know you've been doing these demos, but there's a long way to go. Am I right?"

Jacob shrugged. "Well, yes. We've got to do some gigs really. We need a drummer and bass player for when we play live. And another guitarist as well. I need some new equipment. Effects pedals, some decent mikes. And my guitar's fucked. We need to get into a recording studio to do these songs justice. We need money and we need management to promote us."

"I'll manage you."

Jacob assumed S was joking and laughed. But her straight face alerted him to his misjudgement.

"I don't know, S. It's nice of you to offer, but you don't know much about the music industry do you?"

"Not as such. But I know how to run a business. I know how to organise. I'm hopefully going to be busy when I get some work in London, but I should have some spare time."

"Why would you want to manage us?"

She paused. "Honestly?"

"Yeah, honestly."

"I want this to work for you, Jacob. I want you to get what you want. I know you believe in your music, but I don't think blind faith is going to get you there. I just see you procrastinating when you could be getting on with it."

"That's not fair, I've been working my arse off getting these songs in shape."

"I know. But you have to admit, your plan of attack is a bit vague. And, correct me if I'm wrong, but Reilly doesn't seem to be much use on the organisational side of things."

"Yeah. Fair enough." He held out his hand. "Let's shake on it then. Boss."

"Are you crying, Reilly?" asked Stevie.

There was no point trying to hide it. "Maybe. Yes. So what? This is what music is capable of. This is why it's worth it, not that you'd understand."

"No, I understand. I just don't like this band. As a matter of fact though, I reckon I'm going to start singing again, I've been writing a few lyrics."

Reilly shot Stevie a withering look. "Seriously?"

"Yeah, why not. I enjoy it."

"You're not supposed to *enjoy it* you fucking bimbo. Jesus Christ."

"Of course you are. It's just entertainment at the end of the day."

Reilly held up a hand to Stevie's face. "Just please stop. Stop saying these things, you're making me ill. Let's just listen to this band. You might learn something."

The song finished, a beautiful minor chord coda easing it towards the end. Reilly stood and applauded. Stevie half-heartedly tapped the side of his beer. The rest of the crowd seemed to share Stevie's assessment, clapping out of politeness rather than gratitude.

"Thanks," said the singer. "This is our last song. We didn't write it though, it's a cover." Then the guitarist spoke into his mike. "With you in a moment, we've got to tune up for this one."

A cover. Reilly wondered what it would be. They obviously had taste. It had to be something by the Velvet Underground. Or Nick Drake. Maybe Neil Young? Or something off *The White Album* perhaps?

"Right. We're ready. This is a song written by the Nu-Birds. It's called *Big Sky*."

The crowd went wild. Stevie let out a roar of approval, and as the song built, he stood up and started dancing around Reilly, drunkenly singing every word.

Reilly was silent. He stood motionless, feeling his world collapsing around him.

Radio friendly unit shifter

Mondays were always slow. The slowest day of the week. The weekend's cigarettes and alcohol, successes and failures, were still ebbing through Jacob's system and weighing him down. But he was almost there now, it was three o'clock, and he told himself that Tuesday would be easier. At least he'd been left alone. Phil and Marion were busy with the first 'Cool Workshop' with the sales team, and he had the marketing office to himself.

He sent off an email to Jimmy Reckon, apologising for Reilly's behaviour on Saturday and congratulating him on Cloudfunk's set at Ashton Court. If he'd been honest, he would have told Jimmy that he wasn't keen on their new direction, second-hand white boy funk, but manners cost nothing. The crowd had clearly loved it, and Jimmy might prove to be a useful contact if he kept him sweet. S was right, he needed to be organised, business-like.

He went to Google and typed in "discount recording equipment." The search brought back a few promising links. He scanned through pages of DATs, samplers, processors and amps, cables, tuners and mikes. There was some great stuff. He jotted down some ball-park figures and did a tally. The total was daunting. Five grand. Five thousand pounds, and just for the basics. He'd also need a PC, a new acoustic for Reilly, and that Gibson copy for himself. And then there was studio time. Eight or nine grand all up. He realised that it was an impossible figure, out of reach.

He looked around the office as a wave of despondency descended over him. He looked at the pictures on the wall, Phil's mission statements and motivational art. One picture caught his eye. It depicted a sports car racing along a mountain road, approaching an impossibly tight hairpin bend. The strap line read, "EMBRACE THE CHALLENGE: ADAPT TO SUCCEED."

"I'm fucking stuck here," he said to himself.

He got up and made another coffee as he weighed up his options. He knew there was no point sending the demos to record companies as they were. No matter how good the songs, he knew they only listened to the production. A few seconds of analogue tape hiss and Serpico would be in the A&R's bin, along with all the other crap. He would have to raise the cash somehow.

His credit rating and existing overdraft meant talking to the bank would be a waste of time. And Reilly couldn't even get a membership at the local video shop. He thought of his parents, considered asking for a loan. But they wouldn't stump up ten grand to record an album. He'd have to make up a story, and couldn't face lying to them.

What about Reilly's folks? He realised he knew virtually nothing about them. It was clear that Reilly had had a comfortable upbringing, but Jacob could recall no other details. He realised that Reilly never mentioned his parents, never spoke to them on the phone. This was unsettling, and so Jacob moved on.

Stevie was the next possibility. He clearly had money to burn, and an understanding of the cost involved, but for all his good points, he was the last person Jacob would want to owe money to. He would probably charge interest, penalties for late payment, and although Mirage's implosion was in the past, Stevie would enjoy nothing more than owning Serpico, and having Jacob and Reilly in his pocket.

S. She might have money. There was bound to be some windfall from the divorce. He went back to his PC, swallowed hard and wrote her an email -

'Hey there Manager!
Just doing some sums re: recording equipment, and have hit a snag.
ie - difficulty with finance.
Any ideas?
Jacob.'

He clicked on send, and as the page refreshed, an email popped into his inbox. Finally, a reply from Reilly -

'Jacob. fucking hell, what a day. Think I lost some brain cells over the weekend. Lousy cheap brummie coke I reckon. I'm fucking suffering here. These fucking mongoloids I work with are organising some self-serving charity day where they shave their heads and give a pittance to cancer research to justify their sick narcissism. As if they give a fuck about cancer, stupid selfish fuckers.
Anyway, what's this about a 'band meeting.' Was that a joke?

Jonathon I Reilly
Customer Opportunity Facilitator
Sales Leveraging Unit
Western Telecom - "Let's Communicate!"'

Jacob clicked reply and took a hit of coffee. But Phil appeared in the doorway to halt his progress. "Jake! My guerrilla marketeer. How's it going? Anything new for me? I'm excited."

"Er, yeah, I'm hard at it, Phil."

Phil rubbed his hands together and bolted over to Jacob's workstation, as Jacob deftly minimised his non-work related browsers. Phil sat himself on the corner of Jacob's desk, way too close. Phil was a space invader. As he spoke, Jacob could feel his breath on his face; hot Listerine and cheese.

"What have you got for me? Give me some ammunition so I can fire this gun." Phil made a two-barrelled pistol shape with his hand, and with his other hand, held it upright, James Bond style.

In response, Jacob looked away, trying to hide his embarrassment, and proceeded to rattle off his piece - "Well Phil. I remember reading this thing a year or two ago somewhere. It was basically listing all these terrible things about Coca-Cola, and by association, other soft drinks. Stuff like – 'did you know, if you place a human tooth in a glass of coke, it will dissolve to nothing within three hours?' and, 'did you know, US police use Coke to clean blood off the road following a car crash?' You know the kind of thing."

Phil was nodding eagerly. "Yep. Go on…"

"Well, I thought we could gather up some of these facts, and make it funny. We could even stretch the truth a little bit on some of the points. Then we could add at the end, 'on your next break, are you going to head for the vending machine, or the water cooler?' Then we send it out as an email, making sure it can't be traced back to us. It then starts buzzing around the country as a chain email from office to office…" *Now for the pay-off.* "And it gets people talking about water coolers."

Phil leapt up and punched the air. He let out a sharp squeal as if enjoying a mid-coital loss of self-control. "Yes!" he proclaimed. "Yes! Yes! You are the man, Jacob. You are the bomb! Hit me!"

Jacob considered this offer as Phil bounced from the room, clapping to himself.

Crawling with idiot

Sandra removed her 'Bling Bling, Ring Ring' baseball cap, took a seat and gestured for Reilly to do the same. This was clearly serious. They'd booked the main conference room and Gavin from Human Resources was sitting in, stony-faced. A manila folder lay on the table, the words 'Jonathon Reilly, Sandra Adcock's Team,' scrawled on the front. Reilly sat down awkwardly and ran his hands along his trouser legs, wiping away the cold sweat.

"Jon," said Sandra sombrely. "A matter has come to our attention. A rather serious misuse of company resources."

Reilly racked his brains. Panicking now. He was aware of his breathing, fast and erratic. He tried to hide it. *Show no fear.*

"Gavin is here as an independent witness to our meeting, and I have to tell you that depending on the outcome of our discussions, we may have to take action against you. Now you should be aware that you have the right to have a colleague here with you, if you would like."

Reilly waved the suggestion away - "No, that's fine Sandra."

"OK. Now do you know what matter I may be referring to?"

He didn't - "Honestly. No. I have no idea."

Sandra looked doubtful, and a tight smirk formed on Gavin's face. "Well, Jon. The I.T. department flagged an email sent by you earlier in the week. The email contained foul and abusive language, and in addition, inflammatory remarks about your colleagues."

That fucking email. He never normally read Jacob's emails, let alone replied. Jacob was an e-pest, forwarding on every JPEG, link or joke, regardless of how puerile, pointless or plain unfunny they were. Idiot. He was just thrown by the band meeting thing. And he really wasn't feeling right on Monday, still half crazed by that filthy weekend. Fuck.

She continued. "You also alluded to some recreational activities that cause us concern."

Sandra waited for a reply.

"Right," was all Reilly could muster, still in shock.

"Is there anything you want to tell us Jon?" said Gavin, in a calm voice. "We want to help you if we can." Gavin was clearly a veteran of several people management courses. Courses with titles like 'Effective Dispute Resolution Strategies,' 'Constructive Diplomacy,' and 'Winning With Trust.' He really believed this shit, the oily little maggot.

The anger was burning inside Reilly now. How could they dare to speak to him like this? And how could Sandra of all people talk down to him, given that she was the owner of one of the worst haircuts he'd ever seen? And fucking Gavin. He was receding, and he was probably only twenty-three. It was preposterous that he was having to explain himself to these ugly no-marks. But Gavin was throwing Reilly a rope here, and he knew it. The choice was clear. He could act as every part of his being urged him, and let the expletives fly, or he could play along and keep his job.

Reilly had no fear of being sacked in itself, it was a slap in the face that lost its sting with each repetition. What Reilly feared was having to get another job. Having to write a series of cheesy applications, endure Mickey Mouse phone interviews, then panel interviews involving toe-curling role-play exercises. And all for the prize of a job just as ridiculous and repugnant as the one he currently held. Reilly feared that the effort of feigning interest for long enough to secure his next assignment was now beyond him.

He took the life-line on offer. *Tell them what they want to hear. Tell them what they want to hear.*

"This is a little difficult," he began, eyes down, head bowed. "As you know, I'm a quiet member of the team. But I get results. I can sell these products."

"Yes, of course," said Sandra, "that's not in doubt."

"But I do put a lot of pressure on myself. I want to do well. I want what everyone wants I suppose - I want to own my own home, I want a nice car, wife, children someday. A stable life, no alarms and no surprises."

"Of course," said Gavin, perhaps wondering where this was heading.

"Well things haven't been going so well outside work. I met a nice girl, and we were engaged to be married. Next summer, it was all planned - Edinburgh for the ceremony, Barbados for the honeymoon. My little nephew was going to be best man. He was so excited."

"I had no idea," said Sandra.

"Well I like to keep my personal life separate to an extent. But she left me. She said she didn't want to marry a salesman, that she'd always imagined herself with someone in middle management, someone who could make a difference, a human resources executive or something."

Gavin nodded sagely.

"But that's just not me. I love what I do. I can't change that. So anyway, it all happened rather suddenly and it hit me quite hard. I'm only human and I was weak." Reilly paused, took a deep breath before delivering the pay-off -

"Sandra, Gavin - I have an addiction. That email, it wasn't me. Well, it was me, but it's the part of me I want to fix. I need help."

Reilly looked up slowly and waited for a reaction. Sandra regarded him through narrow eyes, a slow nod and quivering top lip. She'd swallowed the story. And her haircut was still a disaster.

Gavin leant towards Reilly and rested his elbows on the table. "Jon. I want to thank you for your honesty. It's a brave man who can face up to his problems as you have. We have just brought in some new initiatives for this kind of situation, and I'm confident that we can help you through this."

The discomfort clung to him as he rode the bus up Gloucester Road, on the way to meet Jacob. As little respect as Reilly had for Sandra and Western Telecom, duplicity didn't sit well. But he told himself once again that he'd had no choice.

He was by no means off the hook. He'd agreed to start seeing a professional counsellor, and if appropriate, attend a drug addiction support group. Western Telecom were paying, and Sandra wanted regular feedback on his progress. He was digging a hole for himself, and he knew it.

Reilly left the bus two stops later than usual and made his way to the Annex, working up a sweat in the early evening humidity. The Annex was dead as usual, a real backwater of a pub. A couple of fat old locals were talking football at the bar, their urban bumpkin patois colouring the air and setting Reilly's teeth on edge. A couple of kids were shooting pool, and a rough-arse townie couple were snogging in the far corner. Otherwise, the pub was empty. *Witchita Lineman* was playing.

He found Jacob sitting with a pad and a biro, and two fresh pints of Stella. He was bright-eyed and excited.

"Good day at work?" he asked as Reilly sat down and rolled a cigarette.

"Yeah, just the usual."

"Great stuff."

Reilly lit up and took a deep swig from his pint. "So what's all this about?"

"Well, like I said. It's just a meeting. We need to get organised."

Reilly didn't feel like another meeting. "Jesus, what are we? Fucking U2?"

"Not yet, no," laughed Jacob. "But I've got some plans. We need a record deal and we won't get there without being focused."

Where had this come from? When had they turned into a small business? Reilly shrugged his agreement as Jacob scanned his notes.

"Firstly mate, do you know anyone who could lend us ten grand?"

"Eh?"

"I mean, would your mum and dad give you a short term loan?"

Reilly's parents? Fucking hell. His first reaction was to laugh out loud. But instead he replied, "Don't think so. No definitely not. That's not an option."

"Never mind," replied Jacob as he made an adjustment to his notes.

"What do we need ten thousand pounds for anyway?"

"Recording. Gigs. We need a lot of new equipment."

"What's wrong with my demos all of a sudden? It's the best fucking album of all time as far as I'm concerned."

"It's not Reilly, you know that. But it could be. It really could. That's why we need to record it properly. We also need to advertise and get a bass player, a drummer and another guitarist for when we play live. I've already got us a manager. S has offered."

"Woah, hold on. What was that? No way. We can't have your fucking girlfriend as a manager, and I'm not working with someone called Sharon. Are you crazy?"

"She's not my girlfriend."

"No way. What do we need a manager for anyway? They'll only fuck things up for us. And no session musicians either, I'm not playing with strangers."

"Reilly, we need to play some gigs, and we need live drums

and bass. And there's too many guitar parts for me to play alone."

"Why do we need to play gigs?"

"To get a deal. To create a buzz, to get a reputation."

"Fucking hell, you sound like Jimmy Reckon. And ten grand - isn't that what record companies are for? To pay for all that?"

"Yes, but they don't pay for anything unless they sign you. No band's signed from a four-track demo tape alone."

"Well fuck them then. We'll set up our own label."

Jacob laughed as he lit a rollie. "Reilly. This is what we need to do to get signed. We need to play live and get a following, get a reputation around the credible venues. We need to record the album, or at least half a dozen songs as a demo. And we need to pull some publicity stunts, to create a buzz and get us noticed. Record companies will listen to decent demos, but that won't do it alone. They have contacts at live venues who give them tips on who's doing something good and getting a reaction from the punters. And they also want that little bit extra, that commitment to show that you're in it for the long haul. And we need to get in the thick of it. We need to move to London. We have to…"

Reilly looked Jacob in the eye as he continued his mission statement. Without a word, he put his pint down, clasped his hands tightly over his ears, screwed his eyes shut, and grimaced.

The relative silence was lovely. He could still hear Jacob's muffled speech, and beneath that the locals' conversation, but the edge was gone. Bliss. He could've stayed like this for hours, it was great.

He felt Jacob's hand on his arm and a muffled "Reilly? Reilly?" He opened one eye and looked up at Jacob, saw his boyish, clean-shaven face staring down at him. He was looking quite annoyed. Reilly had had enough of annoyed people today, and shook Jacob's hand away. He could still hear him though, so he let out a long, loud "AAAAAHHH!" to block out the muffled questions.

Jacob backed away at Reilly's vocal objection, and looked

around nervously toward the bar, where the fat locals and landlord were gawping in disbelief. Reilly watched through his one open eye as Jacob, embarrassment written over every twitchy movement, gathered his pad, tobacco and pint, and disappeared out the back, presumably to the garden.

When Reilly was sure Jacob was out of earshot, he closed his mouth and removed his hands from his ears. Smiling, he took a sip of lager and waved at the locals - "Alroight moy lovvers? Lovely eve'nen ain't et?"

One of the old guys grunted an acknowledgement and turned around, shaking his head.

Reilly headed for the garden, giggling to himself as he found Jacob.

"What are doing out here, Jacob?"

"You fucking weirdo Reilly. If you ever do that again, I swear..."

"Calm down, calm down," said Reilly as he sat down. "Anyway, you were saying."

"What's the point? You've just got all these stupid punk rock hang-ups, we're not to get anywhere are we?"

"Don't sulk Jacob, I do want to do this album. It's just all the other stuff I can't stomach. I don't want to be a part of *the problem*."

"Well I'm doing all the work here - what are you doing? Just being a prick. I mean, 'let's set up our own label' - that's just a cop out - don't you want to see how well we could do in the real world?"

"I'm serious about the label, Jacob. If you really want to put this album out, let's do it. But let's have total control. Fuck, I'd be perfectly happy to stick it on the internet and give it away for free."

"But no one would know about it. If you want to make money from it, you need a label to promote it and sell it."

Reilly sighed wearily and placed his pint on the table. "How many times do I have to tell you, Jacob? I don't give a fuck about selling it. As soon as it's a job you cheapen it, you're just like all the other sell outs."

"Come on mate, you're not telling me you wouldn't want to make music for a living. That's what we're looking at here. I know you don't want to sell call-waiting for the rest of your life."

"You're not listening. Is this going to be the best album ever made?"

"Well, maybe."

"Then that's the aim. Nothing else is relevant."

"But I want people to hear it," said Jacob. "I want it to have an impact. Otherwise it doesn't count, does it?"

Reilly felt himself getting a little heated at this - "You couldn't be more wrong. Say if *OK Computer* was never released. Say Radiohead recorded it and then a fire destroyed the master copy and then they'd split up, and the album was lost. Would it have been a crap album?"

Jacob thought for a moment. "Well, no I suppose..."

"Of course not. It still would have been a great record. They still would have achieved that, even if it hadn't sold one copy."

"But shouldn't music be heard? So it can change people? Anyway, fucking Radiohead are on a major label, they're making a living from it, why shouldn't we?"

"I fucking hate Radiohead."

Jacob stopped and stared at Reilly. His face was a portrait of disbelief.

"No you don't," he finally said. "You love them."

"Not any more. From now on, anyone with a record deal is a parasite as far as I'm concerned. Just feeding this stupid industry. I can't wait for all the major labels to fold. It's going to happen, it's just a matter of time. Then we can go back to the way it was, people making music because they want to, not to buy into this pop star bullshit and making fat, deaf record company executives rich."

"What about Mazzy Star, Wilco, Sparklehorse, the fucking

Strokes?" asked Jacob, exasperated. "They're all on majors, and if they weren't, you wouldn't have fucking heard of them would you? For fuck's sake."

"True. But I can separate the music and the contract that's signed. That's fine for them. I forgive them."

"You *forgive* them?"

"Yeah," replied Reilly, brightly, "why not. I acknowledge that I've benefited from bands I like signing deals, I can't deny it. And they made a choice, but it's not for me. It's time to do something different. Kill your heroes, you know."

Reilly let this hang in the air as he downed his pint. Jacob's mouth opened, but no words emerged.

"You ready for another, Jacob?"

"Yeah, same again mate."

Reilly went back in to the pub and got the beers. He knew Jacob was shocked, but it needed to be said. And he'd meant every word. He glanced out of the window as he waited for the pints. Jacob was looking seriously pissed off, rolling another fag and staring at his shoes like a lost puppy. Reilly paid the landlord and made his way back.

"Jacob, I don't want to piss on your bonfire here, but it's better that you know now. We're not going to be rock stars, mate."

"Why not? I know you don't give a fuck but this is it for me. It's all I want to do. I'm no good at anything else. And neither are you, come to think of it."

"I just don't want to lose sight of what it's all about. That's all." Reilly thought back to his day at work, and said, "Look mate, I would like a change. I don't want to do my job anymore, and if a label offered to sign us, then I'm happy to take the money. But let's aim to make the best record we can, not to get the biggest advance we can."

Jacob perked up - "Serious? Great. But you've got to let me get all this organised. Let's not fuck this up just out of stubbornness."

"Right. But no manager, and definitely no fucking session

musos moaning about doing what they're told. And I'm never moving to fucking London."

"Reilly…"

"No. Not negotiable. And no gigs until we've recorded the album. And we set up our own label and release it ourselves. That way we have no meddling from outside, we can have whatever artwork we want, whatever track listing we want. And we can do that thing you said with the BPM and no one can tell us different."

"Oh yeah. I'd forgotten about that."

"Then if a label come in for us, then we'll consider the offer."

"OK."

"Where are we going to record it? Which studio?"

"I don't know. I'd like to do it at the Coachhouse."

Reilly looked blank.

"You know, where Massive Attack recorded *Blue Lines*. But money's the problem. We need that ten grand from somewhere. S says she's skint, my parents can't help."

"So who does that leave?"

Jacob rotated his pad and pushed it towards Reilly. A series of names were crossed out, the remaining name on the list being 'Stevie.'

"Fine," said Reilly. "He might as well put his money to good use for a change."

"I don't know. I love Stevie, but I'm not sure I want to owe him money, you know what I mean? Have you got any other ideas?"

"No. Let's get that brummie to stump up some cash, that's fine by me."

"Worth a try I suppose. I can't see another way."

Jacob took the pad back, and as Reilly looked on, turned over to a new page and began writing, underlining and drawing arrows.

"Jacob?"

"Yeah."

"I'm thinking of getting a pipe."

"A pipe?"

"Yeah, you know, to smoke. As a statement."

Jacob looked up from his notes, and considered this for a moment. He shrugged and then smiled. "Yeah, I can see that."

He went back to his note making, and after a moment he said – "You know, Reilly, I know virtually nothing about you."

Without a pause, Reilly shot back, "Jacob, you know everything about me mate. Everything."

I am trying to break your heart

This was it. The final track. Just these four minutes, fourteen seconds to master and the demos were done. Serpico's first album, ready for the studio. Jacob pressed 'record' on the tape deck, and 'play' on the four-track.

A few delicious seconds of tape hiss crackled through the speakers, and the drums came in, low thuds, slow and deliberate. And now the guitar. Just two alternating chords for the intro, notes picked through a tremolo effect, lovely reverb. Almost country, thought Jacob.

He adjusted the levels as he listened, tweaking the treble a little on the guitar, wanting more crispness. Then Reilly came in, vocals delivered quietly at first, as if imparting a secret to a trusted friend -

"I'm watching the lights,
Looking for signs,
Chasing the fear,
Out of my mind..."

Jacob brought up Reilly's acoustic as the bass guitar and snare drums kicked in, building up the depth of sound.

"I'm watching the skies,
Making them mine,

Waving goodbye,
And drawing a line..."

Heavier drums now, and some guitar feedback from Jacob, swirling around in the background. The four-track was showing its limitations, some of the sounds were a little imprecise and muffled, but the overall effect was as intended. Jacob made more adjustments to the levels as the song built, Reilly's vocals now more forceful –

"Am I breaking a chord?
Taking a life?
Pushing my luck?
Or twisting the knife?
Am I losing a friend?
Taking a ride?
Am I testing your love -
Like suicide?"

Jacob felt a rush inside as the percussion built, the volume rising. His slide guitar joined the mix, Reilly now screaming the lines –

"Like suicide,
Feels like suicide,
Like suicide,
Is this suicide?"

The walls of distorted guitar burst into the mix - white noise testing the speakers. And the drums, pounding techno in slow motion. The waves of feedback continued, the levels just right, and Jacob was up and dancing around his room, screaming along. "Like suicide, feels like suicide!"

After four bars the guitars tailed off, and the song broke down to the final coda, Reilly now whispering the hook over the tremolo and high-hat. Jacob was out of breath, his heart racing. What a fucking tune. What a band. And what an album this would be.

He waited for the last note from the guitar and stopped the recording. And it was there, captured on tape. The final of the twelve songs that would become the album. Jacob was elated. The overall sound quality was patchy, and no A&R would hear past it as it was, but Jacob was thrilled. The experience of mastering the songs had been overwhelming. Hearing it all come together, his hard work bearing fruit. The phrase 'religious experience' popped into his head for a moment. But was replaced. With the association, Jacob remembered a middle-aged couple he and Reilly had once known called Terry and Barbara. His thoughts of Reilly the singer, the songwriter replaced by Reilly the nut case.

Terry and Barbara had knocked on the door one night, and Jacob answered, listened to a few words of religious zealotry, then politely explained that he was a bit busy and they should try the next buzzer. Reilly appeared in the doorway behind him with excited eyes.

"Are you Jehovah's witnesses?" he asked.

"Yes we are, I'm Terry and this is my wife Barbara. What's your name, friend?"

"Fucking brilliant!" exclaimed Reilly. "Get your amazing minds inside, let's have a fucking chat about God shall we?"

Terry and Barbara shuffled in and sat down. Reilly was rubbing his hands with glee as they began telling him about their beliefs. They then handed them a pamphlet each, the title of which was 'Are we paying for the sins of a past life?' To illustrate the point, there were two photographs - one depicting a woman talking to a man, a glass of wine in one hand and a cigarette in the other - the second a woman in a wheelchair. Reilly giggled to himself as they continued, waiting for his chance to wade in.

And wade in he did. Jacob sat awkwardly on the arm of a chair as Reilly tore their arguments apart one by one - "How do I know God didn't create the world? There's a fair bit of information about that disproves what you say - like every book on evolution written in the last hundred and fifty years. God exists, but he's man made. And I'm a man, so I made him. I made him, so I own him. Are you with me? I own him so I can kill him."

Terry, Barbara and Jacob looked on with varying levels of concern as Reilly continued.

"It's all internal, just the way humans are wired. He exists in the sense that people like you misinterpret the electricity charging around your brain. Look at every human civilisation, right. Every one. Right through history. Every one of them has more or less the same structure – God or Gods, that live in the sky, get angry and impose a moral code, that have to be worshipped in some way or other. There's your answer - it's humans, we can't not explain something - we have to say to ourselves, 'this or that happened for a reason.' But there is no pattern. There is no fate."

"But I feel God all around me, and he's all around you." countered Babs calmly.

Reilly cut her off - "You feel him? Then you should get yourself to a doctor. You've probably got temporal lobe epilepsy. I'm serious. When psychology stops just scratching the surface, as it's doing now, they'll prove the link I promise. But go and see your doctor. I'm deadly serious about that."

Jacob had jumped in an effort to mediate - "But Reilly, are you one hundred percent sure there's no such thing as God. I mean, isn't there a part of you that worries about what might happen after you die?"

"Of course God doesn't exist. Of course not. There's no question to answer. I have no doubt, none. There's no argument - look at the facts. Life on Earth is an accident, we know that. Evolution can be explained. The notion that we're being watched over by some benevolent force, it's preposterous. It's fucking

Santa Claus or the Easter Bunny. It's just bad science."

Jacob excused himself soon after, and went for a pint by himself. Barbara and Terry stayed for several hours, patiently listening to Reilly and trying to get their message across. Reilly got their home number and for a few weeks he'd call them intermittently, haranguing them with facts, trying to save them from themselves. "Come on, Tez," Jacob had once heard him shout down the phone, "Let's evolve. Let's get onto the next level. Forget your fairy tales, make up your own mind. How do you think you should treat other people, what does your brain tell you?"

Terry eventually asked Reilly to stop calling him, and when the request was ignored, changed his phone number.

Jacob shook the memory away, and brought himself back to the present. He packed up the four-track, leads and his note book, and rewound the tape. Stevie would be here soon, and they were having a World Cup on the Playstation. He grabbed his wallet and headed out to the off licence.

Reilly carefully placed his mug of wine on the side of the sink, turned on the taps and stepped into the shower. He tried to ignore the mould growing on the low ceiling above him. The shower head was old and cheap, the spray spat at him intermittently, testing his patience.

But it felt good to get clean. It had been another scorcher of a day, and he'd spent the best part of it on the sofa, reading the broadsheets and sweating into his suit, half listening to the Serpico demos as they drifted from Jacob's bedroom. The songs sounded good, Jacob clearly had a talent, producing a menacing dub sound filled with clever samples and swooping guitar effects. The album was going to be special, something Reilly would be pleased to put his name on. And the idea of setting up their own label was a masterstroke. It released them from all the crap other bands had to contend with. The suffocating contracts, the thick-headed board members asking for more choruses, the clueless receptionists asking how they thought up the band name.

He washed his hair. Heard the front door close. At last, Jacob was off to get more booze. Now he had a few minutes to himself, a few minutes to prepare.

Jacob had told him to let Stevie win the football, in the naïve belief that he would be more likely to agree to their proposal. Reilly had said, "Yeah, no problem, whatever it takes," but had not meant a word.

He was having England, and he was going to win this tournament, no question. He was going to win it with intelligence, sophistication and an irresistible attacking elán. Now he just had to decide on a starting eleven.

Jacob let Stevie in and gestured towards the lounge. Reilly laid on the sofa, sipping his Valpolicella and listening to Wilco's *Yankee Hotel Foxtrot*. He raised a hand to acknowledge Stevie's entrance.

"Reilly! Still wearing that suit eh?"

"It's a new one," said Jacob.

"Oh right. Good old Oxfam. Let's see today's T-shirt then."

Reilly stood up, opened his suit jacket to reveal the slogan.

Stevie read it out loud. "'Shopping is not creative.' Woah, that's cosmic man," he said in a California stoner accent, "You've like, totally blown my mind, dude."

"Shut up, you're wearing a fucking Birmingham City shirt you artless airhead," said Reilly.

Stevie laughed and kissed his club badge, enjoying the opportunity to add fuel to Reilly's fire. "What have you two been up to today then?"

"I finally got those demos done," replied Jacob.

"Nice one mate. Time to hit the record companies eh?"

"Well…"

"I've been writing some tunes of my own today. Great fun, isn't it, Reilly, making up a song I mean?"

"Fuck's sake Stevie," said Reilly, "stop this sick joke now. Please."

"No, I'm deadly serious. They're good as well. You can use them if you want."

Jacob saw where this was heading, saw the insults forming in Reilly's mind. He jumped in - "Anyway, Stevie, you want a beer?"

"Thought you'd never ask. Thanks mate."

Jacob ran to the fridge and back, handed Stevie a Kronenbourg and said, "Right then, a world cup!"

"Excellent," replied Stevie. "I'm having England."

"Fuck off!" roared Reilly. "I'm England. It's already set up. Can't change it."

"You're always England. Have someone else."

Jacob shot Reilly a pleading look. Raised his eyebrows. Reilly calmed down.

"Fuck it. Whatever. I'll be Italy. Jacob, you're Spain. Now here are the rules. You can only do subs and tactics if it's your team, and the other two players have a half each."

The group stages went by without major incident. Spain cruised through their group in Jacob's hands, with measured, efficient victories over Peru, Japan and Ireland.

Reilly's Italy romped past Romania, Scotland and Saudi Arabia, not a single goal conceded to twelve scored. Reilly was clearly up for this, leant forward on the edge of the sofa, now swigging wine directly from the bottle whenever there was a break in play. Each goal brought a silent clenched fist and nod of the head.

England's progress was more haphazard, Stevie appalling Reilly by playing Beckham as a striker and labouring to a one all draw with the United Arab Emirates. Big wins against Sweden and Uruguay saw England home, Stevie hammering the keys randomly and laughing dementedly as the goals went in.

They broke for food before beginning the knock out stages,

Jacob preparing oven pizzas and garlic bread. The Kronenbourgs and Valpolicella kept coming, and Reilly started DJing, picking single tracks from the CDs on the bookcase. He started slowly with songs from the Telstar Ponies, the For Carnation, Ariel M. He lifted the pace and volume a little, moving onto to Mogwai, Six by Seven and the Delgados. By the time they were all ready to continue the world cup, he was playing Primal Scream's *Kill All Hippies*, Stevie drunkenly pogoing along, shouting, "tune!" over and over.

"Right, let's get on with it," said Jacob, sitting down. "Turn that music off Reilly, you're playing Turkey."

"Nice."

"You and Stevie are due to meet in the semi-final. Looks like I'll be playing the winner."

"We'll see."

Reilly sat himself down, stubbed out his cigarette and picked up the controller. His face was a picture of grim determination.

Jacob picked up the other handset. The evening was going well. Stevie was drunk, and on good form. And Reilly was behaving himself. Jacob thought about just asking Stevie right there and then, striking while the iron was hot. But apprehension stopped him. Stevie was a great friend, and would probably be able to help them. But there was a lot at stake. If he said no, then what then? There were no other options. Jacob decided to wait. "Stevie, you do the first half, I need a slash."

Reilly dispatched Turkey and then Germany to set up the semi-final with Stevie. Jacob was already through to the final. Things were getting tense. After several hours in front of the Playstation, the tournament was taking on an eerie air of realism. The graphics seemed smoother, the players developed their own personalities and traits. And the noise from the crowd was too real, rising and falling with each attack.

Jacob had felt genuine nerves before his semi-final against Portugal, telling himself that the Spanish fans would hate to lose to their closest rivals and he must do everything to avoid defeat at such a late stage. He held the controller with sweaty palms, probing away and trying to avoid defensive mistakes. He talked to his players - "Settle down lads. Keep it simple." "Well played Salgado," "Who's picking up Figo?" "Great vision, Raul." A goal early in the second half settled his team and they were on their way.

And then Stevie and Reilly took up their positions, Stevie shouting, "Come on England, let's beat those dirty Italian bastards."

"Forget about it Stevie, you English thug. We're the form team of the tournament. England have fluked their way here, playing Beckham up front for fuck's sake. You haven't got a clue. You're going to get found out by some Italian class."

Jacob tried to catch Reilly's eye, to remind him to let Stevie win, but Reilly's gaze was fixed on the screen.

Totti scored a forty-yard screamer to open the scoring, and Reilly did a lap of honour around the lounge as the replays showed the detail - "Get in there you fucker! How do you like that, Stevie? I knew Totti would score, he's so up for it, this lad. Say what you like about him, but he plays for the shirt."

"Sit down, sit down," slurred Stevie as Jacob giggled to himself.

Half time came and Stevie announced he was going to make some changes. He scanned through his subs. "Where the fuck's Rooney?" he asked. "Jacob, how old is this fucking game? Oh bollocks to it." He brought Heskey on for Owen, and Dyer for Beckham.

Reilly howled with derision - "You've subbed your two best players, you fool. You're going to get the sack. The worst England manager since Graham Taylor."

"We need height up front," reasoned Stevie, inadvertently knocking over his beer. "Fuck."

They kicked off and it was all Italy, Stevie chasing shadows with his delayed reactions, tapping the keys and trying to steer his team with the controller. But Reilly couldn't score. He hit the bar twice, Inzaghi and then Montella - "Come on lads, let's finish them!"

As injury time approached, Reilly began passing the ball along the back line, keeping possession and running down the clock - "This is how it's done Stevie," he said. Stevie was hammering the buttons as if trying to defuse a bomb, desperately trying to get a tackle in. 'Come on Emile!" he shouted as the Heskey-shaped group of pixels lunged for a pass.

And collected it.

Reilly's Italian defenders were after him, but he was away, galloping towards Toldo's goal. "Fuck no!" shouted Reilly, as his defenders chased. After what seemed like an age, Heskey reached the penalty area and pulled back his right foot for the shot. From nowhere Nesta took a wild swipe, but couldn't stop Heskey drilling the ball into the bottom left hand corner past Toldo.

"COME ON YOU BEAUTIFUL BASTARD!" screamed Stevie, now standing on the ˙ sofa. Jacob, laughing uncontrollably, collapsed backward into his chair, clapping to himself. As the replays started, Stevie pulled his Birmingham City shirt over his face and began rhythmically grunting and thrusting his pelvis towards the TV.

Reilly sat in silence, awkwardly picking up his tobacco and rolling a cigarette, preparing for extra time. He looked on as Stevie, now singing *God save the Queen*, jumped from the sofa and started humping the television.

The TV table creaked, and then split from Stevie's weight - videos and games scattering outwards as the unit collapsed. Stevie, shirt still over his head, landed awkwardly on the fallen TV, his left knee smashing into the Playstation, pulling the power supply from the wall. He lay groaning across the blank screen as Jacob jumped up to help - "Shit mate, are you alright?" Reilly remained seated, calmly lighting his cigarette and taking a drink.

With Jacob's help, Stevie rolled off the television and onto the floor, disconnected leads and broken wood lying around him. "Fuck me," he said as he pulled his shirt down over his face, breathing heavily. "What a goal, eh lads?"

Reilly let out a roar of laughter at this, and Jacob and Stevie joined in, almost literally pissing themselves at the mess they'd made.

Stevie eventually gathered himself, stood up clumsily and dusted himself off. "I reckon I owe you two a telly," he said as Jacob shot Reilly a knowing look. "Heh Reilly, more tunes please, my good man."

Reilly fired up the CD player and slipped in *New York City Cops* by the Strokes. They all sung along. Even Reilly. Stevie started playing air guitar, Jacob supplied the air drums.

This was it, the perfect time to ask the question. As the song finished Jacob turned off the stereo and turned to face Stevie.

"Stevie. Mate. We have a favour to ask you."

"Oh yeah. What's that?"

"It's about the band."

"You want to use my songs? Yeah, no problem Jacob. I'll give you the tape."

"No, it's not that. But thanks. We really believe in the songs we've demoed, and we've been doing some thinking about the best way to get this album out there."

Stevie leant forward, giving Jacob his full attention - "Go on."

"We're going to set up our own label and record and release the album ourselves."

"Oh yeah. Nice one. What's the label called?"

"Erm, don't know, we haven't really…"

Reilly cut in - "Naked Cousin Records. After the PJ Harvey song."

Jacob shrugged his agreement.

"Good name. And you want money right?" asked Stevie.

"Well yes. We want money. But it would be a loan. I'm confident an established label will come and offer us a deal, and then you get your money back."

"And what if they don't?"

"Then we'll pay you back another way. But we'll get a deal."

Reilly interjected - "We don't want a deal though Jacob, remember?"

"Reilly, we've discussed this."

Reilly held up his hands - "Whatever, whatever."

Stevie was silent for a moment, and then standing up said, "Alright boys, the mighty Serpico. I'll help you out."

Jacob also stood up, and moved towards Stevie saying, "Thanks, thanks mate. This means a lot."

"Alright, don't hug me for fuck's sake. How much do you need?"

"Ten grand."

Stevie laughed. "No seriously, how much do you need?"

"We need ten thousand pounds. We need a lot of new equipment, and time in a decent studio."

"Shit. I thought you were asking for a few hundred quid or something. I don't have ten grand."

"Come on Stevie," said Reilly, "Of course you have. Don't fuck us about." He turned to Jacob - "I knew he'd do this."

"Sorry boys, I can't help. I've got money, but it's all invested. Term deposits. Shares. I'd help if I could. Fuck me I'm drunk, got the spins and everything. Why don't you just do a single or an EP, that would be cheaper."

"We're not that kind of band," answered Reilly. "We're like no band ever before. We are too good for all that bass player, drummer, guitarist, frontman shite. We're above the clichés. And we don't do fucking singles."

"Fair enough mate. You don't have to convince me. I've heard your stuff. I know how good it is. I'm just sorry I can't help."

Jacob felt close to tears, this was desperate. He tried to think of something to say, to salvage this. All he could muster was a croaked, "But?"

Stevie swayed on the spot, clearly bladdered now. He clasped a hand over his mouth. "I'm going to be fucking sick," he said as he bolted for the bathroom.

Jacob sat back down and tried to ignore the coughing and slurping coming from the toilet. He put his head in his hands.

After a minute or two Reilly spoke. "Stop moping Jacob. Fuck that brummie anyway. We don't need his money."

Jacob looked up. "Of course we need his money. That's the whole point. Jesus, Reilly, you know everything, but you know nothing."

Jacob's words hung in the air as Stevie returned, breathing heavily. He sat down and picked up his can, taking a long swig. "That's better." He looked up at Jacob, who wore a desolate look. Reilly was loading up his new pipe with tobacco.

"What the fuck is that?" asked Stevie.

"It's a pipe. You smoke it."

"You look like an old man," said Stevie, shaking his head. "Oxfam suits and a fucking pipe. Priceless."

"Well yeah, that's what I want. A reaction."

"Eh?"

"Never mind."

Stevie picked up on the agitation in Reilly's voice. "Look boys, I'm sorry. I simply don't have ten grand. But there is another way, you know. If you're game."

"Fuck this, we don't need you Stevie," said Reilly, standing up and leaving the room.

Stevie waited as Reilly departed, and then continued. "Hear me out, Jacob. I've been toying with this idea for a while. There is a certain level of risk involved, but it could be, let's say, mutually beneficial."

Jacob leant forward, and quietly replied. "I'm all ears."

Less than you think

Jacob straightened his tie again and thought about the sweat forming in the small of his back, prickly and unstoppable. He wondered if it was visible yet through the dark blue cotton of his shirt. Fuck it, he thought, I can't take the chance.

Standing up, he grabbed his jacket from the back of his plastic chair and slipped it on. He knew this action would appear bizarre, and in an attempt to address this, he rubbed his hands together in the manner of a chilly old man and looked long and hard at the air conditioner above his head. Feeble.

Feeling defeated before he'd even begun, Jacob looked around the room and did a quick head-count as the last delivery driver walked in. The canteen was near full now. Forty-five drivers and admin staff, chattering away and occasionally looking towards Jacob, wondering what this was all about, and why it was so important that it could delay them leaving for the day.

He awkwardly flicked through his notes and switched on the projector, Marion twitching anxiously and playing with her hair beside him.

Phil appeared at the doorway, and bounded through the crowd, doling out back slaps and high fives. To Jacob this performance appeared to be impossibly condescending, a facsimile of bonhomie. But Phil was met with a real warmth, broad smiles and even some clapping. Phil soaked it up, snaking towards Jacob and making pistol shapes at a baffled Marion.

He stood at the front and said, "Right people. Great to see you. As you know I'm the marketing manager for this kicking little organisation, Jacob and Marion are my foot soldiers. We work for you. We are the creatives. We're paid to dream, and to make those dreams real. It's what we do, and we're damned good at it. Now listen closely, because something's happening here. Something big. Something challenging. And we've all got a stake."

Jacob watched Phil as he spoke, studied him. It was his sincerity that did it, reasoned Jacob. He could say things that would make your skin crawl, but he meant every word. That's why people listened.

"Now Jacob's got a little something for you. He's going to run it up the flagpole and see who salutes." He turned to Jacob, and leaning in to him, quietly said - "Go for it, champ."

Jacob stood up uneasily and faced the crowd. Pushed the 'enter' key to start PowerPoint, the words "Let's talk," appearing on the screen behind him.

As the words started leaving his mouth, Jacob zoned out, left the scene. He was able watch himself as if a stranger. Totally detached. He wondered who this sweaty little guy in the cheap suit really was. And what the fuck he was talking about.

Phil's words clung to him as he walked through the car park, loosening his tie on the way. "You did well Jacob, really well. You got 'buy-in' alright. You're a great communicator Jacob, there's no doubt. I sometimes think you doubt yourself, but you shouldn't. You were made for this."

Marion was waiting for him at his car, arms folded and shifting awkwardly from foot to foot. "Jacob," she said, "have you got a minute?"

"Er, yeah," he said as he started to roll a cigarette. "I mean, of course. What is it?"

"It's about this whole brand thing. You seem to have a real grasp of it. I wondered if you could answer a couple of questions for me."

Jacob wanted to get home, to forget all about *The Brand*, to have a beer, to phone Stevie, to iron out the plan. He said - "I'm kind of in a rush. You know, things to do."

"Please, Jacob. I think Phil's going to sack me."

Jacob could see that tears were imminent. Fuck it. He unlocked the car.

"Come on Marion, I'll buy you a pint."

"A pint?"

"Or short. Whatever."

"OK."

There were no real pubs for miles, so Jacob swallowed his pride and drove toward the nearby Harvester, Marion filling the car with anxiety and bad vibes. Jacob tried to ignore her wheezy and erratic breathing, her left knee shaking in his peripheral vision. He fought back the pity he felt for her, tried to wrestle it out of mind. She said, "I'm sorry to burden you with this. You are a special and unique person and you don't need to help me, but I had to ask."

"Forget it, I know what it's like in there, with all those changes."

"I'm sure he's going to sack me Jacob, I'm sure."

"Don't be stu..." He stopped himself, started again. "Why would he sack you? You haven't done anything wrong."

"Not as such, but things are different now with this re-branding thing. I don't understand it, I really don't."

"Marion, no-one understands it, not really."

"You do, you just gave that presentation."

"Marion, between you and me right..." he paused, wondering if it was wise to share this with Marion.

"You can tell me," said Marion.

What the hell. "I just got it all off the Ellis and Stead website."

"All that stuff about brand loyalty?"

"Yeah."

"So you don't understand it either."

"Well to an extent I do. I mean I understand why people buy

Heinz baked beans even though they're twice the price of the home brand. I understand why a dentist drives an Audi, a geography teacher drives a Volvo, and a complete wanker drives a Lexus."

Marion didn't laugh. "Hasn't Phil got a Lexus?" she asked.

"Er, not sure. But anyway, my point is: don't worry about it. Phil's not going to sack you. He doesn't really understand this re-branding either."

"Don't be ridiculous, Jacob."

"No, I'm serious. He knows what he's told. He knows how to get everyone excited. But the thing with Phil is, he'd have the same level of excitement whether he was launching a new brand or cleaning his fucking toilet."

"I've never heard anyone talk like this before, Jacob."

Marion seemed a little happier now. But some of her excess unease had transferred itself to Jacob. He felt unsettled having said all that stuff out loud, to Marion. It was risky, stupid. She was likely to either see Jacob as a traitor, or attach herself to him like a limpet.

Jacob cursed himself and pulled into the Harvester's car park. He eased into a parking spot and waited as Marion examined her face in the mirror, making clumsy and ultimately pointless corrections to her make up. He looked away.

Jacob's battered old Saab was the sore thumb here - the rest of the car park contained row after row of formless, shapeless middle-management fleet cars - slippery, metallic, overweight; soulless, sexless, dead.

A chinless, comb-overed accountant type emerged from the pub. The early evening sunlight hit his eyes, provoking a pinched, tooth-exposing grimace from his pasty face. He was looking for his car, a briefcase under one arm. His mobile went off - some crap polyphonic thing - and he stopped dead right in front of Jacob's car to answer it. He had no idea that Jacob and Marion were there.

Jacob felt like David Attenborough, silently studying this

incredible, and at the same time, profoundly unremarkable beast.

The beast let out a nasal clack of laughter. Then his reedy voice trilled - "Yeah, we got the contract. Donald just bought us all champagne, yeah it was a real buzz...hah-ah."

He walked off in the direction of his car, hoisting his slacks and exposing a pair of elephant-grey leather slip-ons. Jacob actually gasped at the sight of the shoes. They struck Jacob as sad. Not sad as in a nineteen-eighties description of uncool, but sad as in sudden and multiple-bereavement. Relentless, bruising grief. The end of everything.

I have got to stop noticing people's fucking shoes.

At this, something gave way, ruptured in Jacob's abdomen, and he felt a tight coiling inside of him. He knew the feeling wasn't physical, not really, however much he felt it that way.

He turned to Marion - "I don't know if I can do this anymore. I feel like I'm playing a part."

"What?"

"This private enterprise thing, all this handshaking, meeting-holding posturing, pretending that anything that we do is of any real consequence beyond office ego - everyone knows it's bullshit, but no-one says so. It doesn't make any sense to me."

Marion looked alarmed, confused. She sat speechless.

"I've got to get out. I can't be this person, do this, for one more year, one more month. Not for one more day."

"Jacob, what are you saying?"

"Marion. I don't know, I'm just...I'm just sick of being in the wrong fucking job."

I'm losing more than I'll ever have

Jacob slipped the shovel under the patio door, and leaning back, levered the door from the frame. He was in. He turned to see Reilly through the darkness, pissing in a flowerpot.

"What the fuck are you doing?" he hissed. "I don't know why you came anyway. I could do this by myself."

"There is no one I'd rather burgle than Stevie," replied Reilly, shaking and zipping up.

"Give me a hand with this door. Put those gloves on."

Reilly tutted in response.

"And put that fucking pipe out."

Reilly did as instructed, and the two of them heaved the metal frame to an inside wall, carefully resting it there.

"Right. What first?" asked Reilly.

"Heaviest stuff first. Go for the TV. I'll get the microwave."

Jacob headed to the kitchen, squinting in the darkness, scanning for anything else of value. He spotted an espresso machine, a juicer and a neat-looking portable stereo on the sideboard. He made a mental note to come back for them. He grabbed Stevie's iPod from the work surface, and stuffed it in his back pocket. Then he grabbed the microwave, and carried it out through the garden and into the back alley, where his car was parked. He looked back up at the house.

In the flat above, the lights were out as expected, it was three in the morning after all. Stevie had assured Jacob that his upstairs neighbour was a heavy sleeper and scatty as hell, unlikely to be a reliable witness if it came down to it. Jacob thought he heard a police siren for a moment, but told himself to reject any thoughts of getting caught, to simply refuse to let them in. He headed back in to the flat, concentrating on his breathing.

To his horror, Reilly had turned on the living room light, and was using a magic marker to write on the walls in huge red letters. Jacob stood in open-mouthed panic.

Reilly turned from his handy work, a broad grin on his face. He'd written "DIE BLUES SCUM," "UP THE VILLA," and "FUCK B.C.F.C." He gave Jacob a nod, as if to say "pretty clever eh?"

Jacob flicked the light off, and struggling to keep his voice to a whisper, said - "You stupid fucker Reilly. What are you fucking thinking?"

"I'm trying to make it realistic. Frame some Villa fans. They won't look for us god-fearing yids then, will they?"

"Jesus Christ. Get that TV in the car, or fucking go home."

"Yeah yeah."

Reilly headed for the TV, Jacob's panic rising as he watched him clonk about among the wires. Jacob grabbed the DVD player, stacked the video and X-Box on top and hurried back out.

He waited by the boot as Reilly stumbled through the garden with the TV. He took it from him, slid it into the car and handed Reilly some bin liners, saying, "Right, get all the CDs. And be fucking quiet."

Another fifteen minutes and they were done. The car was full of appliances, electronics, jewellery, and other trophies. All items carried a cash value.

And crucially, the cargo also included Stevie's music stuff – his guitars, laptop, DAT machine and amps. They would all be put to use.

Jacob's conscience was eased by the notion that Stevie's long neglected mikes, processors and effects pedals would be liberated like the mangy inhabitants of an Eastern bloc zoo.

They drove away through the back streets, away from Clifton and the scene of the crime. Avoiding main roads, Jacob slalomed across Bristol and back towards the flat. The sky was brightening as they sped away. A deep blue, a new day.

He looked over at Reilly, who was now asleep, breathing heavily. His T-shirt read 'THANKYOU TESCO.' His face looked ghoulish in the dawn light, blue-white skin and what appeared to be a tear drying on his right cheek. It was a pitiful sight. *To think I could go to prison for this poor, sad, beautiful bastard...*

Jacob looked back at the road, as a milk float appeared through the gloaming, dead ahead. He slammed on the brakes, and swerving violently, almost clipped the float's wing mirror, narrowly missing a parked car on the other side of the road. "Shit!"

As a reflex, he stepped on the accelerator, and then threw a hard left, down a side street and out of sight.

Jacob phoned Marion, telling her he wouldn't be in. He sat stiffly on the sofa, drank coffee after coffee, and chained cigarettes. The phone rang at ten-fifteen. Jacob pounced on it.

"Hello."

"Jacob. How are you dear?"

"Mum? Good, thanks."

"I just phoned your work, but they said you had a migraine. How are you feeling?"

"Fine. I mean, pretty rough. I'm just taking it easy. You know."

"Well, you look after yourself."

"Oh I will. How are you and Dad?"

"Fine. The shop's not doing so well though to tell the truth. The supermarkets are killing us really. No one wants to go to a little shop when they can buy their books from Tesco along with the weekly shop. It might be time to sell up, cut our losses."

"It's always slow this time of year though, isn't it?"

"Yes it is. If we have a good Christmas we'll be alright. We won't need to ask our only son for a loan just yet." She said the words in jest, but Jacob noticed a hint of desperation in her voice.

"I'll help you out Mum, you know that. I'm skint at the moment, but I might be able to help in a couple of months. I'm going to be recording an album…"

"I know. I got an email from Sharon. Such a lovely girl. So thoughtful of her to drop a line and tell me she was back in England. You two were always so suited."

"Mum."

"I know it's none of my business. I will say no more."

"Good. Look Mum, I've got to go. I'm waiting for a call. I'll give you a ring later, OK?"

"OK."

Jacob put the handset down and rolled another cigarette. The phone rang again as he was lighting up.

"Hello?"

"He heh, Jacob the cat burglar! Nice work mate."

"Stevie. How did it go? With the police?"

"Oh, no sweat. They were fine. Very polite. Always a pleasure to deal with the police." He paused. "You wore gloves right?"

"Yeah, of course. Why?"

"Oh, you know. They were dusting like mad."

"Sorry about your wall."

Stevie laughed. "Yeah, what was all that about? Didn't look like your writing."

"Reilly thought it would be a good idea to drink a few bottles of wine beforehand. He was doing my head in. What did the police say about it?"

"Oh they weren't too arsed. I've got that picture of St Andrews on the bedroom wall remember? They told me it was probably some kids on crack or something! I had to keep a straight face. Hey, is Reilly there? Put him on."

"He's gone to work. Still pissed I think."

"What a guy."

"Yeah. Stevie, did your neighbours hear anything?"

"I don't know. The police didn't mention it anyway."

"What about the insurance?"

"They're sending some bloke 'round this afternoon. It'll be cool."

"I hope so."

"Don't worry Jacob. Be calm. You did a good job, it'll be fine. You even remembered to grab my Tag Heuer. I loved that watch, make sure it goes to a good home."

"Very funny mate. Look, I've got to go. Speak to you later."

"Nice one Jacob. Ta ra a bit."

"Bye."

Jacob put the phone down. He exhaled. Almost there now. He downed his coffee and looked for his car keys.

The sales meeting was painfully slow, a drawn out toothache of an hour. Reilly fought to hide his indifference. But it was nearly over, Sandra handing out 'Ring Ring, Bling Bling' coffee mugs to the team. An unexpected thought hit Reilly midway - maybe there was more to life than this. Maybe it could actually work, this Serpico thing.

What if they got a deal with a good label, Domino or Chemikal Underground or Big Cat. A label that understood artists like Reilly. Maybe it could be a job, maybe you didn't need to be a sell out. Perhaps Reilly could have full artistic control, and the respect he deserved. Then he could fuck up the industry from within, make his mark in some worthwhile way. Use it as a platform to speak out about the Bush junta and the danger of the American neo-conservatives.

He imagined himself at some future Brit Awards, waiting backstage with Jacob, ready to go on and present an award. They would stride out together, a respectful hush as the invited guests recognised them and made the connection, start whispering among themselves - "It's Serpico. They brought out that amazing album, changed the face of British music. They funded it themselves apparently." "Yeah, that's right. I heard that the shorter guy's a total freeloader, the singer's the genius."

Jacob would calmly approach the mike. "Good evening. We are Serpico. We're here to present the award for Best International Female Artist. And the nominees are…"

Reilly would talk next, and he knew just what he'd say - "Ladies and Gentlemen. Let me just say that I believe that any artistic endeavour carries a level of risk. The risk that the outcome cannot be known. The creative process is always an experiment, and I think it's fair to say that the instigator of the experiment is the recipient, rather than the creator of the end result. Maybe the experiment works, maybe it doesn't, and ultimately, what fucking difference does it make anyway? I mean, really?"

The audience would no doubt gasp at this point. But Reilly would push on - "You see how pointless the whole notion of an award for music is? Why are we congratulating people for performing experiments with lucky outcomes? Music is not the Olympics, you fucking morons. And further to that, I just want to add every single man, woman and child in this room makes me physically sick. You are all self-regarding wankers."

Reilly would probably have to pause again here for another gasp. "Anyway, the stupid, ugly, pointless nominees are…"

"Jon, can I have a word?"

Sandra put a hand on Reilly's shoulder, as the rest of the team filed from the sales meeting, smiling and whispering among themselves.

"Yes Sandra, how can I help?"

"You look a bit, unwell. I saw you nodding off in the meeting. I know you're having a hard time, and I don't want to put any more pressure on you. I think you should go home, and get some sleep. I'll see you tomorrow."

Reilly waved an arm at her. "No no, I'm fine. I want to sell stuff. I need to sell stuff. I'm going on the phones."

He made a movement towards the door.

"Jon, I really think…"

"You think too much," he said and pushing her away, ran from the room to find his desk.

He sat down and slipped on his head set. A wave of laughter alerted him to his mistake. The other desks were empty, the rest of the team having formed a loose circle in the middle of the sales floor, in the centre of which sat snivelling little shit Michael, wearing a smock. Mary stood over him, electric clippers in her hand.

"Come on Jon," said Mary, "You're next!"

Everyone laughed.

"Oh, it's this cancer thing, is it?" he said as he staggered over to join them. His team mates ignored him, and looked back to Michael who wore a sit-com grimace and was mouthing "No, no, no," as Mary fired up the clippers and started removing clumps of hair. A couple of girls shrieked, one lad shouted, "Mister Potato Head!"

Mary sheared away, and after a couple of minutes, and much laughter, Michael was bald. He stood up, and removing his smock, looked at himself in a vanity mirror, touching his head gently as if it were not his own.

"Who's next?" asked Sandra.

"Jon!" shouted Mary, and the team turned to face him. A couple of others seconded the motion - "Yeah, Jon!" "Let's get that hair off you!"

"No," replied Reilly. Quietly but firmly.

"Come on," persisted Mary.

"No," said Reilly, more forcefully this time.

"It's really rock and roll you know," said Mary, "my bass player and drummer both have number one cuts."

"Shut the fuck up about your stupid fucking crap fucking band, you clueless fucking cow," said Reilly before he could censor himself. He felt a pleasant jolt of surprise at how easily the words left his mouth. It felt natural and right.

Everyone was looking at him now. A deathly silence filled the floor. Reilly filled it - "And shaving your head to support Cancer research! Could you be any more fucking crass? You fucking pigs. You make me sick. And *you*..." he turned to Michael. "You had your head shaved because you *wanted* to, not to help anyone. You fucking love it, you did it because you wanted to have your head shaved but are too much of a fanny to go to the barbers and ask for it. You mark my words everyone, his head will still be shaved in a year's time."

He paused for breath, and was still met only with silent disbelief. He felt duty bound to continue. An idea struck - "Michael, here's a challenge for you." Michael shifted uneasily, looking for Sandra. "If you want to do something to show you care about cancer, a real sacrifice I mean, then let's do it. What do you reckon?"

Michael did not reply.

"Let's cut our little fingers off. Come on, you and me. I'm sure everyone will put in a hundred quid to see that, it's a great cause after all. That's got to be what, two grand for charity just like that. It'll show how much we care, let's do it Michael. Who's got a knife?"

Michael was now refusing to look Reilly in the eye. Sandra stared open-mouthed, the clippers shaking in her hand. Reilly looked around at the rest of the team. The anger drained from him. And was replaced by a guilt. He suddenly felt very tired. He thought about his bed, rubbed his eyes.

"Sandra. I don't think I want to work here any more."

Waiting for engines

Jacob followed the road out of the countryside and through the edge of the town, and looking down at the passenger seat, read the directions again -

"Centre of Taunton, Ford Street is just off the High Street. The shop's called 'Millennium Pawnbrokers.' The owner's called Reg, and he asks NO QUESTIONS.

Good luck mate, Stevie."

He found his way and parked up outside. He went to unlock the boot, but rethought. He reasoned that it would be better to go in empty handed at first, just to check the lie of the land.

The shop was empty, save for an old fat guy with Wurzel's sideburns sat behind the counter. He stood up, radiating an easy confidence. The confidence that Jacob had noticed people past fifty often had. *Is that how long it takes to accept yourself and become comfortable in your own skin?*

"Reg?" stuttered Jacob.

"The very same, sir. How can I help you today?"

"I've got a few things to sell. I'm emigrating to Australia and can't take it all with me. Will you have a look?"

A broad grin spread across Reg's face - "Australia eh? I get a lot of people saying that. Must be a great place. And getting very crowded I'd say. Whereabouts are you heading?"

"Oh, er. Sydney."

"Sydney. Very nice." Reg was just about containing his laughter. "What have you got for me then?"

"Various things. They're in the car. I'll show you."

"Better drive 'round the back," said Reg with a wink. "We don't need my nosey neighbours seeing our transactions now do we?"

"Right."

Jacob did as instructed, and following Reg's hand signals, reversed up to the shop's back door. He opened the boot and removed the blanket covering Stevie's possessions.

"Well, you really are travelling light," said Reg as he scanned the merchandise with eager eyes. "Let's get all this inside, eh sir?"

Jacob pulled up a chair as Reg went through each item in turn, plugging them in, checking they were in working order, flicking through catalogues for prices. The jewellery and Tag watch took longer, Reg making a couple of phone calls and stroking his chin dramatically.

To Jacob, the process seemed to take an age. He imagined the local constabulary dropping by for a surprise inspection. Strutting in with handcuffs and smug one-liners at the ready. What would he do? He could bolt for the back door. But no. He couldn't leave the gear.

He took a look around the shop to distract himself. He spotted a couple of guitars at the back. The first was a flying V, a real cock-rocker's delight. He shivered at the thought of the macho riffing it had surely been subjected to, and turned his attention to the Les Paul copy lying next to it. As he walked closer he could see it had a couple of strings missing, and the body was heavily scratched, but it looked well made. He picked it up.

This was no copy. It was fucking real. It was covered in dust, and the pick ups were a little rusty, but the logo was unmistakable. An original Gibson Les Paul. Did Reg know this?

"See something you like sir?" asked Reg, making Jacob jump a little.

"Maybe." Jacob put the guitar down.

"Anyway, I've got a figure for you. Tell me what you think."

Reg led Jacob back to the counter and, using a biro, pointed to his note pad. On it he'd circled, "6K."

"Six grand? This stuff's got to be worth almost thirty thousand new."

"Well, sir. It's not new is it?"

"No. But, six grand's no good to me. I need ten," he pleaded, appalled at the desperation in his own voice.

Reg sucked his teeth. "You seem like a nice young chap. And you're going to need some money for your new life…"

"My new life?"

"In Australia."

"Oh, of course. Yes."

"I can offer you seven. And that guitar."

"Eight. And the guitar."

"Done." Reg held out a hand. Jacob shook it, and while Reg counted out the fifties, he headed for the Les Paul, sucking in his lips to stop the broad smile that threatened to form across his face.

Jacob stashed the cash in the glove compartment and feeling elated and energised, powered out of town and into the Somerset countryside. He rolled down his window to get some air flowing through the Saab. The summer air was thick with pollen and humidity. And it felt great to be out of Bristol, the contrast as dramatic as land and sea. Jacob felt healthier, he looked at his arms and realised he'd caught a bit of sun, he had a hint of a tan. The Chemical Brother's *Pioneer Skies* pounded from the stereo, and the steering wheel became a drum kit, Jacob banging along maniacally. He pulled off the main road, and checking his atlas, headed for Thrall.

A few miles of gently winding country roads and unreal looking patchwork fields and Jacob reached the village. He pulled in at the Post Office to ask directions to Sennen Farm.

"Keep going for about half a mile, there's a left turn just after the Wheatsheaf. You can't miss it," a shrivelled but warm old lady told him.

"Thanks very much."

"You in a band are you?"

Jacob thought for a moment, and then shooting a smile, replied, "Yes. Yes I am. We're called Serpico."

The woman nodded, and then said - "Can't say I've heard of you. Sorry. My granddaughter's probably got your poster on her wall though."

Jacob laughed. "I doubt it. But she may have one soon."

He found the Wheatsheaf easily enough, and took a left as instructed. A half-mile dirt track led him up a hill to a huge renovated farm house, dark wooden beams and white walls, a pristine thatched roof completing the picture.

He parked up and killed the engine. He stuffed the cash into one back pocket, the demo tape into the other, and rang the doorbell. The door opened, and Dave Wilson himself stood in front of Jacob, wearing nothing but a ridiculously small pair of Speedos. Dave Wilson.

"Yes?" he said.

"Oh, hi, er, Dave. I'm Jacob. I've come down from Bristol. I'm going to be recording an album, wondered if I could have a look at the studio?"

Dave, noticing Jacob's unease at his state of dress, laughed, and said, "Of course mate," in a slow Somerset drawl. "By the way, I was just getting into the pool, I'm not just some perverted ex-rock star. Come in, I'll get changed."

Dave led him through to the lounge, and gestured for him to take a seat on one of the huge leather sofas.

"You want a beer, Jacob?"

"Yeah, lovely."

"Good man."

The walls were decorated with gold and platinum discs, photographs of a young Dave with David Bowie, Lou Reed and Andy Warhol. Jacob was bowled over - this was how to decorate a lounge room.

Dave returned with a couple of bottles of Stella and was now dressed in a loose cotton shirt and jeans. He looked like Howard Marks. *I hope I look as cool as this when I'm forty-five.*

"Right, I'll show you the studios then. Follow me."

They walked out the back, past the pool where an exotic young model type was doing lengths. "That's Madeleine," said Dave as they walked on through the landscaped gardens.

The view was incredible. Miles of undulating farmland and copses, villages dotted around the landscape, little church spires announcing each one.

"What's your band called, Jacob?"

"Serpico."

"Serpico. I like that. The Al Pacino film, right?"

"Yeah, that's it."

"Band names are important. When Mechanical Sundial split up, I wanted to get away from all that prog-rock stuff and I formed a couple of bands. We used to argue for weeks about the name."

"Well, Serpico wasn't my idea. It was Reilly's, the singer. He said he liked the idea of being a misfit battling against stupidity or something."

"Nice. How many are in the band?"

"Oh it's just us two. We're not your average outfit."

"Fair enough. Nothing wrong with that." Dave pointed using his beer. "The studios are just up here. There's two of them. The smaller one's probably better for you if there's only two of you. More cosy."

At the top of the garden, hidden amongst the trees, was a huge shed. Dave unlocked it and flicked on some lights. "I'll get this air conditioning on," he said. Jacob followed him in to the sound booth. The booth had a large fridge, a kitchenette and a couple of sofas facing a TV. It was bigger than Jacob's lounge. He looked around in awe. At the end of the booth was a huge mixing desk, an unfathomable amount of buttons and knobs spread across it. A glass panel separated the booth from the studio proper, and Jacob approached it, peering in. It was a fantastic space. High ceilings and floor space enough for a brass band.

"This is the small one, Dave?"

"Yep." He laughed.

A large Persian rug was spread across the floor, and dark drapes hung from the soundproofed walls.

"You can change the décor obviously. There's dimmer switches for all the lights so you can change the atmosphere. What do you reckon, Jacob?"

"I reckon this is fucking perfect. Really is."

Dave smiled. "What does Serpico sound like then?"

"Er, well it's guitar based, but we use loops and samples. It's a bit like Death in Vegas, the later Radiohead stuff maybe. I've got the demo tape here, can I stick it on?"

"Yeah great." Dave took the tape and put it in a deck, flicking various switches as he sat down at the mixing desk. "Pull up a chair," he said.

"This one's called *Summertown*," said Jacob, as the monitors filled with noise. Reilly's voice came in, and then the drums. Dave nodded along.

He shouted to make himself heard, "This is great. *That* voice. Wow."

Jacob grinned. The song finished.

"It's pretty raw," said Dave, "but you've really got something to work with here. I like the way you've absorbed dance music, the way it's written, the way it builds, rather than just sticking loops over a normal indie song. That's what Bowie was all about, back in the day. What label are you on?"

"Oh. Er, Naked Cousin."

Dave looked blank.

"It's our own label." Jacob felt a twinge of embarrassment. He was reminded of the time he'd filled up a trolley at Sainsbury's, gone through the check out before realising he'd left his wallet at home.

But Dave wasn't bothered. "That's cool. As long as I get paid! When are you thinking of recording?"

"Well, the August Bank Holiday weekend if that's possible."

Dave thought for a moment. "Next weekend? An album in three days? That could be a bit full on. But it's possible I think. Yeah, we can do that. I've actually got another band in the big studio then, so yeah, that could work. Hey, have you got a producer?"

"No."

"Well, I'll engineer it if you like, and we'll mix it together. What do you reckon?"

Jacob could have kissed him. Dave Wilson, offering to produce his album. What a guy.

"That would be just great."

Dave laughed and slapped Jacob on the back.

"I almost forgot Dave. What's the cost?"

He tapped his chin for a moment, and then said. "Oh, I don't know, call it fifteen hundred?"

"Great." Jacob started counting out the fifties.

"Shit, you came prepared didn't you?"

"Yeah."

Dave pocketed the cash and led the way back to the house. Madeleine was lying on a sun lounger, her lithe young limbs soaking up the sun. She flashed Jacob a warm smile and a wave as he strode past, which he awkwardly returned.

"Dave. I want your life," he said as they reached the front door, and Dave bellowed with laughter.

"It's all there if you want it, mate. You just need to take it."

"Is it that easy?"

"Of course it is. I'll see you next weekend."

"Thanks, Dave."

Jacob turned and headed for his car. Dave shouted after him.

"Oh, one other thing Jacob. Just so you know - it's going to be busy around here next weekend - this other band are booked in the bigger studio.

"They're only doing B-sides but their A&R reckons they'll probably bring a load of hangers-on. But they're paying me twenty times what you are and bringing some big shot producer with them, so it's best to indulge them."

"Fair enough. Who are they?"

"They're called the Nu-Birds."

Shocker in Gloomtown

Jacob got to the conference centre half an hour early, and made his way to the entrance. Phil had detailed him and Marion to greet each coach load of employees, to hand out welcome packs and, "get those mothers excited!" Marion was waiting for him, wearing another bad trouser suit with terrifying shoulder pads. She was looking less and less like a busy executive, more and more like a posh beggar.

"Jacob! Good to see you. I was worried you weren't coming. What with the crisis you're having. If you want to talk, I'm here. Do you want to talk?"

"No, thanks though."

"Fine. That's fine. Because if you ever want to talk... You know I may come over as quite calm and together. But it's because of these groups I go to. I've had some hard times too."

Fuck. Marion now had him down as a kindred spirit. She was nice enough, he told himself, but Jacob knew that people like Marion were quicksand. However harmless and golden hearted they appeared, you couldn't get too close because you'd never get away.

He changed the subject - "Today should be interesting, don't you reckon?"

"Yes. I'm so nervous. I lay in bed last night just, just... visualising. I just want it all to go well. I can't wait to see the new brand."

"Yeah," was all Jacob could muster to this. He'd spent last

night writing drum loops on Stevie's laptop and cursing the inconvenience of today's launch.

They were both in business dress, and thankfully the heat wave had abated slightly. The day was grey and nondescript, the temperature a pleasant twenty two degrees. Marion relayed her latest personal disasters as they waited for the first coach. She'd somehow allowed herself to be sold a timeshare in the Canaries, and the company had gone under, leaving her three grand out of pocket and with nothing to show for it. She'd also fallen off her bike in the park, breaking a finger in the process, and was compiling a case against the council for not erecting warning signs. She was hoping the two things would even out somehow. Jacob nodded and made sympathetic noises while he waited, internally appalled at the harmful decisions Marion made for herself.

Christyn and Stefan from Ellis and Stead arrived, pulling up in an aggressively expensive BMW Coupe. Jacob waved eagerly, thankful for the respite.

"Jacob! Marion! How's it going?" asked Stefan.

"Great," said Jacob.

"I'm nervous as hell," offered Marion.

The contrast between the two couples couldn't have been more marked. Jacob was acutely aware of the disparity. *They are so slick, they don't even need to talk themselves into belief in their work. They are their jobs. We are scruffy, nervous, neurotic fuckwits, and they know it.*

"Don't be nervous," said Christyn, placing a reassuring hand on Marion's arm. "This can't fail. There's too much invested in it."

Stefan winced theatrically - "You're not wrong there." They both laughed.

"How much?" asked Jacob.

"Sorry?"

"How much is invested? I'm just curious what this sort of thing costs."

Stefan and Christyn looked at each other for a moment. Stefan spoke - "I guess we can tell you, but don't go spreading it around. Some people aren't as clued up as you two. You realise that the cost of building a brand is a great investment in terms of future returns."

"Oh yes, we understand," said Marion, her pained expression contradicting her words.

"Just under eight and a half million all up."

Jacob and Marion were speechless.

"But think of it like this - it's eight and a half million that will return maybe a hundred million over the next ten years. That's a good return. And the launch alone is massive, it has to be."

Christyn took over, "And you get what you pay for. We know about branding. We've had some of the finest minds in the industry, in the world, working on this. Some real geniuses."

Eight and a half million was beyond Jacob's understanding. He felt flush with eight grand in his glove compartment. Impossibly excited by what it could buy.

The first coach pulled in, and Jacob and Marion set to work, handing out the packs and giving directions to the hall. Christyn and Stefan headed for the conference centre, shaking hands and dispatching cool welcomes as they went.

Phil was first on the bill. He strutted out across the stage, his legs shrouded in dry ice, the chorus of *Let Me Entertain You* sound-tracking his big entrance. Jacob stood at the back of the hall, arms crossed. Marion was still at his side, shadowing him like a hangover.

The music faded out and Phil began, his words booming enthusiastically through his lapel mike and out of the PA.

"Hi, everyone!" he said, spreading his arms in a Christ pose.

"My name is Phil Jessop. Some of you know me, I'm sure, but for those who don't, I'm the marketing guy!"

Marion clapped enthusiastically.

"It's my job to make dreams real. To tell the world what we're all about. To get people excited. And let me tell you, today I'm the one who's excited - and all of you should be too!"

Jacob zoned out as Phil continued. He thought of the drums he'd been sequencing the night before. It had really flowed, everything was falling into place, and his idea of building the pace of the album track by track was working fantastically. He ran through the track listing in his mind, savouring the song titles, imagining them on the CD artwork - *Satellite Town, Swoon, Lower Maudlin Street, Analogue Soul, Summertown, Misplaced Coda, Junta, Biological Control, Lost Soul Music, Lactic* and *This Is Not An Exit.*

Oh yes - *Life and How to Live* it - the greatest album ever made.

"And so," said Phil, "to tell you more, please give a warm welcome, to my boss, your boss - Geoff Lieberman."

Applause filled the hall.

"Thanks Phil, and hello everyone. Now this really is a big day. It's huge…"

Where should Serpico play their first gig? Jacob knew he had to get moving on this. He wanted to keep the momentum going. He was afraid that when the recording was done, they'd slip back into the usual pattern of procrastination and over-preparation. And now that Reilly had more time on his hands, maybe he'd even start writing some new songs.

"In a moment I'll be showing you a short video presentation to announce the new brand, and it's going to blow your minds, I promise…"

They couldn't make their live debut in a back room of the local pub. It had to be professional. It would have to make an impact. To set out their stall. Would it be possible to set up a video screen like the one behind Geoff here? That could really set them apart from the hobby bands. Get people talking.

"This is a new era for our industry, and as promised, the moment you've all been waiting for." Geoff stepped aside and the screen sprang to life. An expectant hush fell over the room.

Jacob had heard a lot about this film, Phil had been banging on and on about it, without giving away too many details. Jacob tried to concentrate, told himself to take all this in -

The screen was blank, white. There was nothing there. After a few seconds Jacob thought maybe there was a problem, but no. Now some activity - two animated figures walked on from the right, and stopped centre screen. A stick man and a stick women. Strange.

"Sometimes we have an idea," said a saccharine sweet female voiceover. A light bulb appeared over stickman's head. "...And we just have to share it."

Stickman whispered in his companion's ear. A love heart appeared over stickwoman's head, and her cheeks flushed red. The audience laughed as the couple rushed off screen hand in hand, presumably for a stick shag.

The screen was, for a moment, blank once again. Another stickman appeared, this one stroking his chin, a question mark over his head. "Ideas are good," continued the voiceover, "ideas are what make us human." A light bulb appeared over his head, and the stickman rushed around the screen, assembling pipes and valves into a huge structure.

Once complete, the pipes began to rumble and shake, stickman placing a bottle under a big tap. The pipes swelled to bursting point and then fell silent, a drop of liquid fell into stickman's bottle.

With a satisfied smile, he slapped a label on the bottle, and held it up. It read *"Love."*

"Sometimes ideas give us more than we could have possibly imagined," explained the voiceover.

Marion tugged Jacob's sleeve - "What is this?' she asked. Jacob shrugged, and the low murmuring around the hall suggested the rest of the workforce shared their confusion.

"Imagine the power of ideas. Of all our ideas combined," said the voiceover, as a million stickmen and women danced around the screen, light bulbs appearing above each head. The stick people excitedly chatted among themselves.

One big light bulb now filled the screen. The voiceover said, "This is what our organisation is all about. And we have given it a name. We call it..."

There was a pause. And a tangible expectation in the hall. Like Jacob, everyone wanted to see what came next. What was it? What was this name? This brand.

The words were now on the screen, in thick italics, dark blue. Jacob read them - *Sex-U-up*™.

There were gasps around the room. Jacob took a moment to digest it. Marion looked up at him, as if waiting for some kind of reassurance.

The voiceover continued - "Yes. Sex-U-up. Say it to yourself. It's different, that's for sure. But great ideas are." And the film was over. The sounds of whispering, giggling and confused swearing began to fill the conference hall, slowly rising.

Marion went to the bar as Jacob got stuck in to the complimentary buffet. A perk of being in marketing, free food and booze with the managers. Jacob slugged back his champagne, happy with the free refreshment, but the mood of his fellow VIPs was best described as sombre. A collective brave face was being displayed, but it was obvious that senior management had expected a more enthusiastic response from their workforce. And the managers here who, like Jacob and Marion had not previously known the new company name, were in the main, utterly baffled. Jacob eavesdropped on a couple from finance -

"I know what you're saying, but, what does it mean?"

"As I understand it, it doesn't really *mean* anything. It's designed to get people talking."

"But we still sell water coolers, don't we?"

"Yes. I think so."

"What the hell is sexing you up got to do with it?"

"I don't know."

"Shit."

"I guess they know what they're doing."

"But, but it doesn't make any sense."

For his own part, Jacob couldn't really give a shit what they called their company. Made no difference to him. The whole episode, the absurdity of Sex-U-up was a mildly amusing distraction, something to relay to S next time they spoke, it would make her laugh.

Phil bounced around the room, slapping backs, shaking hands and winking indiscriminately. He spotted Jacob, and excitedly rushed over.

"Jacob - how about that eh? Quite an impact. Just what we want." There was something in Phil's expression that Jacob had not seen before. A desperation? No, a sadness. A moisture in his eyes.

"Yes, Phil."

"What are your thoughts then, Jacob? Shoot from the hip."

"Erm, well it's different. Edgy. It will get people's attention. I guess it also means it can be used for other products, because it's not specific to our current product."

"Yes! Yes! Bull's-eye Jacob. I love it. What's the feeling from your colleagues?"

"Pretty positive, I think. It'll take time."

At this, Phil looked over both shoulders, and dramatically leant toward Jacob. He stage whispered - "You may have noticed a bit of resistance from certain people."

"Really?" said Jacob, trying to sound surprised.

"Oh yes. Some people fear change, Jacob. They fear being challenged. They're scared of big ideas, creativity. They'll never understand people like you and me, but we are the future. I see big opportunities for you and me within Sex-U-up. Some people may snipe about the name, they may even leave the organisation. But it's their loss. It just leaves more room for people like us - stick close," he said, moving away from Jacob, slinking back into the throng.

Everything in its right place

The Flyer was about a quarter full, quiet in the early evening lull between afternoon and evening drinkers. The day had progressed from overcast, to muggy, and now the air hung heavy and damp. Rain was surely on the way.

Jacob, glad to be back in the real world, put his pint down on the usual table and pulled up a seat. It was time to slow down, to take stock and to drink beer. Reilly clumsily sat down opposite him, patting tobacco into his pipe with a deliberate forefinger, his eyes fixed on the task at hand, this evening's T-shirt, "SCARED OF AMERICA."

Jacob, ignoring Reilly's strange demeanour, downed half of his Stella, the cold, almost unbearable prickle of fizz tickling his throat on the way down - deliciously well deserved after today's extra-curricular activities. The first pint is always the best, he thought, as he rolled a cigarette. Reilly was still fiddling with his pipe.

"You alright, mate?" asked Jacob.

"Oh, yeah. Bit pissed actually."

"Is that what you did today? Get drunk?" laughed Jacob.

"Yes," replied Reilly candidly. "Well no, not just that. I had a look at some of that new equipment you got. Played some guitar. Played with the effects pedals. But anyway I got a bit bored with that, so I cracked open a bottle of wine. It wasn't like an all day thing."

"Shit, why didn't you get out and about. Don't know how you can just sit in all day. It's summer."

"What the fuck would I do outside? This is Bristol for fuck's sake."

Jacob laughed.

"Anyway, it's not like you're some kind of fucking outward bounds rambler or something is it? Fucking hell, Jacob."

"Alright, calm down."

Usually, Reilly's state of sobriety and mind would have Jacob concerned, but tonight he was immune. He was buzzing. This time next week they would be recording the album. In a real studio, with a real producer. It was all coming together and Jacob could not stop smiling.

"Big week, eh?" said Jacob.

"What? Yeah. Suppose it was. Glad to be out of that job."

"Reilly - fuck that! I'm not talking about your job. We cracked it. We're recording next week. With a real producer, in a real studio - fucking Serpico, Reilly. We're not a pretend band anymore. We're going to do it."

Reilly considered the words, finally sorting out and lighting his pipe. A smile spread across his face. Jacob had not seen this kind of smile in so long - a clean smile. Not caused by the misfortune of another, or the promise of revenge. A very un-English kind of smile. He thought immediately of S.

Reilly spoke - "You know, you're right. We are going to make this fucking album aren't we? The greatest album of all time, nothing more, nothing less."

"Too right. Cheers." Jacob offered his glass. Reilly, still smiling, lifted his own and their pints met, clinked.

"But Jacob, just remember, whatever happens – remember why we did it in the first place."

"What do you mean?"

"I mean never buy in to this *success* shit." The smile was now gone.

"Reilly…"

"No, it's important."

"We can sell records and be decent people, the two things aren't mutually exclusive. It doesn't have to change anything. You're just afraid to be good at something, Reilly. Think of... I don't know, the Pixies, Joy Division, Nirvana, fucking Radiohead - all these people you love. They played the game, sold a few records, but you can't call them sell-outs exactly."

Reilly thought for a moment. "I know what you're saying, mate. I hear you. I love those bands I really do, but there's just something so... repugnant about successful people, you know what I mean?"

Jacob sensed something forming in Reilly's mind, he was building up to a rant. Jacob sat back a little, got ready.

"...whether it's a scientist, TV presenter, dotcom entrepreneur or whatever. I mean who gives a fuck? I mean who really gives a fuck? People like that, they start believing that the slice of luck that put them where they are was really just some part of a grand plan. They might start out as good people, but they mistake luck and timing and a slice of skill for something else, like destiny. They become ugly, distorted, fuck-up human beings who are morbidly self-satisfied and what's more, have the audacity to pity anyone who's not them.

"They start saying that they wish that everyone could just have that drive that put them where they are - as if where they are is really so impressive anyway - I mean really who gives a fuck if your record sells, if you're the new queen of rom-com, or if you build a chain of shops up from a Sunday market stall. All so you can buy some fucking car and wear it like a medal."

"Right," offered Jacob, riding it out.

"There's something fundamentally vulgar about doing well in this society as it is, and the values it represents - success on these terms is failure, Jacob. Success. On. These. Terms. Is. Failure."

Jacob let the words hang in the air for a moment, and then, knowing it was easier to ask the question than not, said, "Why is it a failure then?"

"It's a failure because you're validating and perpetuating these values that you know are fundamentally ridiculous and lack integrity and lack any foundation or moral weight."

Reilly took a drink, and laid his pint down on the table.

"This fucking pipe," he said, "can I nick some Rizlas, mate?"

"Yeah, sure."

A couple of hours passed, Reilly and Jacob getting steadily drunker. Reilly systematically and methodically slated various bands, celebrities and belief systems, Jacob nodding along, playing devil's advocate and taking the resultant abuse on the chin. It was a good night. Although neither addressed it directly, they were celebrating.

Stevie arrived at about eight, got the beers in and sat down rubbing his hands together, a broad, seemingly fixed smile on his face.

"Guys, guys, guys..." he said, shaking his head in mock disbelief, "You will never guess, never..."

"What?" asked Reilly.

"Is it the insurance?" asked Jacob.

"No, no. Not that. " His smile faded as he recalled the scam, breaking the glee for a moment. "That was all sweet by the way. The bloke from the insurance company, the er, Loss Adjuster. He was a scary bastard though. Fuck me. Much worse than the police. He really grilled me, suggested all kinds of stuff like I'd done it myself! The cheek of it. I mean do I look like the kind of person who'd pull an insurance scam?"

Stevie laughed long and hard at his own joke.

"So what is it, what's your news?"

"Oh right. Well." He paused again. "Sorry guys - I'm being rude. I haven't congratulated you - fucking Serpico, in the studio. Like big boys! That's great stuff, it really is."

"Thanks mate," said Jacob, "and we're playing the Louisiana two weeks today."

"Fuck off! You're doing a gig?" Stevie shook his head. "I

never thought I'd see the day. Fucking Serpico getting off their lazy arses. Fair play."

"It's just a case of keeping up the momentum."

"You and your mission statements," said Reilly.

"Shut up. We talked about this."

"Who's that guy who's producing?" asked Stevie.

"*Co*-producing," corrected Jacob, "a bloke called Dave Wilson." He loved saying it.

"Who is he again?"

"Dave Wilson. Was in Mechanical Sundial! Huge in the seventies. Had that big hit - *Apple of my Eye.*"

Stevie was blank, shrugging.

Reilly jumped in - "Dave Wilson. Was in Mechanical Sundial, a very dodgy progressive-rock band. All pompous drum solos and crap album sleeves, sub-Salvador Dali surrealist crap with magpies and shit. Terrible. Horrible. Anyway, they had one big hit, which Dave Wilson wrote. A radio song. It goes '*I love you baby, you're the apple of my eye.*' Fucking Boyzone or Westlife or someone did a cover of it, which was Christmas number one a couple of years back. Inane, anaemic crap it was."

"Serious? That bollocks!" laughed Stevie.

"Yeah. And in the eighties he grew a terrifying mullet and wrote songs for David Hassellhoff - *Crazy For You*, that was it. Huge in Germany."

Stevie laughed hysterically at this.

"Fucking bollocks, Reilly," said Jacob, offended. "That's not true."

"No, you're right. About the Hassellhoff bit anyway. The rest is true."

"Fucking hell," said Stevie, still baffled. "I know the name, but…"

"He was on *Shooting Stars* once. They made him get in a pram and eat four bananas."

"Oh yeah!" Stevie finally got it. "They were taking the piss out of him for shagging girls half his age. He looks a bit weird, like he's made out of leather or something. Talks like a bumpkin."

"That's him," said Reilly, slumping back into his chair with relief.

There was an awkward pause.

"Fucking hell, Reilly," said Jacob. "Why do you have to be so fucking negative? He really knows his stuff. And he was really into Serpico, you ungrateful prick. He's not just some numpty you know, he's a really nice bloke. Really down to earth, not an ounce of pretence about him. And just because someone does a shit cover of a song he wrote thirty years ago, so what? Jeff Buckley used to cover *Apple of my Eye* when he was first gigging. It's a good pop song."

Reilly held up his hands, and in a rare display of humility, said, "I know Jacob. You're right. I'm just being, well, provocative. Truth be told, I'm amazed he's producing us. I love that PJ Harvey album he engineered."

"There you go then. And wait until you see the studios, man. You'll fucking love the set up there."

"Studios? More than one?"

"Yeah. Two actually."

"Two? Is the other one being used as well then?"

"Erm. Don't know. Dave said they might have another band in. Or not. Too early to... anyway, I need a piss."

Jacob bolted from the table, disappearing in the crowded pub, Stevie and Reilly raising eyebrows to acknowledge his strange exit. Reilly rolled and lit a cigarette, took a deep swig of Stella and looked around the pub. It was a depressingly familiar Saturday night crowd - overly made-up women, overly eager men. Townies, yuppies, trendies. All yapping, all saying nothing. Reilly knew this landscape so well now - The Flyer and the interchangeable but ultimately unchanging human traffic within. But tonight as he surveyed it, a creeping, irresistible feeling rose in him. A sense that something was drawing to a close. That a line had been crossed and non-negotiable ending of some kind was upon him. That events bigger than Reilly were piling up, ensuring that he would never, ever drink in this pub again. The feeling found him well.

"Oh yeah. I was going tell you some news," said Stevie with a jolt.

"That's right. What was it?"

"Well, you know those songs I wrote?"

"Oh, for fuck's sake."

"They're good mate. You shouldn't judge what you haven't heard."

"Oh, come on. Stop fucking about, Stevie. Is it Jacob's round?"

"Well I saw this ad in NME right? *'Frontman required for new band with major deal: send tape and photo to'* blah blah. So I thought what the fuck? Sent off a letter saying what my influences were and that, and I got a call this afternoon."

Reilly sat in astonished silence for a moment, his cigarette hanging from the corner of his still mouth. He spoke - "What are you saying?"

"They're really into it."

"Who? Who's into it?"

"They want me to head up to London this week to meet them, they're really keen."

"London! Don't go to fucking London, Stevie."

"London's cool mate. You know what they say - if a man's tired of London…"

"Please shut up."

"The bloke who phoned me, the guitarist, him and the drummer were in that band. What were they fucking called? Brit Pop band, back in '96 - they sounded like Blur. Always toured with them."

"Menswear?"

"No. Girl singer."

"Elastica?"

"No, no."

"Sleeper? Echobelly?"

"No. It wasn't them. But they were like them. Catchy tunes, on

TFI Friday all the time. Anyway the bass player was in… er. You know, that lot from Manchester."

Reilly held up a hand, laughed. "I get the picture Stevie."

Jacob reappeared, setting a new round of drinks on the table. Noticing Reilly's exasperated look, he asked, "What's going on?"

Reilly started laughing uncontrollably - "You're going to love this Jacob. This is fucking priceless. Stevie's beaten you to your precious record deal."

The rest of the evening disappeared in a wave of alcohol, drunken argument and congratulations. Stevie purchased cigars and tequila and the three of them, the three *musicians*, smoked and drank and rambled. Reilly could not stop laughing at Stevie's news. At the very idea. At the band name - Accelerator. At the way Stevie had absolutely no idea what this band sounded like yet, had no interest in the artistic value of their work, but had wholeheartedly pledged his future to them. Estate Agent to Indie Pop Star on a whim.

Jacob was pleased. Pleased for Stevie. But his pleasure was fused with a hot, incessant jealousy. This was just the latest episode in Stevie's charmed life. His innate knack of being in the right place at the right time.

Not for the first time, Jacob felt that life was mocking him. Making light of his own efforts by handing reward free of charge to others. Jacob felt like his adult life thus far had been spent running to simply stand still.

But Jacob's self pity was not Stevie's concern. And Jacob had no desire to punish Stevie for his good fortune. They drank and talked, shouted and boasted. They made pledges and plans until last orders interrupted, calling them out of the pub and onto the Bristol streets. Out into the warm summer rain.

Each time I bring it up it seems to bring you down

Back at the flat, Jacob fetched beer from the fridge as Reilly perused the bookcase. Standing no more than three inches away, he gently swayed on the spot, scanning the CDs and rubbing his hands together. Stevie, however, was several steps ahead, having spotted a Virgin Megastore bag on the coffee table with Jacob's latest purchase inside. While Reilly pondered, Stevie hijacked the stereo, and with his confidence boosted by his sudden elevation in the musical hierarchy, put the first Streets album on.

Reilly listened to a few bars, nodding gingerly to the beat. But then the vocals came in - Reilly's face turned, he looked disgusted, then genuinely nauseous, then enraged. "What the fuck is this? This sounds like a fucking school music lesson. Jesus wept."

Stevie was laughing. "Brummie class mate, brummie class."

"It's so... ugly," said Reilly, "it has no artistic weight. It tells us nothing. Fucking turn it off."

Stevie, laughing loudly, did as instructed, and in a move of appeasement, slipped in a Velvet Underground CD. *Sunday Morning* began chiming from the speakers. Reilly, very drunk now, stood up and literally applauded Stevie's choice - "The only band from the sixties worth listening to, Stevie. Listen and learn."

"What about the Kinks? What about the fucking Beatles?"

"Fuck the Kinks and fuck the Beatles. They didn't write *Sunday Morning*, did they?"

"You love the Beatles," said Jacob as he entered the room holding three beers, "everyone does."

"Kill your heroes, Jacob."

"What? Stop saying that."

"Is this Kronenbourg? Again?"

"Why does *everything* disgust you Reilly?"

"Because it's only right and proper that it should. What other reaction could there possibly be?"

Jacob didn't answer.

"And besides," continued Reilly, slurring now, "I cherish my disgust. It's the most valuable thing I own. If I ever lose it I'll be dead, because it's my weapon..."

Stevie interrupted - "Hey, shut up a minute. Look, since we're all fucking pop stars and that, and since we need to fucking sober up..." He pulled a wrap out of his back pocket, tapping his nose with the index finger of his free hand.

"Fuck off!" Reilly roared. "You and your fucking crap coke. It's probably cut with Vim."

Stevie laughed as he cut out a line, and gave Reilly a wink.

"Oh, go on then," said Reilly.

The phone rang. Jacob left the lounge to answer it.

"Hello?"

"Jacob, how are you?"

"S! Good to hear from you. It's been mad here, it's all happening."

"Oh, yeah?"

"What?" Reilly and Stevie were arguing in the background. "Hang on, S, I can't hear you. I'll get the phone in my room. Hang on a minute. I'll put the phone down."

"OK."

Jacob clumsily replaced the handset, and weaved along the hallway, pulling his tobacco, filters and papers out of various pockets as he did so.

Once in his bedroom he flicked on the light and jumped on his bed, rolling to the phone on the other side.

"S? Are you still there?"

"Yes, I am. Where have you been then? Flyer?"

"Yeah, how did you know? Been celebrating actually."

"Wow, what's happened?"

Best to sound cool - "Just band stuff, you know. But how are you? Are you working yet?"

"So thoughtful, Jacob. Such a caring, sensitive modern man."

"Shut up."

"Well, yes I am working actually. Friend of a friend of a friend edits one of those free commuter type papers, and I've done a bit of stuff for them. Not riveting, but it could lead to something bigger. You know I was hoping for a new career in music management, but some ungrateful git said no."

"I'm sorry, S. I really am. He just wouldn't have it, nothing personal."

"Bloody hell, Jacob, how drunk are you? I'm joking."

"Oh."

"So what's happening then, what's your news?"

"Well, we're recording the album next weekend. And we're doing a gig at the Louisiana the Saturday after. I really thought about what you said, about being organised and all that. So I got on to it."

"That's great Jacob, it really is."

"Thanks. I mean, between you and me, I'm nervous as fuck. I'm really on the verge of something here, I know it."

"Jacob. Just enjoy yourself."

"I don't want to fuck it up."

"You won't. Just take a step back. Drink it in. Laugh at it."

"Right. It's just all moving pretty fast. It seems to be falling in our lap, it makes me nervous. Like I don't deserve it."

"Jacob. You've been leading up to this for ten, fifteen years or something. You deserve it. Just be calm."

"You're right, you're right."

"I'm always right, you know that. Anyway, next weekend's the bank holiday isn't it?"

"Yeah."

"It's too bad. I was going to ask if I could come to stay next weekend. Never mind. Another time. I wanted to see you."

"Why?"

"Jacob. You make me laugh."

"What?"

"Nothing."

"S. I know what you're doing. I do." Emboldened by alcohol, Jacob added, "If you want us to get back together, just say so."

She was silent for a moment. "It's not that simple, Jacob. As you well know." She paused again. And then asked, "Do *you* want us to get back together?"

"I don't know. Yes. Maybe. It depends."

Jacob's words hung in the air, and a heavy static hummed down the line, building up. S was silent again, in thought. Jacob jumped in before she could respond - "No, it's not a good idea. I mean, I'm going to be really busy. You too. You're in London, I'm not…"

"You're right, Jacob. You're right. I'm sorry, I've waltzed back to England and expected nothing to have changed. I'll leave you alone. All the best with the recording and everything."

"S?"

"I'll see you Jacob."

"S, wait a minute."

"Goodnight, Jacob."

Click.

Fuck, fuck, fuck, fuck.

Jacob forced himself upright, as regret washed over him like an early hangover. He wandered back through to the lounge.

There he found the singer of Serpico and the singer of

Accelerator, wrestling. Stevie was winning, and deftly swung Reilly around and into a headlock.

"Get off me, you bummer!" screamed Reilly, utterly stuck now.

"Say it then," said Stevie calmly.

"Never."

"Say it."

"Never!"

Stevie noticed Jacob in the doorway, and casually nodded a greeting, rolling his eyes at the sight of Reilly's reddening face under his arm.

"Say it."

"Let go, I can't breathe."

"Then say it."

"Fuck off."

Stevie tightened his grip.

"Alright, just give me some air."

Stevie loosened slightly. Reilly muttered something.

"Come on, I can't hear you. Say it properly. Repeat after me - I promise. Not to wear. This suit. Ever again..."

A pause, and desperate struggling from Reilly.

"Never, you bastard! Never!"

The spark that bled

Jacob drove, nudging ninety in the fast lane, keeping an eye out for police. His law breaking was flagrant, but he was not alone, nestling mid-way in a chain of ten or twelve other speeders. A flock of co-conspirators, all silently agreeing to let Darwinism take its course should a patrol car appear.

Reilly slouched in the passenger seat, chaining roll ups and glancing regularly at the Oddbins carrier bag at his feet. On the car stereo - one of Reilly's mix tapes - Nirvana's *Scentless Apprentice* currently playing, and sounding tense, angry, utterly glorious.

"Just open a bottle if you want," said Jacob.

"What? Oh yeah. The Valpolicella. Yeah, why not?" Reilly pulled out a bottle and attacked it with the corkscrew.

"Oh fuck - look at this traffic," said Jacob as he piled on the brakes, flicked on the hazards.

"Told you, didn't I? August Bank Holiday. All those caravaners can't help themselves, it's Pavlovian. Three days off in a row - they just have to head down to Cornwall before it gets dark, leaving behind their neat little red-bricks in neat little rows. Drive their flabby arses down to some campsite and park their neat little stupid caravans in neat little rows. Really get away from it all. Fucking morons."

The Saab slowed to a crawl, and then a stop. Jacob took the opportunity to roll a cigarette, his first since they set off. The tobacco crackled deliciously as he lit up and inhaled. He drew the smoke down, deep down into his lungs and held it there. Reilly offered him the bottle of wine. He exhaled, holding a hand up.

"Reilly. I'm driving."

"Oh right. Yeah."

"We'll get off at the next exit, go the back way. Should still be able to make it by nine. I want to dump our stuff and get to the studio as soon as we can. Hopefully get a fair bit done tonight if we can get all this stuff set up." He gestured towards the boot and back seat of the car, which was packed with equipment both old and new - both Stevie's stolen goods and the newly purchased gear.

"Which song are we doing first, Jacob?"

"I think we should do it in the sequence they're going to be on the album, so we know where we are. Start with *Satellite Town*, then track by track from there. We'll get a better feel for the pacing of it that way. And the songs get a bit more, er, *technical* later on."

"What are you talking about? Technical." Reilly spat the last word out, as if a pube.

"Well, like the guitar parts on *Lactic* for example, I tuned down a couple of notes for those, but the rhythm guitar has a capo, so it's going the other way. Sounds good, but it all gets a bit complex. A bit of a juggling act."

Reilly shrugged - "I'll leave all that to you. As long as it works. As long as it does what we want."

"Don't worry. It'll work."

"You know what I mean though - I'm trusting you with my life here, Jacob."

"Reilly. It's my life too. I won't fuck up mate."

Reilly smiled. Drank some more wine.

They pulled up outside the Wheatsheaf at 10.15, Jacob stiff and testy, Reilly warm and drunk, heading straight for the bar as

Jacob sought out the Landlady.

Reilly perched on a barstool and ordered a couple of Stellas. The barmaid clocked and read his T-shirt - 'MISOGYNY AND HETEROSEXUALITY ARE NOT THE SAME THING' - and looked away, puzzled. The Nu-Birds were on the juke box, jangling in their inane, postured way. Reilly involuntarily tutted his disapproval. He looked around to see who might have chosen the song. An obviously underage couple, young farmer types, seemed the most likely culprits. The lad was wearing a fleece, supping cider and drumming along with his fingertips, his girlfriend pulling on a Silk Cut.

An oldish guy sat alone under the bay window, reading *Mojo*, a barely touched pint of Guinness on the table in front of him. Reilly clocked the leathery skin, unusually unkempt hair for a man his age, and made the connection - Dave Wilson. Without thinking, he walked over.

"Dave?"

"Er, yes?"

"I'm Jon Reilly. Serpico."

Dave thought for a moment, and standing up, said - "Hey, Reilly. Nice to meet you. I've been listening to your demo tape all week. It's very good, if you don't mind me saying so."

Reilly fought the smile, telling himself that this guy was a dinosaur, a prog-rock clown for whom punk never happened.

Dave continued, "Your vocals Reilly - very special I must say. What really struck me was the honesty. I don't mean the lyrics were honest, I mean your voice itself - there's nothing forced in it. It's a beautiful thing, you can't learn that."

Reilly now wore a broad grin, despite himself. "Thanks. Thanks a lot."

"Not at all. I can't wait to see what sort of album we can make. Nice T-shirt by the way."

"Thanks."

Jacob appeared at Reilly's shoulder.

"Dave. Good to see you." They shook hands.

"And you, Jacob."

"Thought you'd be at the house."

"Madeleine's away until tomorrow, thought I'd treat myself to a pint. How's your room?"

"Oh yeah. Fine. I'm thinking we'll be in the studio most of the time anyway. Twelve tracks in three and a bit days, it's going to be tight. We should get going really."

"You've got time to have a pint," said Dave. "Pull up a chair."

"OK."

Reilly fetched the Stellas from the bar and the three of them settled down at the table. Dave held court, relaying anecdotes from his *Shooting Stars* appearance.

Jacob had never seen anyone connect with Reilly so effortlessly before. Dave disarmed him, charmed him. Reilly tried to fight it, but he kept forgetting to be cynical and on guard, and found himself laughing long and hard at Dave's jokes. The pints soon disappeared and after a couple of whiskeys, last orders arrived.

"Time to go," announced Dave. "Let's make this album of yours then, eh?"

Jacob carried the gear in to the studio, Reilly studying the mixing desk as Dave attempted to explain why hundreds of dials and buttons were necessary.

"It just looks overcomplicated to me, Dave. I hate all that muso shite."

"It's not actually that complex when you know what it all does. A lot of it we won't use anyway. Do you want some more whiskey?"

"Wouldn't say no."

Jacob carefully positioned the equipment as he brought it in. Along one wall, he put all the guitar stuff - the Les Paul from the pawnbrokers (now restrung and reconditioned), a new Telecaster copy and Stevie's Stratocaster (great for feedback). There was also an array of pedals, both digital and analogue.

Two new amps, and Stevie's effects processor went in the far corner of the studio. Stevie's keyboard and sampler went by the fire exit, the new bass and amp opposite. Jacob put Reilly's new acoustic guitar, vocal mikes and lyric sheets in the centre of the studio, and headed back out for the laptop and iPod.

On his return, he found Dave and Reilly in the control room adjusting the lighting levels.

"What do you reckon, Jacob?" asked Reilly. Jacob looked around. The studio was bathed in a soothing half-light, the instruments around the edge lit up by small downlights above.

"I love it," he said. "Let's get in there."

Reilly watched from the control room as Jacob built up the guitar parts to *Satellite Town*, one by one. There were no drums in this song so Dave played a click track through the speakers to keep time. After thirty minutes, Reilly was utterly bored. Jacob seemed to be playing just two notes at a time, stopping and starting, adjusting and readjusting. It was painful to watch, the detail so tedious. He downed another whiskey.

"When do I do my vocals, Dave?"

"Not for a while. This is going to take a bit of time I think."

"I'm sure this song wasn't so fucking fiddly when I wrote it."

"A demo's different, Reilly. This needs to be just right. At the end of this track, the drums for *Swoon* start and it needs to sync perfectly to work. Wait and see."

"Right. Fascinating. I'm going out for a cigarette."

"You can smoke in here," said Dave, but the door was already closed.

Razor pilot

Reilly woke up. On a sun lounger, by a swimming pool - Dave's swimming pool. Alone, save for the whiskey bottle in his hand, and a screaming, angry headache.

The sun was up. He looked at his watch - 8.38am. And it was already getting warm.

He sat up, cross-legged, and rolled a cigarette. He looked down the hill as he smoked it, the studios amid the trees at the bottom of the garden, and the valley going on forever in the background. It was an incredible setting, without doubt a great place to make great music.

The warm breeze blew up the hill, and Reilly heard beats from the studio, a steady, low thud. Unmistakably Serpico. Dave and Jacob were still at it, or had they been to bed and just re-started? He'd missed the whole thing. He listened closely, trying to work out which track was playing, how far they'd got.

"Hi," said an unfamiliar voice. Reilly jumped, dropping his cigarette in the pool. He turned around. Stood over him was Madeleine, laughing.

Reilly knew immediately that she was a model. She was tall, near six foot, with an obvious model's frame, her movements filled with easy grace. She wasn't wearing make up, and she looked so fucking healthy that Reilly felt he should be in a hospice. She spoke - "I'm assuming you're not a burglar or a stalker or anything similar. If you are, you should know that I'll kill you."

"You're Dave's wife?"

She laughed long and hard at this - "Wife?"

Reilly was not in the mood for games. "Girlfriend, wife? Whatever. I should go. I'm supposed to be doing my vocals."

"I like your T-shirt."

"Er, thanks."

"You look like shit. Do you want a coffee or something?"

"Yeah," he said, taken aback. "Thank you."

"My name's Madeleine," she said, offering a hand. Reilly shook it.

"I'm Reilly."

"Right then Reilly. Stay here."

Madeleine drifted off to the kitchen, as Reilly rolled and lit a replacement cigarette. He tried to think where he'd seen her face before - what she'd been selling. He reckoned it was one of those high street shops skirting around the edges of credibility with their edgy slogans that certain demographics found irresistible - FCUK CHRISTMAS, FCUK SHOPPING, that kind of thing.

She was probably about twenty-three he judged, a full five years younger than himself, and near enough a full hundred years younger than fucking Dave Wilson. She returned with a cafetiere, two cups, milk and sugar.

"Dave is really excited about your band. He never says anything about the bands he has in the studio, but he's been listening to your tape non-stop. He's really into it."

"Really?"

"I had a listen as well. I thought your singing was very good. And I thought you'd be an interesting person to speak to."

"Me?"

"Yes. I've always been fascinated with singers. You know I've met quite a few, being a model and that. Move in the same circles."

"Who have you met?"

"Some real greats. I know Mick Hucknall quite well, and…"
Reilly almost choked on coffee. "Fuck off! Fucking hell. Mick fucking Hucknall. Jesus Christ."

"What? What did I say?"

"How could you… why would?" The words wouldn't form. "Look, this is a big mistake. Fucking hell. I can't talk to you anymore. I just can't." Reilly stood up and marched down toward the studio, muttering "Mick fucking Hucknall" to himself, indignant. Over his shoulder, he distinctly heard Madeleine chuckling.

Jacob sat down at the mixing desk, his coffee in one hand, cigarette in the other. It had been a long night, but for Jacob an immensely satisfying one. He'd thrown himself into the recording, switching between guitars, bass and keyboards without any real break.

He'd been in a studio once or twice before, but this was something else - playing every instrument himself, the drum loops he'd programmed on the laptop pounding around the studio as he did so. For Jacob, being here was a culmination, a vindication, and he was utterly at home.

Dave was great to work with, gently coaxing the songs out of him, never rushing or criticising. While Jacob had found Reilly's disappearance selfish and faintly embarrassing, Dave had laughed it off, calmly advising, "We only need him to sing like he did on those demos. Makes no difference when or how he does it."

Jacob lit his cigarette and with a nod, gestured to Dave, sat alongside - "OK. What am I listening for then?"

"It's a small thing, but it's bugging me," said Dave. "The feel of it as it comes into the second verse. It sounds thin. I think we may need to do something with the bass, distort it a bit, fuzz it up maybe. Just to give the sound some depth. See what you think."

Dave pressed play and *Lower Maudlin Street* began, and a swirl of guitar feedback over a warm wall of keyboard filled the monitors. The hi-hat came in, clicking a rhythm and creating a shape. And now the bass. Just a note each bar for the first verse.

"Sounds fucking good to me, Dave," said Jacob.

"Oh yeah. It does. But it's just this bit... now."

The second verse came in and with it, Jacob's bass line. Dave was right, the bass was weedy.

"I don't understand," said Jacob, "it sounded great when I played it."

"It's not an exact science," said Dave, pressing stop, the playback ceasing. "Do you want to have another crack at it now?"

"I'm fucking knackered, Dave, to tell the truth. But I suppose we need to keep going. We've been up all night and we've only done two and a half songs."

"Two and three quarters. And you're doing well. This is good stuff."

"Well, yeah."

"What time is it now?"

"Ten to nine."

"Have your coffee, then we'll re-record that bass line. And *then* we'll get some sleep."

"Fair enough, Dave."

The door swung open, and into the booth walked Reilly. Looking dishevelled, and more than a little riled. Without saying a word, he headed for the fridge and removed a can of Coke. He sat down on the sofa, away from the mixing desk, and rolled a cigarette.

Dave stood up, and with an enthusiasm betraying his lack of sleep, said - "Reilly, my son. You are just in time. We need some vocals."

"Well, *Dad*. You'll have to wait while I smoke this fag."

Dave laughed. Jacob tutted. "Where have you been? You look like you slept in a fucking hedge. Did you get back to the pub alright?"

"Er... yes. I did. I slept at the pub. In our room."

"Right. How did you get back?"

"Walked."

"Why didn't you get changed?"

Reilly paused for a moment, and then stood up - "Let's do these vocals then."

Reilly stood in the centre of the studio and glared at Jacob and Dave on the other side of the glass, awaiting further instruction. Jacob pointed to the headphones at Reilly's feet, which he eyed suspiciously before picking them up and slipping them on. "They'll help you hear your pitch," said Dave over the intercom, reassuring him.

Next, Reilly adjusted the mike stand, trying to get the microphone at a comfortable level, before angrily giving up and holding the mike in his hands, "Fucking thing."

"Be calm, Reilly," said Jacob.

"Fuck off, Jacob," said Reilly.

Dave interrupted - "Reilly. We need a level, just sing the first line into the mike for me please."

"I'm not comfortable. Can you turn the lights down a bit, Dave?"

"No problem." Dave gestured for Jacob to dim the lights. "How's that?"

"Yeah, good."

"Do whatever you need to do, Reilly," said Dave, "move around, sit down, lie on the floor, whatever works."

"Thanks, Dave," he replied, looking around the studio before deciding to stay exactly where he was.

"Dave?"

"Yes, Reilly?"

"Can you just play the track, I'll sing over it."

"No problem, we'll use it as the guide vocal."

"Don't know what that means, but yeah."

Dave laughed. "Here we go." He pressed play.

Jacob sat back, arms crossed as his guitar playing from last night filled the studio. He was amazed by how good the song sounded played through the Les Paul, through a decent mixing desk, in a real studio. The notes chimed beautifully in the background. No drums on this first track. Reilly started to sing -

"I think I feel like letting go,
Walk into the ocean,
Let the waves decide which way I go,
Don't you see?
None of this means a thing..."

Reilly's voice filled the control room, and Jacob, half-crazed through lack of sleep and the night's effort, was hit.

"...I can change my name,
Or my address,
But those old ghosts still walk around,
And break my bones,
Sit on my chest..."

Something in the grain of Reilly's voice, *that ache*. It hit Jacob on a primal level, starting a rush. His reaction was non-intellectual, a reflex at the base of his spine. A shiver ran up his back, prickles on the back of his neck. This is what music could do.

Jacob looked into the studio, from where this sound was emerging - at Reilly, eyes clenched shut, one hand holding the mike, the other over his right earphone. Such a difficult, awkward human being, standing alone in the half-light of the studio. Jacob didn't know if he was a genius or a fuck-up. Could he be both?

The song moved towards the end, Reilly delivering the pay-off lines -

"...Will I ever be free?
Do I even want to be?
My hands are tied,
And I'm so tired,
I need to sleep,
Please let me sleep."

The track finished, Reilly opening his eyes and searching for his cigarette stuff. Dave was silent.

"What Dave, what's up?" asked Jacob after a moment, assuming a technical problem had ruined the take.

Dave shook his head, and checking the intercom was off, said, "Nothing's wrong, mate. This guy. I swear, he fucking floors me. You don't know what you've got here, you really don't. You two are going to be gods."

So fast, so numb

By ten o'clock the vocals on *Satellite Town, Swoon* and *Lower Maudlin Street* were complete. Dave pulled three Heinekens from the fridge and they headed outside, blinking as they emerged into a glorious summer's day.

"I'm fucked," announced Jacob, downing his beer. "I've got to go back to the pub for a sleep."

"Good idea," said Dave, "I'll see you back here at what, four o'clock?"

"Make it three. Still got loads to do, haven't we?"

"Fair enough," said Dave, and with a wave he walked up the hill towards the house.

Jacob waited until he was out of earshot, and turned to Reilly - "What a guy, eh? He's been brilliant."

"He knows his stuff, I suppose," said Reilly grudgingly. But Jacob knew Reilly was as bowled over as he was.

"I've got to go," said Jacob rattling his car keys. "Or I'll fall asleep standing here."

"Right. I'll catch you up. I'm going to see if I can remember the chords to *Analogue Soul*."

"OK. See you later."

Jacob walked up the hill, leaving Reilly alone. He sat down on the grass in front of the studio, and rolled a cigarette. He laid back and smoked it, watching the trees swaying gently above his head. He finished his beer and realised he was bored. He ducked back into the studio to fetch a bottle of Valpolicella.

He found a set of tumblers in the sound booth and taking one, headed back outside. He sat back down on the grass, and poured himself a generous glass of wine. He drank it down, feeling the familiar blue-black fuzz settling on his teeth. A calm came over him, and his mind wandered.

He thought about Madeleine. About how the hell she could have ended up with Dave Wilson. Had she ended up with him? There was certainly something strange about the arrangement. And that Mick Hucknall thing? In retrospect, it seemed clear that this was designed to wind Reilly up. Why would she bother?

A low roar from behind the house broke Reilly's train of thought - an engine. No, engines. Two large black trucks emerged over the hill, and inched down the dirt track at the side of the garden, towards the studios. Reilly stood up. *Who the fuck is this?*

The trucks edged closer, and turned toward Reilly, the driver of the first giving him a stiff nod as he passed. Reilly drank some more wine and watched the trucks pull up outside the other studio.

Two men emerged from each truck, a driver and a roadie for each truck full of equipment - who was this, fucking Guns 'n' Roses? The driver of the truck nearest Reilly was a rake thin, serious-looking specimen. Had a side-parting - very odd. It made Reilly laugh involuntarily.

His passenger was a wide, squat bloke - had a rugby frame. He waddled, holding his arms away from his body as he walked, as if impeded by the bulk of his own muscles. As he walked closer, Reilly was amused to note that it wasn't muscle that impeded him, but the fact that he was a fat bastard.

Reilly walked towards the back of the truck, and was greeted by a withering look from the thick-necked roadie. The look said, "Stay right where you are, freak." Reilly knew this was a fair reaction - he was, after all, wearing a slept-in suit and drinking wine at breakfast time.

But he ignored the warning and moved closer. He peered into

the back of the truck - amps, guitar cases, and lots of other expensive-looking muso gear.

"Can I help you?" asked Thick-Neck.

Reilly looked at him for a moment. He had that ex-forces dullness to his eyes.

"Army or Navy?" asked Reilly.

"What? Oh," he said, but seemed to instinctively understand the question - "Er, army. Years ago now though. How did you know?"

Reilly wanted to say, "your eyes give you away. You're obviously very neat and tidy, but haunted by some of the darkest thoughts imaginable." But he didn't. Instead, he said - "Who are you a roadie for then?"

"I'm not a roadie. I'm a sound engineer."

"Same thing."

"Look. We're pretty busy here. So if you don't mind…"

With that, Thick-Neck hauled a guitar case from the truck. Reilly read the words stencilled on the side - "THE NU-BIRDS."

He started jumping up and down, laughing hysterically and spilling his wine. Thick-Neck regarded him with concern.

"The fucking Nu-Birds. This is brilliant. Brilliant!"

Thick-Neck looked at his colleague and rolled his eyes, as if to say, "Another fan."

Reilly stumbled away, laughing to himself. He went back in to the studio and shaking his head with disbelief, picked up his guitar.

Reilly spent the next two hours sat on the studio floor, playing his acoustic and mumbling the lyrics to himself. And one by one, and by trial and error, he remembered the chords to his songs. *Analogue Soul* didn't take long, having only two chords throughout. *Junta* was trickier though, it had a stupid and unnecessary middle-eight that he now had no recollection of writing. But he got there in the end.

He worked out *Misplaced Coda* pretty quickly, and on a whim, plugged in the guitar, microphone and switched on the P.A. stack. Standing up now, with the microphone stand in front of him, he played a chord. The sound came back at him through the monitors, fantastic in its volume and clarity. He played another. And then tentatively, the opening chords of *Misplaced Coda.*

This track was intended as one of the heavier ones on the album, towards the middle where the BPM and volume rose. But Reilly was playing it differently today. Gently and slowly. A country waltz - a Saturday morning song, a hangover tune. He leaned into the microphone, eyes shut, and sang the first line -

"Let the night,
Wrap you around,
Gently,
Fill your lungs..."

The sound of his own voice, framed against the acoustic guitar, coming back at him through the speakers and all around, was glorious, overwhelming. He played on -

"...This is how to,
Feel it,
What it is,
To be alive..."

He opened his eyes, leaning back. In the control room, staring intently, was Madeleine.

Reilly stopped playing. Just stood there silent. She reached for the intercom - "You can sure sing Reilly. Just amazing. But those lyrics?" She took her finger from the intercom button, and holding her nose, wafted a metaphorical bad smell with her other hand.

"Cheeky fucking cow!" screamed Reilly, removing the guitar and heading for the booth. Madeleine was laughing to herself as he opened and marched through the door. "Don't kill me!" she said, still giggling, "I was only joking."

"Well, don't," replied Reilly, wandering why he was so annoyed. He stood perfectly still now, trying to think of what to do or say next. Madeleine saved him - "Can I have a glass of wine?"

"Help yourself."

He looked her up and down as she filled a tumbler, looking for a flaw that would make her real. But none was forthcoming. An inch of smooth, tanned belly between her hipster jeans and T-shirt caught his eye.

"So what's your story, Reilly?" she asked.

"What?"

"Where do your songs come from? Who or what is your muse?"

"I can't answer that."

"Why?"

"Because your question is faulty."

She laughed. "You pretentious twat."

"Fuck off. Who are you anyway? A fucking model?"

"Yeah. So what?"

"It's got to be the most vacuous, vulgar, empty profession there is."

"Well, you're not exactly curing cancer yourself."

Reilly was silent. Stumped. Madeleine topped up her glass, offered the bottle to Reilly.

"Thanks," he said. And then not knowing why, he told her something he'd never told anyone. "I don't know where my songs come from. I really don't. They just kind of, *arrive*. I…" He looked up to see her reaction.

"Go on," she said.

"Well, when I'm playing, and writing, I feel like I'm wrestling with the music, working out who's boss. It's not much fun, it's hard. Not enjoyable at all. It makes me not want to do it anymore. But eventually I get to a beautiful point where it becomes this living, breathing thing, bigger than me. And when I get to that point, I can just sit back and do what I'm told, it tells me where to go. It doesn't feel like your own creation, but more like something given to you. A gift. Yeah, that's it - a gift. Does that make any sense?"

Madeleine considered Reilly's words for a moment. Reilly wondered why he was telling her. And then she said - "Not really, sounds like bar room philosophy to me, but then what do I know? I'm just a model."

"Right," said Reilly, lost for words again.

"Can I bum a fag?"

"Sorry?"

"Can I have a cigarette?"

"Er, yeah, here you go." He handed her his tobacco and papers.

"Thanks."

"Are they here yet?" asked Reilly.

"Who?"

"The Nu-Birds."

"No. They'll be here later today apparently. They're playing Reading and Leeds this weekend so we don't know exactly when they'll get here."

"Why are they recording here?"

"Who knows. Are you a fan then?"

"Fuck off. They're the worst British band since Toploader."

"Toploader were alright."

"Oh for fuck's sake. The worst British band since Kula Shaker then."

"Oooh. That's low. But they're good. I love that song in the charts, what's it called?"

"*Big Sky.*"

"Yeah, that's it."

"Fucking hell."

Madeleine laughed - "You're a funny bloke, Reilly."

She flicked her hair away from her face and lit her cigarette. Reilly studied her, trying to put her in a box, to head off an unpleasant feeling rising within. She was a model. She was not creative, could not understand art. She liked the Nu-Birds for fuck's sake. She'd no doubt lived a closeted and protected life, promoting the vapid and pointless fashion world.

To Reilly's disgust, he also found himself wondering how she'd be in bed. He hated himself for a reaction so obvious, so *everyman*. Reilly was better than that, wasn't he? Incorruptible by such superficial concepts as beauty, money, fame.

"That Mick Hucknall thing?" asked Reilly.

"I was joking," she said.

"Right."

Die in the summertime

The alarm clock woke Jacob at two-thirty. He was straight out of bed, anxious to get back to the studio. He slipped on his trainers, washed his face and did the sum again - twelve songs, divided by three days. Four songs a day. They'd already done three, but it had taken all night. But that wasn't so bad, three songs done, and it was still only Saturday. *But you must allow time for delays, problems. But at the same time, you can't rush it. If a song takes two days, then it takes two days.*

But it can't take two days. You've got work on Tuesday. You can't phone in sick after a bank holiday - too obvious. And anyway, deadlines are good - give you focus. And even if you do miss it, then the studio will still be here next weekend - but next weekend's the gig. Fucking hell, the gig. It's too soon. Shut up shut up shut up. He went downstairs, to the bar, and ordered a pint of Stella.

He pulled up a stool, rolled a cigarette and lit up. A familiar voice drifted across the pub - "All I'm saying is, there's got to be some level of danger in anything artistic, there's got to be a darkness, or what's the point? It must provoke in some way to be of any real value…"

Reilly and Madeleine sat at the bay window table, a half-empty bottle of wine and a full ashtray between them. Jacob picked up his pint and walked over.

"Reilly, how's it going?"

"Jacob, excellent. Tell her why the Nu-Birds are so shit. She doesn't understand."

Madeleine laughed, and reaching over the table, pushed Reilly playfully on the chest. "I understand, you dickhead. I just don't agree."

They were both drunk, and the obvious frisson between them embarrassed Jacob. He gulped down his beer, and said, "I'm driving back down to the studio, do you two want a lift?"

"No, no," said Reilly, "I'll see you there later. When do you need me?"

"If you're talking about doing your vocals, then I suppose we'll have something for you to sing over in three or four hours. But you're very welcome to come now and help me set the guitars up for *Analogue Soul*. If it's not too much trouble."

Reilly didn't pick up Jacob's sarcasm - "No, fuck that mate. You know I'm no good with all that guitar-monkey side of things. You do it."

Madeleine giggled and Jacob's humiliation was complete. Without another word he turned and left.

Once at the house, Jacob parked up and walked down the hill. The studio building was now a hive of activity. Outside the larger studio were three trucks and a people carrier, the windows blacked out. Roadies scurried around, carrying cables and monitors, shouting and receiving orders. The activity excited Jacob, and suggested a future where all this manpower might be put to use for Serpico.

Dave was standing in the doorway of the smaller studio, talking to a tall, weary looking guy in a tartan suit. A record company type, his hair was impeccably unkempt, highlighted. His glasses were thick-rimmed and serious. Jacob approached.

"Hey Dave, Nu-Bird's here yet?"

"Jacob. You're back. No, not yet. We were just talking about that. This is their A&R, Liam. "

"Hello."

"Nice to meet you." His accent was southern Irish - posh Dublin. He turned back to Dave - "The silly little fuckers don't know what they're doing. They're playing Reading tonight, and the Leeds festival tomorrow. They insisted that we book studio time and a helicopter so they can do some B-sides instead of waiting around backstage. But when it comes down to it, they'd rather hang out with the cast of fucking Hollyoaks than do some work. Fuckwits."

Jacob and Dave nodded their understanding. Liam continued - "So they're not coming today, I can tell you that."

"What's the deal then? Are they at that stage where they start believing the hype?" asked Dave.

"Too right they are. One fucking hit and they think they're the fucking Beatles. Obnoxious little bastards. A year ago they were begging me to listen to a demo, now they're ordering me to set up meetings with Rod fucking Stewart. Who, incidentally, is a complete twat. And they have the cheek to send me out to the fucking sticks to sort out this studio that they picked on a fucking whim..." He checked himself, seemed to realise he'd said too much. "Anyway, no offence intended, it's not your problem."

Jacob knew this was an opportunity. He was no networker, but the chance to introduce Serpico to an A&R from a major label could not be passed up. He swallowed hard and went for it.

"Liam. If you get a chance, do you want to come and have a listen to our stuff? I mean my music. My band. We're called..."

Liam held up a hand, and cut him off - "I really don't want to appear rude mate, but we're not looking at the moment. I'm sure your band's great, but I've got to tell you straight - no. I'm not going to have a listen. But I'm sure you're a nice person and your mum loves you and I wish you all the best and all that." He'd clearly delivered that speech before.

"But..."

"It's been nice talking to you guys, but I've got to go and sort a few things out in case the little fuckers decide to turn up. I'll see ya." He walked off, pulling a mobile from his pocket and dialling.

"Don't worry about it," said Dave, "it's not your kind of label anyway."

"Yeah."

"Come on. Let's get back to it."

The tracks fell into place layer by layer, beat by beat. Jacob found a satisfying rhythm to the recording process. He'd play a guide track, and then a real take. After a playback in the control room, he'd go back and correct mistakes or change some settings. He was chipping away at the songs, and almost imperceptibly the music widened, as a tapestry emerged from the single threads.

Analogue Soul became a grand, moving torch song, bigger than Jacob had imagined it could be. Immediate and affecting, even at this stage it was the obvious centrepiece of the album. As they listened to the final playback, still without vocals, Dave turned to Jacob, grinning, and said, "This is something. Really something."

They pushed on and *Summertown* and *Misplaced Coda* were complete by eleven thirty. Jacob was elated to be back on schedule, and the music had been flowing effortlessly - doing what it was told.

Dave produced a bottle of Jack Daniels and a can of Coke, and they sat for a while in the control room, unwinding, a leather sofa each.

"I'm sorry about Reilly, he's a selfish bastard," said Jacob.

"What do you mean? Not turning up? Doesn't worry me. He only needs to do the vocals. People work in different ways, you have to respect that. And correct me if I'm wrong, but I reckon it's easier for you to work without him hanging around."

"Well, yeah."

"There you go then."

Jacob stubbed out his cigarette, and fully aware that he didn't need another, rolled one anyway.

"Yeah, you're right. I just feel like it's really going to happen for us, and he's missing it. I mean when we send these tracks round the record companies, one of them's going to sign us, aren't they?"

"Well I think so. In fact, Jacob, I know some people who may be interested. I can't promise anything, but when we're done I'd like to send the album to a bloke I know at EMI. With your permission, of course."

Jacob sat bolt upright. "Shit yeah. Thanks Dave, that'd be fucking great."

"Well, you know. Could be a way in."

"Thanks for all your help with this Dave." He waved away Jacob's gratitude - "Don't be daft. I'm a fan."

Dave got up and headed to the fridge, retrieving another Coke for the next round. Jacob watched him and was hit by an uncomfortable notion, that while Dave was doing everything for Serpico, Reilly was quite possibly at this very moment cuckolding him by way of thanks.

But surely Madeleine was way too good for the likes of Reilly? In the time they'd shared a flat, Jacob had seen some undoubted beauties tiptoeing short-changed out of Reilly's bedroom in the morning. But Madeleine was something else. Surely several leagues above Reilly's undeserving and unappreciative clutches. Surely.

I want you like an accident

Madeleine slowly sat up, and holding her breath, passed the joint to Reilly. She exhaled, flicking her hair away from her face and blowing a white cloud up and across the pool, into the night sky. "I fucking hate weed," said Reilly.

She laughed and watched him as he took a long drag of his own. The joint whizzed and popped unevenly as he pulled on it. He filled his lungs and held it just there. When he could bear it no more he let the breath out, through his nose at first. The hit was surprising smooth, a warm buzz. He took another drag, and passed the joint back to Madeleine.

They were lying on loungers by the pool, watching the lights reflecting off the water in the foreground, and the Nu-Birds' roadies scuttling around at the bottom of the hill. Distant village lights twinkled around the valley beyond. The sound of Serpico drifted up the hill on the warm breeze, Jacob adding layered guitar parts to *Misplaced Coda*, by the sound of it.

"Shouldn't you be in the studio, Reilly?"

"What for?"

"Well, you're in the band as well, aren't you?"

She was right of course, but the prospective boredom of watching Jacob pick away at the songs note by note had kept him out of the studio.

"I'll go down later."

She laughed, and reaching over, took the joint back.

"Sounds like you've got a good deal here, Reilly," she said.

"What do you mean?"

"Jacob does all the work, and you go down the pub."

"It's not like that. The songs are mine. Jacob can't write music - you know, songs. And I can't stomach all the technical stuff. It works this way."

"It's just not the way bands usually work, is it?"

"Well, we're unlike any other band ever. Always have been."

Madeleine paused for a moment, and then said - "You like absolutes don't you Reilly?"

"What of it?"

She shrugged and pulled on the joint, closing her eyes as she held the breath. Reilly stole a sideways glance, and studied her face for a moment. Her beauty was alien, beyond his understanding. He wondered for the first time if he was out of his depth.

She opened her eyes.

"What do you think?" she asked.

"What? To what?"

"This skunk."

"Oh. Nice. I mean yeah. Best smoke I've had in a long time."

Reilly was feeling it now, foggy and woozy, the studios at the bottom of the hill suddenly seemed to be miles away. Even the distance to his feet now seemed so very far, as if viewed down the wrong end of a telescope. But it wasn't totally unpleasant.

They talked some more and suddenly Reilly was ranting about the Nu-Birds again - "Fucking hell, I mean, the singer - he's very talented. You could almost say he's got too much talent - talent to spare." The volume of his voice began to rise - "The man has talent coming out of his arse." He laughed at his own joke. "Stick on your Nu-Birds CD and just sit back and listen to all that talent flowing straight out of his arse. And into your home."

Madeleine was laughing as well, the weed taking hold of them both - "Reilly, you'd make a hell of a pop star. You know that?"

Reilly stopped laughing.

"We'll have to keep in touch," she said. "I mean, I travel a lot and you will too with the band. But maybe we'll be able to meet up now and then."

"I'm not sure you understand what kind of band we are."

"Reilly, come on. Stop being coy. You can drop the punk rock thing now. You know you're on the verge of something here. Maybe you and me can hang out, go to things together - awards ceremonies, premieres, all that stuff. We'll have a laugh."

There was a heavy silence. The spliff was now almost at the roach. Something snapped in Reilly's head, came loose. He was spinning suddenly, adrift.

"I'm having a… turn," he said. "It's the, er, smoke I think. I'm going to bed."

"I'll come with you."

"What?"

"You need some help Reilly, you look terrible."

Reilly coughed, fighting the nausea. "Madeleine," he said, standing up, swaying. "I shouldn't be here."

"What?"

"I'm not what you think at all."

"What are you talking about?"

"I would disappoint you, utterly."

"Reilly?"

He left the words hanging in the air, and staggering a little, set off alone, slipping away into the darkness.

Blame, etc

"Wake up, Reilly." He sat up and took the coffee from Jacob, blinking as he looked around the room - the twin-bedded, country pub, B&B room. Floral wallpaper in various browns suggested serious sickness ahead. Jacob drew the curtains, and a blizzard of white light hit the back of Reilly's eyes. He gasped involuntarily, and spoke to his pupils through narrowed eyes - "Constrict, you lazy fuckers, constrict."

"Sorry?"

"Nothing. What fucking time is it?"

"Ten. Come on, get that coffee down you."

"Right. Throw me that T-shirt would you."

Jacob picked it up, held it up, quickly read it - "THE WAR AGAINST CLICHÉ." He threw it dismissively at Reilly.

In the car, bouncing down the dirt track towards the house, Jacob was full of information - "...we've got loads of it down now Reilly, it's really coming together...and I'm thinking that with *Biological* we could maybe stick the guitar bits for the verses through that program on the laptop, give it some reverb, a kind of churchy, hollow sound, you know? Ghostly. But Dave's keen on how we did it first take..."

Reilly, coffee still in hand and first cigarette of the day just lit, turned to him, cut him off - "Yeah, but don't overproduce it. It can't be perfect, you know what I mean? There's got to be space and little mistakes, or it sounds dead. That's where the soul is,

Jacob. In the spontaneity - it's the imperfections that are beautiful."

Jacob thought of S, swallowed hard. He knew that he should call her. He said - "I know, I know. You're right."

Jacob parked up and they walked around the house, over the crest of the hill, down toward the studio. It was Jacob who saw them first. He wondered if he could get Reilly in the studio before he saw them too. A howl of laughter from beside him was his answer.

"Fucking hell," laughed Reilly, "could it be? Could it really be them?"

The Nu-Birds were soaking up the morning sun outside the studio, the singer and guitarist deep in discussion with the posh Irish guy. The drummer and bass player sat on the grass, smoking and waiting for instructions.

Reilly approached, Jacob hovering at his shoulder. They stopped just within earshot, Reilly rolling another cigarette as he eavesdropped, a big grin on his face.

"I say we make it more fun, a summer song, you know?" said the guitarist.

"Yeah, I can see that, la," said the singer, nodding.

"I don't know, lads. I don't know," said Liam.

"Come on, Paddy."

"Don't call me that."

"Sorry Liam. Let's just get in there, make some fucking music man," suggested the singer.

"Yeah, lets rock 'n' roll," said the guitarist.

"Woo-hoo!" said the drummer, punching the air.

"Well, we need to get something out of this weekend. Eighty fucking grand for a fucking cover version." Liam shook his head.

The guitarist turned to the bass player and drummer - "Come on lads, we're doing it." They stood up and followed their bandmates and A&R inside.

Jacob turned to Reilly - "They look different somehow, don't you think?" This was true, the drummer's pudding basin cut was gone, shaved off. The singer and guitarist now had Paul Weller mops, brushed forward. All four wore flared jeans, the guitarist had a beautifully fitted leather jacket. They all now had the intimidating gleam that famous, instantly recognisable people have up close. And Reilly had to concede that they looked fucking cool, like real rock stars.

"Yeah - they've got a fucking stylist now," He said.

"You reckon?"

"Of course. You're not telling me those fuckwits could dress themselves are you? Stevie'll be the same in a month or two, wait and see."

"Serious?"

"Come on, let's go in." Reilly started walking for the door.

"Reilly. We can't just walk in."

"Why the fuck not?"

There were perhaps fifty other people in the cavernous studio, some professionals, others hangers on, and Reilly and Jacob were not challenged or even noticed. Roadies and technicians were scattered around the periphery, chatting amongst themselves. Half a dozen *Hollyoaks* cast members milled around outside the control room.

There was just one guy in the control room itself, presumably the producer, checking levels. It seemed that The Nu-Birds were happy to have everyone in the studio with them. They were at the opposite end of the room, facing their ad hoc audience, picking up instruments, plugging in.

Jacob noticed a table lined with canapés, glasses and bottles of champagne - all opened, like a wedding. Reilly was already there. He swiped a bottle and started downing it. He stopped for air, wiped his mouth with the back of his hand, shot Jacob a smile and grabbed another bottle, came back.

"Here you go, mate," said Reilly, handing Jacob the bottle.

"It's ten-fifteen in the morning."

"Hair of the dog. Kill or cure. You know."

"Right." Jacob put his bottle on the floor, and watched Reilly swigging.

"Reilly?"

"Yeah?"

"You didn't… last night I mean, you didn't…"

Reilly cut him off - "Not my type."

"Good. I mean, right."

The singer picked up his mike, clicked it into the stand and spoke - "Alright, people?"

A cheer from the *Hollyoaks* crew was his reply.

"We're going to have a go at this song. We're gonna have some fun with it. Don't be afraid to make some noise, we like that live atmosphere, you know? Let's have some handclaps."

Reilly laughed and leaning toward Jacob said, "This is too fucking funny Jacob. They've no idea. We're like Trojans mate, *Trojans*." He went back to his champagne, giggling. Jacob looked on.

The drummer nodded to the bass player, and kicked off, striking up a slowish rhythm, all rimshots and pattering hi-hat. Reilly sniggered. The bass player came in, a lumpy, loping bass line in between the beats. The singer pursed his lips and snaked his hips like a *Stars In Their Eyes* Jagger, prompting Reilly and Jacob to cringe in unison. *Hollyoaks* cheered.

A couple of bars in and the guitarist joined in, hitting and then stroking the chords out in a reggae rhythm. Reilly roared with laughter. This was reggae alright - white boy reggae. UB-fucking-40. The singer bobbed up and down, bending his knees in time to the beat, loose-limbed. "Fucking reggae!" said Reilly, delighted. "Priceless."

Reilly's laughter slowed and then stopped, as the chords tumbled out. He recognised the song. *Surely not, surely not*. He actually shuddered at the awful realisation of what was unfolding before his eyes.

"This is fucking *Teenage Kicks*," he said. "You can't cover this song, you can't cover this song." He shook his head, and all

Jacob could muster was - "Shit, you're right. This is... just horrible."

The singer came in, delivering the opening lines in a Jamaican accent –

"Are teenage dreams so hard to beat?
Every time she walks down me street,
Another girl in me neighbourhood,
Wish she was mine,
She look so good... "

Reilly turned to Jacob, resting a hand on his shoulder, as if for support - "I... I don't... I..."

"Reilly?"

"You...you can't cover this song Jacob, you just can't. What are they doing to it?" He looked like he might cry. "Make it stop," he said.

Reilly started groaning, as the singer continued toward the chorus, his Bob Marley accent getting thicker -

"I wanna hold ya,
Wanna hold ya tight,
Get teenage kicks right through the night,
Oh yeah!"

"This is horrible," Jacob said again, to himself really. He looked around the room to gauge the reaction - the technicians were mostly staring at their shoes in embarrassment, but *Hollyoaks* were loving it, grinding along to the rhythm. The Nu-Birds played on, plowing their reggae field -

"I gonna call her on me telephone,
Have her over cos I all alone,
I need excitement oh I need it bad,
And it's the best me ever had..."

Reilly's groaning grew. He was shaking. And then he started to scream. To really scream. Jacob backed away from him, alarmed.

Bottle still in hand, Reilly started to run, run at the band, sprinting across the studio floor - arms flailing, still screaming as he went. The guitarist saw him coming, and stopped playing. The drummer slowed down, as did the bass player. The singer never saw a thing.

Reilly leapt at the singer, his limbs whirling, and in mid-air, twatted him across the head with the champagne bottle. The band stopped playing as Reilly stood over the unconscious singer, screaming, "Stop it, stop it, stop it!"

Like spinning plates

Dave was brilliant. Dave sorted it all out.

After he knocked the singer out, the rest of the band went for Reilly. Really went for him. He took a few blows to his head and body before he struggled free and bolted for the door. They chased him to Serpico's studio where he locked himself in, refused to come out. Jacob slunk out of the studio and up the hill, to raise Dave.

When they got back to the studios, the conscious Nu-Birds and some of their roadies were still banging on the studio door, demanding that Reilly open up. Reilly had queued up *Analogue Soul* and was blasting it from the speakers by way of reply.

Dave headed for the bigger studio first, Jacob following. Some of the *Hollyoaks* kids were attending to the singer, who was now awake but still laid out on the floor where he fell, stroking his head and muttering. Dave spotted Posh Irish and approached - "What's happening, Liam?"

"It was terrible, mate. Some nutcase comes running out of nowhere, straight for the singer and bottles him. Then he runs off and locks himself in the other studio."

"You phoned an ambulance?"

"Yeah, on its way."

"Is he OK?"

"Think so. It was a hell of thing. Never seen anything like it. Poor bastard." He looked like he was trying not to laugh.

Dave leaned in closer, and said, "This is a bit delicate, Liam. The guy, the nutcase. He's the singer for the band I'm recording next door."

Liam turned to Jacob - "He's with you?"

"Er, yeah."

Liam *was* laughing now. This attracted the attention of the singer, now sitting up - "It's not funny, la. It's Lennon all over again. But it's me. Some deranged fan, probably been stalking us for months like..."

Liam ignored him.

"Thing is, Liam," said Dave, "there's a mob outside the other studio... it's not going to help."

"Dave, Dave, they're just playing at being Oasis. They'll get bored pretty soon. All this just gives me an excuse to get the little fuckers out of here, up to Leeds for tonight. Don't worry about it. Done me a favour."

"Thanks, Liam," said Dave.

"Yeah. Tell you what though. Better get this bloke - what's your name again?"

"Jacob."

"Yeah, better get Jacob out the way for a couple of hours, just in case someone makes the connection."

"Thanks, Liam," said Jacob this time.

Jacob drove Dave to the Wheatsheaf, where they sat out front, killing time with Guinness and planning - "What have we got, three tracks left? And we've got the complex ones done now. We're almost there."

"Yeah, Dave. Apart from the vocals."

"Well, yeah. But he'll do those in no time."

"I admire your optimism, but he's probably in that studio now, trolleyed on whatever booze there is. I know him."

"Cross that bridge..."

"Fair enough, fair enough."

A taxi drove past the pub, coming from the direction of the

house. Dave waved at it. Madeleine waved back. "Always working, she's always working." He said, to himself really. Jacob sat silently, wondering if Reilly had lied to him, what he had really done last night.

"You got anyone, Jacob?"

"Got anyone?"

"A girl?"

"No, no. Not for ages. I mean, well I thought I might have for a bit, but you know, it all went a bit...well, I think I fucked it up actually. But now I'm too busy with the band, I don't even have time to think about her."

Dave considered Jacob's words for a moment, And then leaning back, laughed heartily - "You're a shit liar, Jacob," he said, "Life's too short - just phone her, eh?"

Reilly was asleep in the control room when they returned. Laid out on a leather sofa, the contents of an ashtray spilt across his chest.

"Wake up, Reilly," said Jacob.

"Eh?"

"The coast's clear. They've gone now."

"Right, great." He sat up, brushed the ash and fag ends off himself and rolled a cigarette.

Dave headed for the desk, flicked a few switches, and said - "Reilly, you up for some singing?"

"Done it," he croaked.

"What?" asked Jacob.

"Well I was bored. I didn't know when those scousers were going to leave me alone, saw the DATs lying on the desk there - found a spare track..."

Dave was beaming.

"What about the levels, Dave? Will they be alright?" asked Jacob.

"They were already set, so yeah. Should be. Let's have a listen."

Dave queued up the tape. There was a knock at the door. Jacob went to answer it

It was Posh Irish - "Jacob," he said, "How are you?"

"Oh, not bad, not bad." Jacob was a little taken aback. Liam exchanged greetings with Dave, told him the remaining crew were moving on imminently, and then turned his attention to Reilly, sitting himself on the sofa opposite. Reilly shifted uneasily, sucking on his cigarette. Was he here to serve some kind of writ, make an arrest perhaps? Do A&Rs have these powers? Probably.

"The man himself," said Liam.

"Er, yes," said Reilly.

"My name's Liam. I just wanted to say hello. I thought what you did was fascinating."

"What I did?"

"You were prepared to use violence to defend the honour of a song. A song. Genius."

"Of course I was."

Liam laughed, and said it again. "Genius."

"Who the fuck are you?" asked Reilly.

Liam laughed louder. "I work for Subside Records."

"That's one of those pretend indie labels that's really owned by a major, isn't it?"

"Yes, that's fair." Liam stood up, and turned to Dave - "This guy's hilarious, really."

"Fuck off," said Reilly.

Liam laughed again and went to shake Dave's hand - "I'm off now. Thanks again Dave." He turned back to Reilly and Jacob - "Lovely to meet you gentlemen. All the best."

Dave grabbed his arm. "Before you go mate, have a listen, eh?"

He sighed. "Dave."

"Have a listen. Just this one song."

He sighed again, and shrugged his acquiescence.

Liam sat back down on the sofa, opposite Reilly again. Reilly glowered back, cracking open a beer as he did so. Dave dimmed the lights for effect, Jacob hovered nervously over the desk, checking levels and settings. The opening bars of *Analogue Soul* rose from the monitors.

Elevate me later

"I'm telling you, we got him. He loved it," said Dave, who was looking very excited indeed. Reilly wore a furrowed brow, sceptical. Jacob felt close to tears - "What do you mean? How the hell can you tell? How can you tell?"

"Trust me."

Liam had been silent as the song played, head cocked slightly, listening closely but betraying no emotion. As it finished he stood up and walked, still silent and deep in thought, to the door, pulling his mobile out as he left the studio.

"Who cares what he thinks anyway? He doesn't know better than us," said Reilly.

"Fuck's sake," snapped Jacob.

"What? I don't need him to tell me that's a great song."

"Subside Records Reilly - fucking Subside!"

"Never heard of them."

"Don't be ridiculous."

"Guys, guys," said Dave. "Calm down eh? This is a good thing. Let's have a breather." He went to the fridge. "Now sit down, have a beer." They did as they were told.

Liam re-entered the studio. Smiling slightly now. "Can I have a word, lads?"

"Sure." Replied Jacob. Liam sat down.

"What to say, what to say? Sorry, I'm a bit thrown to be honest. It's just I didn't expect this when I woke up this morning, when I walked in here. Thing is, you're sitting on something here." He looked up for their reaction. "My god, you don't even know, do you? You don't even know what you've got."

"We know," said Reilly.

"Listen, I just made some phone calls. And this isn't how I usually do this. But I want to sign you. I'd like to offer you a deal. I love what you're doing."

Jacob's throat was very dry, he gulped down some beer. But he couldn't speak.

Reilly did - "But you've only heard one song."

"That's all I need. I know that what you're doing is very important. Now, my boss, I've just been speaking to him. He has a policy - never sign a band until you seen them play live. So I've got to go along with that. Fair enough I guess. Have you got any gigs planned?"

"Yes," piped up Jacob. "Saturday - Louisiana in Bristol. By the docks."

"Great, I know it. I'll see you there."

"Great," said Jacob.

"Oh fucking hell, what are you called?"

"Serpico."

"Serpico? Right. Do you have management?"

"Well that would be me, I suppose," said Jacob.

"Right. Well, Jacob, I've got to go. But, here's my card. I'd like to hear this album when it's done. Can you courier a copy to me?"

"Er, sure, no problem."

Liam shook hands with everyone, and made his exit. Once he'd left, Reilly started laughing, while Dave stood back and applauded them both. Jacob couldn't speak. He drank some beer, tried to smile. But his head was spinning. He sat down on a sofa, put his heads between his hands and began to cry, uncontrollably.

Heaven is a truck

Jacob sat in the meeting room, nodding occasionally and trying to look interested. Phil entered the room whistling *Eye of the Tiger*, and was now banging on about the new brand and the level of buy-in they'd enjoyed from each department thus far and Jacob and Marion were his sounding board. Despite the volume of Phil's oratory, Jacob could think of nothing but Serpico. And the offer. Liam's offer.

And the album was all there now - they had it - it was completed, mixed, mastered and sitting on Jacob's iPod. And what an album it was, what a thing of beauty - full of Mazzy Star whimsy, My Bloody Valentine soundscapes. Beats both delicate and punishing. And Reilly's voice - in, around and over the music - that voice, that broken, desperate voice - like a drowning man.

Jacob knew he was too close for any real objectivity but he could feel the power of this thing they'd created - and what it could mean for him. He'd been in a daze since the weekend. Was this how it felt to finally get what you want? He felt close to tears again.

"What are your thoughts on this, Jacob?"

"Sorry, on…?"

"Where your own values lie in relation to our new brand values? Do you feel that you are aligned?"

"I'm sorry, I…"

Marion cut in - "Jacob, how can you communicate this to others, if you're not in touch with yourself?"

"Great point Marion," said Phil, eyeing Jacob suspiciously.

"Well," stuttered Jacob, "I assume that…"

Phil cut in, wagging a finger - "That's not a *Sex-U-Up* word Jacob, is it?"

"Sorry?"

Phil explained, writing on the whiteboard - "When you ASSUME, you make an ASS of U and ME. So we don't say assume."

Fucking hell.

He took a deep breath - "I feel, Phil, that I do have a real commitment to communication. Which I believe is intrinsic to what *Sex-U-Up* is all about. So I am feeling quite well aligned at present."

Phil considered this for a moment - "Good, good," he said.

"And Phil," added Jacob, "while my own values are important, I think it's vital to remember that there is no 'I' in 'TEAM.'"

"Excellent Jacob, excellent! Write that down, Marion. I like that. Can I use it?"

Jacob started composing his resignation letter in his head.

Wednesday night and Jacob made some calls. He phoned the Louisiana and confirmed the details. He booked a PA system and lights. He called the Drumbank and booked a rehearsal studio for Friday (he was planning a migraine for that day). He called Jimmy Reckon to tell him about the gig. Jimmy seemed genuinely enthusiastic and said he'd have a word with a friend of friend who wrote for Venue, see if he could drum up a bit of press interest. It was almost certainly bullshit but Jacob thanked him anyway.

Jacob then called Dave to thank him again and confirm he was coming on Saturday. Dave said yes and to Jacob's delight asked if he could engineer the live sound.

Everything was coming together. He was on a roll. He dialled

S's mobile but hung up before it rang. *Idiot, idiot.* He grabbed his coat, headed out for last orders.

The following evening Jacob walked across Bristol to Stevie's, retracing his steps from earlier in the summer - Gloucester Road, the guitar shops at Cotham, Whiteladies Road and on to Clifton. He listened to the finished album on the way, and remembered how he'd walked this route before, Reilly's raw demos providing the soundtrack that time. Another change - there was a chill in the air, signalling the end of summer. As he walked past a Back to School display in the window of WH Smith, Jacob was briefly overwhelmed by September dread - that annual curse. But he chased the feeling away. Not today, not today.

Stevie was loving it. The pop star thing. And it was really happening. He and his new bandmates had spent the bank holiday at the Reading Festival, being seen and getting trolleyed. Stevie was a natural, born to do it.

He was back in Bristol to pack in his job and tie up loose ends before moving to London to record the album. Stevie's flat was full of new equipment and gadgets courtesy of the insurance company. Jacob tossed a CD, a copy of the album, onto Stevie's coffee table, and noticed a huge bag of cocaine lying on it. Jacob ignored this detail and headed out into the garden, where he told Stevie about the offer.

"That's fucking great, Jacob," said Stevie.

"Yeah."

"What sort of advance are they talking? Have they talked about publishing percentages - that's where the real money is, you know."

"Well nothing's concrete yet. He didn't give us any figures. But he's coming to this gig on Saturday."

"Wicked."

"Yeah."

"What's Reilly make of it?"

"Fucking hell, I don't know."

"Is he working again yet?"

"You must be joking. He's just started drinking full time now, I don't know what he thinks. I tried to get him to come over tonight but ITV are showing *Pearl Harbour*."

"What about the gig? Is he ready?"

"Think so. But I've just put all the loops and samples, some of the guitar parts on a track for the iPod, and all he's got to do is sing and do the acoustic guitar - he can do that pissed."

"You sure?"

"Yeah. He did it in the studio. We've got a rehearsal studio for tomorrow so we'll hammer it all out then."

"You phoned S yet?"

"No."

"Do it."

"I know, I know."

Stevie ducked inside and emerged a few minutes later sniffing dramatically, eyes wild. He held a bottle of Moet and two glasses.

"Jacob, mate. Can you believe what's happening to us?" he asked as he uncorked it. "I mean, can you actually believe it?"

Jacob thought for a moment, downed his champagne - "You know what? Yes, I can. I can totally believe it. It feels right, I actually think I... I mean we, deserve it. And I'm fucking ready."

Ego tripping at the gates of hell

Reilly really wanted a drink. But he was disciplined. He sat, patiently chain smoking on the rehearsal room floor as Jacob rushed around him, setting up. He watched his bandmate scuttle around, plugging in, tuning, a look of grim determination on his face. He seemed to be taking this rehearsal very seriously indeed.

Jacob was saying something - "So we'll play the album in order, track by track. It's tempting to mix it up a little but I think it'll work better if we do that - build the tempo up, then let it all fall. It should work really well. All you need to do is play the acoustic on the tracks that need it and do your vocals obviously. I'm going to set up two mikes, one naked straight to the PA and one through a guitar amp to fuzz it up. I'll have my own mike for backing vocals. I've put the bass on the backing track and I'm going to play the lead guitar, some keyboards and I can set off some of the samples with my pedals, so it should sound pretty much live, there's room to improvise a little bit."

It was a funny little studio, a soundproofed Portacabin with a damp dog smell to it. A knackered old drum kit sat in a corner, and it bothered Reilly. He kept glancing at it, and as he did so, an unsettling thought formed. It had the shape and posture of a fat arachnid. He pictured it moving a leg, then another, inching toward him. The image became too much to contend with, and he stood up, scanning the room for his Oddbins bag.

Without looking up, Jacob pointed to the bag, by the door - "Here, mate," he said.

"Nice one. Thanks." Reilly picked up the bag with a shaking hand. Jacob noticed this and turned to face Reilly, concerned.

"Reilly. You're a big boy now and you make your own decisions and all that, but you know, you really don't look too good. I mean, you look so pale."

Reilly smiled weakly by way of reply. "I'm fine mate, just a bit hung over. A little hair of the dog is what I need."

"Fair enough, fair enough," said Jacob, laughing it off, "we all have phases mate, and I know you're in between jobs at the moment."

"Yeah, that's right." Reilly opened the bottle and took a mouthful of Valpolicella. He felt his anxiety ease as the liquid flowed down his throat. He walked over to the drum kit, gave it a good kick and said - "Right then."

They rattled through the set in one take. It was messy, Reilly missing his cues, singing into the wrong mike and, during *Lactic,* inadvertently pulling Jacob's lead out. He could tell Jacob was pissed off, but he kept a lid on it. At the close of the final track Jacob leaned into his mike and said simply, "again."

The second run through was better, Reilly getting a better feel for the demands of playing the songs live. He was on his second bottle of wine now, and the music achieved a magical clarity for him. He looked around at Jacob during *This is Not an Exit* and watched him wrestling with his guitar, pulling a series of beautiful shapes and colours from it. He was overwhelmed, in awe. And Jacob seemed happier too.

They broke for lunch, grabbing pasties and sausage rolls from a bakery, and after a quick trip to Oddbins, they were back in the studio for another run through the set. Jacob was getting better, tighter, in and around the songs, driving the music along. But the wine was making Reilly clumsy. He forgot the chords to *Analogue Soul*, and stood staring at his guitar waiting for the information to come back to him. Jacob lost it, pulled the plug, stopped the iPod - "It's two fucking chords Reilly! Two chords. Jesus," he screamed.

"Alright, alright. Fucking hell."

Jacob removed his guitar, flicked off his amp, and said - "Let's have a break. A little break." He rolled and lit up a cigarette, his breathing slowing, returning to normal.

Reilly drank a bit more wine, and turning to Jacob asked - "Do you ever think maybe you've got it all wrong?"

"No. We've just got to concentrate a bit more."

"No, no. Not that. I know we're great. I'm talking about something else. I've been thinking about the way I live. I've been questioning a few things. My approach, if you like. Maybe I need god. Or *a* god. Of some kind."

Jacob laughed.

"I'm serious, Jacob. I'm fucking serious."

"Reilly. Shut up."

He ploughed on - "It makes no sense of course. Religion. Scientifically I mean, it's beyond argument. But if we're hard-wired for it, then maybe it's best not to fight it. Maybe it's best to dive in, and satisfy it, because if you've got a physical need, then you've got a physical need. Haven't you?"

Jacob stopped laughing - "Reilly. I'm really not comfortable... I don't want to get into it." He stood up, and self-consciously started checking his guitar cables.

"And another fucking thing," said Reilly, "I've realised I can't hate Arsenal - just for being Arsenal, even though I really want to - I mean, bigotry's bigotry isn't it? However you dress it up."

"What the...? Huh," asked Jacob, now exasperated, "what the fuck is happening to you?"

"Nothing."

"Shit."

"What? What did I say?"

Jacob sighed, sat down - "I just think… you know, we've got this gig and it's our big chance to get out of here, do something special. Do something more than most people get to do. Look, I just think you need to look after yourself. Lighten up for fuck's sake. Please. Let's not fuck this all up."

"This gig, Jacob. It is a big opportunity. I realise that. But it's got to do what I want it to do. Artistically, I mean."

"Fucking hell, Reilly. Don't start."

"I think I want to use the platform, to make a statement. An artistic statement."

Jacob was exasperated again now, shouting - "What are you talking about? Why do you have to do this to me? Why can't you just play your fucking guitar and sing like every other fucking front man?"

Reilly sat still, let Jacob calm down for a moment.

He answered calmly - "Because I'm not every other fucking front man. And we're not every other fucking band. That's why what we do matters."

Jacob sighed, let his shoulders drop. He sat down next to Reilly, defeated. "You're right. Fucking hell. I know you're right." He offered his hand. Reilly smiled, and shook it.

Panic on

6.30pm, and with his guts wound tighter than a magnet's coil, Jacob loaded the Saab and began the drive down to the docks, to the Louisiana. Nerves had gripped him from the moment he woke that morning - choked him. A painful knot of anxiety had pinned his stomach rigid, stopped him from eating all day. And his limbs were not his own, palsied by fear.

But now he was doing something, finally on the move, taking control, and the tension eased a little. Just a little.

He drove with the windows down, through the city evening miasma. Breathing in the deluge, breathing in the air that rushed into the car, that September chill again. He turned up the stereo to break the feeling - Elbow's *Newborn* distracting him for a few glorious moments.

Through the city centre, and Bristol was coming alive. Saturday night cranking up. He passed kebab shops, fun pubs, taxi ranks. And people, people everywhere. It made him dizzy.

He turned off toward the docks, parked up and walked into the Louisiana. The bar was quiet, just a smattering of well-dressed drinkers lining the bar - stopping in on their way to somewhere flashier, black ties and ball dresses, shit-eating grins. A poster behind the bar listed gigs scheduled for September - Jacob scanned for today's date: "SERPICO - no support - on stage 10.00pm. £6.00, £3.00 conc." He nodded at the barman, pointed skywards and headed up the stairs.

He pushed the door open, surveyed the empty room. Dave wasn't there, but sitting on the stage, the PA was. And the lights.

Excellent. He looked at his watch – 6.53 – he had time for a pint. More than enough time. And he deserved it.

Reilly hopped out the shower, grabbed his towel and mug of wine. He'd taken it easy today to placate Jacob, and had waited until five before opening a bottle. The delay had made his first drink all the sweeter.

He headed for his bedroom, gulping wine on the way, catching up. Laid out on his bed was a new suit from Oxfam and the T-shirt for tonight's gig - "OVERNIGHT SUCCESS."

Jacob was midway through his second pint of Stella when Dave walked in, all espadrilles and loose cotton. And to Jacob's surprise, Madeleine was with him. She was looking too good as usual, wearing a cool little dress, Adidas stripes up the side. She walked over to Jacob's table as Dave went to the bar. Heads turned. She didn't notice.

"Hi, Jacob," she said, pulling up a chair.

"Hello. I didn't expect to see you here. Assumed you'd be working."

"Couldn't have missed this, it's the hottest ticket in town. Hey, where's the singer?"

"He's coming later."

"You doing all the work again, are you?"

He laughed. "Yeah."

Dave arrived at the table, set down a couple of pints. He slapped a firm hand on Jacob's shoulder - "Jacob, the son I never had. How are you feeling?"

He thought before answering. "Dave. I have never been so scared. But I'm ready, it all feels right."

"Good man. All the sound stuff here?"

"Yeah."

"And Reilly?"

"I made him stay in the flat. I've got a taxi booked for half nine. I don't really want him here before we're on."

"Oh."

"I thought it best, Dave. You know, there might be quite a few people here tonight that he'd like to argue with. Or who'd buy him drinks. And I don't need the worry, frankly."

"Makes sense," said Dave, nodding. "Let's get upstairs then shall we, get on with it?"

Madeleine sat on the edge of the stage, smoking and drinking, chatting on her mobile, as Jacob and Dave unloaded the Saab and started to set up. Once everything was inside they set up the lights, the PA, and then the amps. They plugged in processors, mikes, taped pedals to the floor, tuned the guitars. Jacob's nerves were easing now that he was busy. His panic was now alternating with intense excitement, as he remembered what this all meant, what this gig could mean. He wondered when Liam might arrive.

He stood on the stage, and looked out across the room, trying not to stare at Madeleine's legs below him. It wasn't a large space, it would probably only hold two hundred at a push. The stage was low, and he'd probably be eyeball to eyeball with the front row. At the back of the room was the bar, and behind it a little kitchen which also served as the dressing room.

Dave was now behind the mixing desk. "Are we ready for a sound check, Jacob?"

"Er, yeah. Let's do it."

Jacob picked up the SG, feeling its familiar weight as he slung the strap over his head. He pulled a plectrum out of his back pocket and stroked it across the strings, the fingers of his other hand forming an A minor on the neck. He let the chord ring, adjusting the guitar's dials with the plectrum between his teeth. It sounded right, alive, and for the fun of it he stamped on the fuzz pedal, and attacked the guitar, playing the riff from *Paranoid Android*. The guitar's growl filled the room.

Reilly sat on his bed, rolled a cigarette. He drank some more wine, and out of boredom, opened his bank statement, scanned it. Disgusted, he threw it away, and watched it glide to the floor, where it nestled next to the job section of the newspaper. He laughed at the cruelty of the landing. He picked up his notepad from the bedside table, and started to write -

"Would it be possible for me to do it and to live with the consequences? Would it be possible to sign with a major record company and not simply perpetuate everything I know to be wrong - to strengthen that which I believe should be dismantled? How can I make money from something that I know shouldn't be for sale?"

He stood up and walked to the window, and cutting a gap in the curtains, took a glance at the world outside. It didn't look right.

He went to the living room, and put Nirvana on the stereo. Turned it up. He wondered how Kurt Cobain felt when he signed his band to Geffen, how he levelled it.

By half past eight the sound check was complete and, hyped up and ready for more beer, Jacob, Dave and Madeleine headed back down to the bar. The barman from earlier intercepted them on the stairs - "Jacob, isn't it?"

"Yeah, that's right."

"Is everything ready up there now?"

"Yeah."

"Great, we need to start letting people in. It's getting a bit crowded downstairs."

"What? Why, what's on?"

Dave laughed - "You are, you fool."

The barman laughed and pushing past, headed up the stairs. Jacob, puzzled, negotiated the final steps and entered the bar.

What he found took his breath away - the bar was rammed, bursting with people - drinking, talking, making noise. He turned to Dave for reassurance. "Jacob, looks like you got a sell out for your first bloody gig."

"What? It sold out? How?"

Dave smiled. "I don't know how much it had to do with it, but I did make a few phone calls."

"Dave? I don't understand…"

"I know a lot of people, and I thought some of them might like what you do. They know I don't make a habit of doing this. They listen to me, they have other people who listen to them, and well, here you go."

"Who are these people?"

"You know, people who like new music. Pluggers, reps, other bands. Just people in the loop."

"Fucking hell!" said Madeleine, pointing. "Is that Massive Attack over there?"

Reilly paced around the flat. He didn't know what to do with himself. His mind alive with thoughts that the Valpolicella failed to suppress. All thoughts led to a single question. He tried without success to block it out. Despairing, he ran to his bedroom, back to the notepad, where he wrote his question down, in an effort to remove it from his consciousness -

"Do I even want to do this gig?"

He held the pad up and read the words back, over and over again.

Jacob stood in the doorway of the little kitchen, the little dressing room. He was watching the room, watching it fill up. Tasteful dance music played on the PA - Zero 7 or something. He was alone, Dave and Madeleine having headed downstairs with some record company types. He gulped nervously from his pint, running through the set list in his head. He remembered what S had said - "Drink it in. Laugh at it." Why hadn't he phoned her? Fucking idiot.

The crowd parted, and Stevie appeared. He shot Jacob a wink, and ducked into the kitchen. He was glowing, a broad grin across his face, a sweaty forehead. He bear hugged Jacob - "Mate," he said, "this is fucking incredible. What a turn out, it's fucking mad."

"Yeah, it's amazing," replied Jacob, still dazed that a pub full of people would want to see his band, and very pleased to see a familiar face.

"I fucking love the album, mate. Can't stop listening to it."

"Thanks mate."

"Jacob, don't want to freak you out. But Polly Harvey's here."

"Bollocks. Fucking bollocks."

"Serious. And someone said Thom Yorke's coming down."

"Fuck off."

"Well, I might have misheard that, but Polly Harvey's definitely here."

"Where?"

"I didn't see her myself, but Jim did."

"Jim?"

"Oh, my drummer. They're all here." He pointed at his bandmates, all three still semi-recognisable from their Britpop days. They were chatting to some excited looking indie kids. Stevie beamed with pride.

"I saw Jimmy Reckon earlier," he said. "He's brought his whole band by the looks of it. Bit of a dick isn't he? Is your A&R chap here yet?"

"Not yet. Well, I haven't seen him."

"When are you on again?"

Jacob checked his watch "Er, shit. In about twenty-five minutes. Fuck, I'm scared."

"You'll be great mate. You'll be great." He hugged him again.

Reilly lay on the sofa, eyes shut tight, listening to the tape. The original tape, his demos. The raw songs, sketched out all those weeks ago on the four track. He listened closely, wanting to feel every strum on the old acoustic, every scratch across its strings. He wanted to feel every word leaving his mouth. He was trying to get back to something, back to somewhere he'd once been. He was trying to remember why he wrote these fucking songs in the first place.

Outside in the street, below the music, a taxi idled. The driver leaned on the horn, checking his watch.

Put the freaks up front

Dave appeared in the kitchen, and patting Jacob on the back, said, "Five minutes." Jacob nodded in response, and lit another cigarette. He held up his empty hand, and watched it shake in front of him. He was a mess again, all nerves.

"Dave," he said, "any sign of Reilly?"

"No, not yet."

"Shit. Can't he even get in a fucking taxi by himself?"

"Relax, Jacob. No need to panic yet. We've got a bit of time."

Dave turned and left the kitchen, went back to the mixing desk. Jacob lowered his eyes, staring at his shoes as he dragged on the cigarette.

"Jacob?" asked a familiar voice. He looked up to see S standing in front of him. She spread her arms, offering a hug. He stood up, cracked a huge smile and dived into her. "I can't tell you how good it is to see you," he said.

She broke off and playfully pushed him away. "OK, OK. Enough emotion." She laughed. "How are you?"

"Absolutely crapping it."

"Not surprised. It's a huge crowd, amazing atmosphere. I saw Stevie, he told me about the record company bloke. He looked absolutely spannered by the way. Stevie, I mean."

"He sort of just does these days."

"Oh, right."

"What are you doing here? Where are you staying?"

"I got a hotel room."

"You could have stayed at mine."

"I just thought, you know. It was better if…" She trailed off.

"OK."

"You should see this hotel. One of those Travel Lodge things, I feel like Alan Partridge."

"How did you know we were playing?"

"You told me. Remember?"

"No, I…"

"Well anyway, I'm here." She paused for a moment, and then smiled - "It's good to see you too, Jacob."

Just then Reilly stumbled through the door, a bottle in each hand - "Fucking hell, it's only wine," he said, holding the bottles up. "They didn't want to let me in. Tight arsed…"

"Reilly!" said Jacob, "I was starting to think…"

"Yeah, well, Mum. I'm here now." He noticed S, sent a nod her way. "Alright, Sharon?"

"Yes, thanks," she said, wincing at the sound of the name on her birth certificate.

"Is there a corkscrew about?" asked Reilly.

Jacob started laughing. It was relief. He handed Reilly the corkscrew, patted him on the back.

"I'm surprised you're here, Reilly," said S, smarting a little. "I mean, not really your scene is it? Record companies, minor celebs. All these people that want to hear your music. If you're not careful, you might end up being successful."

Reilly laughed. Laughed at S's uncanny powers of perception. Laughed at himself. "Well, it's funny you say that. It really is," he said, putting one wine bottle down on the table.

"Why are you here?" she persisted.

He paused, gripping the remaining bottle and turning the corkscrew. "Well, since you asked. I was thinking about this. Long and hard. And in the end, I just want to hear this album live. That's all." He pulled the cork out, looked around for a suitable glass. "Sorry about calling you Sharon by the way. I forgot."

She smiled. "Not a problem."
Jacob checked his watch, took a deep breath - "Mate, we're on."

Reilly grabbed the corkscrew, a glass and the other bottle and led the way. They left the kitchen, and nudging through the crowd as if just any other punters trying to get a better view, they inched their way to the stage. Jacob's nerves were gone now as he followed Reilly through the crowd - their crowd. He was beaming. This was fucking great. What he'd been working towards for so long.

Reilly jumped on to the stage and not looking around, poured himself a glass of Valpolicella. Jacob followed him, picked up the SG and with a little squeal of feedback, plugged in. The stage lights were down and Zero 7 were still pumping from the PA. The audience hadn't even noticed their arrival. Jacob looked for Dave, who he now realised wouldn't know Reilly had made it. He tried waving, but he could barely see the sound desk through the darkness. Then he realised - the mike, his mike. He approached it - "Dave!" he yelled, not knowing if he'd been heard. A couple of seconds and the music stopped, the stage lights came on, bathing Jacob and Reilly in deep blue. Jacob was unprepared for this, and was gripped by panic all over again. "The iPod, where's the fucking iPod?" he said to himself. "This wasn't supposed to happen."

They now had the attention of the audience, and all eyes were on the stage, but baffled by the unconventional entrance, they were strangely silent. Reilly, oblivious, nonchalantly rolled himself a cigarette. A ripple of laughter went around the room, and there were a few sarcastic whistles from the darkness as Jacob found the iPod on the stage floor and started searching for the playlist. He looked up at Reilly, hissed - "Fucking talk. Fucking say something."

"Oh, right," replied Reilly, surprised by the panic on Jacob's face. He lit his cigarette and looked around for his mike. Jacob cued up the first track and stood up, took a plectrum from his back pocket. Dave, no doubt now alive to the predicament, brought the stage lights down again.

Reilly, now in darkness, took a long drag, exhaled and leaned into the mike - "We are Serpico. And we're here to save your lives."

A cheer went up, a roar coming out of the darkness and at the stage. Even Reilly was taken aback by the response, smiling and looking for Jacob through the darkness. The click track started and Jacob began plucking the notes from his guitar, forming the first song. A beautiful chime echoed around the room, delicate. There were more cheers.

Reilly, eyes closed, stepped back to mike, and started to sing -

"I think I feel like letting go..."

The noise from the audience died slightly at the sound of Reilly's voice, as Jacob knew it would.

"...Walk into the ocean, let the waves decide which way I go..."

Jacob played on, listening to Reilly sing. Still an awesome sound. That grain, that ache. The song built, Reilly instinctively stretching the notes just so, understating the lines as he went.

"...I can change my name, or my address,
But those old ghosts still walk around,
And break my bones,
Sit on my chest..."

They built the song, formed it, and gently slid it to its conclusion, the stage lights coming down once more. And the crowd had *got* it, they had loved it. They cheered.

A low keyboard buzz from the backing track announced the

second track, the first with drums. Jacob played an improvised lick and stamped on the sampler pedal, starting a distorted looped echo of what he'd just played. Reilly strapped on the acoustic and announced, "This is called *Swoon*." And the drums came in, a slow BPM. A waltz. Reilly strummed the opening chords, and sang - told his story.

Jacob looked out into the audience, to see what he could see. He was surprised by how little. He could make out faces in the first couple of rows, but the rest was a dark mass, heads silhouetted against the light from the kitchen and bar at the back of the venue. He shifted his focus back to the front row, and was drawn to a speccy indie kid in a Breeders T-shirt nodding to the beat, vacantly staring at him. He was no more than a metre away but was glaring as if at a TV. He didn't flinch as Jacob caught his eye. Strange. Jacob blinked first, turned to face his amp, and as the drums built, lost himself in the guitar parts as he slipped them into the song.

The next song was *Lower Maudlin Street* and as the beats per minute increased, Jacob changed guitars, slipping on the Stratocaster. He edged towards his amp, tugged on the whammy bar and rode the squeal of feedback as it came back at him, trying to control it. Reilly, across the stage, slugged some wine, and sang -

> "*Am I breaking a chord?*
> *Taking a life?*
> *Pushing my luck?*
> *Or twisting the knife?*
> *Am I losing a friend?*
> *Taking a ride?*
> *Am I testing your love -*
> *Like suicide?*"

Analogue Soul arrived and as Reilly stroked out the intro on the acoustic, Jacob looked once more out into the audience. He wondered where Liam was, and whether he was getting this, whether it was coming over. Dave worked the lights, spotlighting Reilly in a purple beam, and turning on a backdrop of fairy lights behind the amps, on the wall behind the stage. The crowd roared their approval, seeming to sense that this was something special, reacting to the plaintive, classic shape of this song.

And over the minor chords, Reilly sang -

"Heaven can wait,
It's just not me,
I can't accept,
What we'll never see,
I'll leave you dreams,
Broken toys,
In a letter,
Leave this noise..."

Jacob clicked a pedal and slowly dragged the plectrum up the bottom string, the fattest string of the guitar, letting the reverb drawl and bounce all around. The sound fattened, widened, the reverb swirled, and Reilly sang on -

"Forgive these songs,
They're just misled,
Why even let them,
Leave my head?
So loveless and torn,
And underused,
So infantile,
So what?"

Jacob looked again at the front row and in the faces there, saw a reaction, saw that this song was more than the sum of its parts. He looked at the speccy indie kid, saw him staring at Reilly now, transfixed. A couple of girls, really young, gawped at Reilly, star-struck. And Reilly was staggering around his mike stand, eyes clenched shut, feeling the chords as they left his guitar, feeling this song, bleeding this song. Every bit the star - a real star, the sort you'd fucking die for.

"I used to know,
But I strayed,
Misplaced the address,
Memory fade,
So I'll steal it back,
Let no one see,
Who is this for,
If not for me?"

Jacob jumped on the pedals, letting the distortion fly from the speakers. Dave punched on the lights, white light filling the room, illuminating the faces therein. Just for a few seconds - just for a moment. Jacob was sure he'd seen Liam, arms folded and smiling.

Jacob put his head down, and powered toward the end of the song, the drums building and hammering all around him. *Analogue Soul* finished in an apocalypse of screaming feedback.

The audience erupted, the noise was incredible from such a small room. And the heat coming off them! Reilly walked over to Jacob and drenched in sweat, still wearing his suit jacket, half-seriously mouthed, "How am I doing?" Jacob could only laugh in response.

Summertown was next, the BPM moving up another notch as Jacob strapped on the bass this time, and Reilly the SG. They were starting to have fun, jamming, improvising around the rehearsed structure.

Then they launched into *Misplaced Coda,* the drums pounding and the crowd moving, really moving. Fucking dancing, having it - they were coming with them, coming with them on this experiment, the building pace. The song built, grew and changed direction into a minor key and with a sampled wall of keyboard. Reilly's soaring vocals morphed into *Junta,* his anti-Bush and Blair song.

Jacob, now covered in sweat, looked over at Reilly, who, with a desperate expression, seemingly close to tears, was hammering the acoustic, stamping on every pedal he could find, jumping up and down on the stage. He started to shout at the crowd, soundlessly under the white noise - the pounding drums, the walls of distorted guitar, the looping, hypnotic bass. The white noise. Reilly approached the mike and screamed his message over the wave of sound -

"You wouldn't understand,
We're here to save you from yourselves,
We have the moral high ground,
And this is the only language you people understand..."

Reilly removed the acoustic and slung it over his head, slamming it down on the stage. The guitar smashed with the first blow, the female curve of the body splintering across his pedals and feet, fragments hitting the kids in the front row. He grimaced, arching his back and brought it down again across the cold black surface of the stage. Somehow, the strings held the neck, the spine, of the instrument in some kind of shape. He flung the lifeless shell in to the crowd, and exhausted, fell backwards on the stage, landing next to his second bottle of wine. He took a swig, smiled. The song finished.

The audience responded again, applauding as the beats faded, and in a haze of feedback, *Biological Control* began. The beats per minute eased a little, slowing and pointing the way towards the set's conclusion. Jacob breathed, took off the bass and strapped on the Telecaster this time. Reilly stood up.

"This is a song about science," he said, as Jacob played the riff. The percussion less frantic, but Reilly's vocals no less urgent this time. Jacob felt the crowd, still transfixed, willing to follow, willing to trust.

Biological Control died and kick-started *Lost Soul Music,* a quiet and slow drum loop over which Jacob played a vibrating wall of guitar turned up through the tremolo pedal, played as full chords through the effect, utterly and joyfully against how the pedal was intended. Jacob was delighted with the full, spectral sound he created. The change of mood together with Reilly's deliberately ambiguous, repeated hook - *"Am I holding you up?"* brought a hush through the Louisiana.

This led into *Lactic*, and the pace slowed once more. The audience seemed to sense the change, that the set was coming full circle. Over Jacob's plucked notes, Reilly intoned -

"This could take a while,
But it's not what you think,
Should I get this said?
Or is it best to just –
Get in the car,
I need to drive you there,
To show you what,
What I was before..."

A monotone wall of distorted keyboard brought Jacob and Reilly to the closing track, and as with the rest of the set, the continuous playlist prevented extended between-song pronouncements. However, Reilly did manage to announce, "This is our last song. It's called *This is not an exit."* He was clearly now exhausted, or drunk, swaying around the little stage rolling a cigarette.

Jacob could not stop smiling, delighted with how the set had gone down. He slipped on the Stratocaster for the final track. Reilly, stumbling over to Jacob's side of the stage, asked, "Where's my fucking acoustic?"

Jacob didn't answer, and smiling, grabbed Reilly's freshly

rolled cigarette and in exchange, handed him the SG.

Reilly, confused, strapped on the guitar and began to play the final song. Jacob carved out a slide solo over the top of Reilly's gently building chords. Despite Jacob's gently swathing guitar lines, the song had a conventional structure, an irresistible classic country lilt. The song built. Reilly leaned into the mike and whispered the lines -

"Dear Friend,
One thing – what I thought I should be,
Hotel, Motel – what's the difference?
It's not enough, to scream it,
To fuck it all, outside and loud..."

Jacob explored the guitar line a little more, breaking away from the rehearsed structure, as with a chord change Reilly brought the song toward its climax, its conclusion -

"But I couldn't look,
And I couldn't stand myself,
The smile on my face – and the pain in my chest,
I can't write this hard enough –
Hotel, Motel – will you follow me on this?
I don't need anything, that I don't already have,
So keep it safe,
And I'll keep it safe..."

The song trailed to its end, and with the backing track cutting out and the guitars fading, the set was over.

Dave killed the lights and the audience went wild, a huge roar engulfing the room. Jacob stood motionless, unsure what was supposed to happen next. He looked over at Reilly, who was equally stumped, stood staring into the middle distance. The audience continued cheering. Reilly turned and met Jacob's eye. Jacob shrugged. Reilly shuffled over. "I'm looking for a way off the stage, but I can't see one," he said. Jacob stood in the dark, smiling by way of reply.

A chorus emerged from the crowd, slow and muffled at first, but building, becoming clearer - "More... More... More..."

"I think they liked us," said Jacob.

"What the fuck do we do now?" asked Reilly.

"Well, I suppose we play another. Except we don't have any more songs."

"I've got one," said Reilly, moving back toward his mike.

Jacob grabbed his arm. "What?"

"Don't worry, you know it. Just do your feedback thing over the top. With the Stratocaster, that'll work. Improvise."

Jacob swapped guitars and looked on, baffled, as with the audience still chanting, Reilly approached the mike.

"We've got another." There were cheers. The stage lights came back on.

"But this isn't ours. We didn't write this. The Smiths did." More cheers.

Reilly picked a plectrum off the stage and started to roughly sketch out the chords, the chords to *I know it's over*. He sang, and the Louisiana sung along -

"Mother, I can feel,
The soil falling over my head,
And as I climb into an empty bed
- Oh well,
enough said,
I know it's over,
Still I cling,
I don't know where else I can go..."

Jacob approached his amp, let the feedback squeal, around the song, as those in the audience that knew the song joined in, sung along.

> *"...And if you're so clever,*
> *Then why are you on your own tonight?*
> *If you're so very entertaining,*
> *Then why are you on your own tonight?*
> *If you're so very good-looking,*
> *Why do you sleep alone tonight?*
> *I know..."*

Reilly, eyes shut and mouth resting on the mike, never leaving it, played on, more of the crowd joining in as he sang -

> *"It's so easy to laugh,*
> *It's so easy to hate,*
> *It takes strength to be gentle and kind..."*

Jacob turned and approached his amp, increasing the intensity of his feedback and guitar line as the song built toward the end. Reilly hammered out the chords as he delivered the closing lines, the volume of his voice rising -

> *"...Mother, I can feel the soil falling over my head,*
> *Mother, I can feel the soil falling over my head..."*

And suddenly everything was quiet. The stage lights went off and the audience roared again. Reilly slung his guitar to the floor and leapt into the crowd. They pushed their way through bodies, heading for the kitchen. Strangers patted their backs, ruffled their hair. Reilly kept getting his arse grabbed. Eventually they made it.

Liam was waiting for them, sat on the sideboard, wearing a tartan suit again, but in a different pattern. He leapt up as they entered - "Fucking hell, lads. Fucking hell," he said, shaking his head.

Jacob, not sure what to make of this, approached him and

shook his hand. "How are you, Liam?"

He waved the question away, "Lads. Lads. Where have you been hiding? It's a beautiful, beautiful noise you make, you know that?"

"Thanks," said Jacob.

Reilly sat down, shattered. He said nothing.

Liam pressed on - "I've been listening to your album all week. I'm just... how can I say this? I've been doing this job for a while. And this is the first time... I mean, what you two do, it's... cinematic.

"And what a show - I mean it really was special. Controlled but out of control when it had to be, you know? You're real. And that sound - I hear Berlin-era Bowie, The Triffids, The Stone Roses, Sigur Ros, Snow Patrol..."

"Jesus wept," muttered Reilly.

Liam ignored him - "I'm serious - your record - it's like The White Album *and* The Black Album *and* the fucking Grey Album. I mean it."

"Fucking idiot," said Reilly, shaking his head.

"And you," said Liam, turning to Reilly and smiling, "you're very welcome to call me names, because you are the real thing - a full on, freeze-your-shit, star. I love you."

Jacob, full of confidence now, pushed him - "Liam? Are you saying you want to sign us?"

Liam paused, and smiled - "Fucking hell. Of course. Of course I want to sign you." He started laughing. Jacob laughed back. They both looked toward Reilly, now silent on his chair, rolling a cigarette.

"Reilly?" asked Liam. "Aren't you going to call me a parasite or something, tell me to fuck off back to London?"

Reilly smiled weakly. "Liam, I'm too tired to argue with you at the moment."

"You alright, Reilly?" asked Jacob.

"Yeah, I'm fine. I just need some sleep. I'm going to get a cab."

"Stay for a bit, Reilly. Let's celebrate."

"No. You celebrate. I'm going to get a cab."

"OK, mate," said Jacob, knowing there was no use is pursuing it, "see you later."

Reilly lit his cigarette and slowly stood up. He shook Liam's hand, patted Jacob's shoulder, and headed out.

Liam and Jacob spent the next half hour drinking beer and discussing the gig. Various people popped into the kitchen to interrupt, to tell Jacob that they'd loved the gig or to ask when the album was coming out. Some Jacob knew, some he didn't - he thanked them one by one. They all asked where Reilly was.

Liam said lots of things about the deal he could offer. Lots of things that Jacob missed, but he did memorise the phrase, "healthy six figure advance and guaranteed status as a priority act." They agreed to meet during the week to hammer out the details.

Liam eventually made his excuses and, with much handshaking, left. Jacob headed back out into the now emptying venue itself, looking for S.

Instead, he found Dave propped against the bar, nursing a Jack Daniels and Coke. "Dave, the sound was brilliant. Thanks so much."

"Oh, forget it. My pleasure. One of the best gigs I've ever seen, I mean it. And the crowd loved it, didn't they?"

"Mate, it was amazing."

"Liam seemed to be into it."

"Yeah. He's going to sign us. I can't believe it."

"That's great, mate. Just great."

Although Dave was talking to Jacob, he kept glancing over his head at something else. Jacob turned to see what. Madeleine was across the room, flirting overtly with Jimmy Reckon, who was showing her a tattoo in the small of his back. The rest of Cloudfunk looked on in awe.

"He's a singer, apparently," said Dave.

"Er, yeah," said Jacob. "Look, I'll see you later."

He found S downstairs, sat alone at a corner table, a pint and a fag on the go. She saw him and smiled. He sat down.

"You haven't been sat here by yourself, have you?"

"No, no. Stevie and his friends just left. They're going clubbing."

She flicked her hair away form her face. She looked really good, really well.

"Tell me, S," he said. "What did you think?"

"You were great Jacob. Really."

"We've got a record deal."

"You're kidding. That's amazing." She leaned over the table and hugged him again. She went to kiss him on the cheek, but Jacob, surprised, backed away and the kiss missed.

"Sorry," she said, as she awkwardly sat down.

"What? No, don't…"

"Fucking hell Jacob, we're not very good at this are we?"

"At what?"

"Communicating."

"Oh, right. Is something wrong?"

She laughed. "You idiot."

"What?"

She laughed harder.

"What?" he asked again.

S was now in a fit of giggles, unable to reply.

Eventually she stopped. Took a breath. "It's like this, Jacob. I'm going to spell this out. So it's really clear." She started laughing again.

"What?"

"Stop saying that."

"OK."

She composed herself, and eyes down, suddenly quite serious, she ran a finger around the rim of her pint glass. "I would like to be with you. In a relationship I mean. I want us to be boyfriend and girlfriend. I want us to be how we were." She looked up at him, met his eyes, "Does that make sense?"

"Yes," he said.

"And?" She was laughing again.

"Oh. And I would like that too. I really would."

She looked him in the eye - "Come on you idiot, let's go." She stood up.

"Where are we going?"

"My hotel. There's a minibar."

Switching off

It was dark when Reilly woke. But he was wide awake. He slowly rolled over and looked at his alarm clock. He lay very still and watched the time moving - 4.47, 4.48, 4.49, 4.50. He had a thirst, and had a slight headache, but the wine had left him relatively unscathed.

He got up, slipped on some jeans and a T-shirt and walked through the flat to the kitchen, flicking on lights as he went. He walked past Jacob's room and noticed the door ajar and bed empty.

Reilly filled a glass from the tap and downed it. As he wiped his mouth he noticed a bottle of Valpolicella standing next to the sink. He picked it up, and felt its weight in his hand, so familiar. Almost by instinct, he started to look around for a corkscrew, but rethought. He placed the bottle back on the sideboard and made himself a coffee instead.

He sat at the table and watched the steam rise from the mug, sitting quiet and still. He rolled and lit a cigarette. Outside, dawn was breaking, and a red half-light crept into the kitchen. He thought about last night, tried to recall some details. He remembered standing on stage at the end of the set, and out of nowhere knowing that he should play *I know it's over*. That it was the right song. It was an amazing moment, he thought maybe he'd dreamt it.

The cigarette burnt down a little and he reached over the table to flick the debris into the ashtray, inadvertently knocking over his mug. "Shit!"

The coffee shot out across the table and onto the floor.

"Fucking hell." He grabbed a cloth from the sink and slapped it down on the table top. He let the cloth soak up the coffee and then wrung it out over the sink. He rinsed the cloth and repeated the process.

When the table itself was clean, he turned his attention to the lino beneath. Four repeats of the soak/wring/rinse technique and the coffee was gone, but with his focus now on the linoleum, he noticed that the floor as a whole was littered with small crumbs, mysterious marks and stains.

Reilly found the bucket and mop in the bathroom cupboard, and some kind of orange-based cleaning product under the sink. He set to work, mopping away as the sun came up.

He was delighted with the result, the floor now really looking as good as new. He set to work on the cupboards and sideboards – the outside surfaces first and then the inside, carefully removing the contents first.

By 6.00am the kitchen was done and, finding the hoover in Jacob's room, he set to work on the hallway and then the lounge. He threw all the old newspapers and magazines into a bin bag, put CDs back in their cases and onto the bookshelf. He even dusted the stereo and TV.

He was staggered by how different the flat looked after a little bit of cleaning. So much better. On a roll, he headed for the bathroom.

He found a scouring pad and using the orange-based cleaner again, started attacking the mould on the showerhead, the screen, and the ceiling above. He moved to the taps and stopped dead. This was a moment of clarity. He suddenly knew what he had to do.

Reilly dropped the scouring pad and walked purposefully to his bedroom. He found the notepad and pen on the floor and picked them up. He took them with him back to the kitchen and sat down once again at the kitchen table.

And he started to write -

"Jacob,

I don't want to insult your intelligence. I think you already know what I'm going to say. And that you already understand why I'm doing this. But maybe it's better if I write it down anyway.

These songs, this album, this thing we created, I've realised that it's all done. That at this moment, it's perfect. And so - this is where it ends, not where it starts. All this other stuff, this success stuff, this car advert version of achievement we get fed for so long that we can't even see another way: I can't play along. I don't believe in it, and I can't dirty myself with it.

I've reached a dead end, so I'm going away. I don't know exactly where, but it'll be somewhere new. And I'm going now, before things can get fucked up. Before those who don't understand and don't deserve to be involved get their teeth into it, before we start selling shares in what we've we done, and by extension, in ourselves. This way, it remains ours.

It's best this way, tidy. I know this letter will not make you happy, but please trust that I'm doing what's right.

And don't ever forget that we did it - it really is the greatest album ever made.

What I'm trying to say Jacob is this - stop worrying about whether you're going to 'make it,' because you already have.

See you mate,

Jon."

Reilly put the pen down, and calmly walked back to his room. He pulled on his trainers, threw some clothes in a bag and without looking back, opened the front door, left the flat.

He walked out into the street, and in the clear September morning, he stopped for a moment, breathed in and kept walking. Just kept walking.

Life and How to Live It

Epilogue: No Surprises

Time passed. The days turned into weeks, and September into October - the chill in the air turning to a bite, the skies closing in. Bristol began its seasonal descent into greys and blues - rain and early darkness. Autumn took hold, summer's promise now long gone.

Jacob got on with things. He went to work, he listened to Phil. He told him what he wanted to hear, Phil loved him for it. He saw S at weekends, mostly in Bristol but a couple of times Jacob got on the M4 and, with great relief, headed for the bright lights.

He listened to a lot of music. Every night after work he'd get in, head straight for the bookcase. He drowned himself in his old comfort albums - The Manics, Smiths, Radiohead. And many times, despite himself, he listened to Serpico. He turned it over and over in his mind - the pain raw, a knife wound in his chest.

Liam stopped returning his calls in November. Always left a different excuse with his P.A. But Jacob was persistent. And resourceful. One Sunday morning he borrowed S's mobile, and Liam, not recognising the number, answered. He cornered him, made him say it - "I'm sorry Jacob, I really am. You know I love the album and I feel for you, I do. But mate, I don't think he's coming back. And there's a not a label on earth that can sell a band with no singer. Sure it's an interesting story, but... look maybe you should try some of the indies..."

In a fit of pique, fully aware that he wasn't thinking straight, Jacob got a VAT number, and finally set up Naked Cousin Records. He spent the last of the burglary money pressing a thousand CDs, a strictly limited run. He numbered them all by hand and drove around Bristol, offering them sale-or-return to every record shop he could find. The staff were generally enthusiastic, many of them having been at, or heard about the gig. He shifted a couple of hundred copies, made his money back.

Things settled down for a while. Jimmy Reckon called in December, said Cloudfunk got the deal they wanted and were off to Los Angeles to record the album. Jacob said, "Yeah, Jimmy," a lot, but after putting the phone down got online and checked it out - and feeling a lack of jealousy that surprised him, found that it was true.

In the run up to Christmas, Phil made Jacob an offer. Sex-U-Up needed a Marketing Manager for the South-East, to be based in London. Jacob jumped at the chance, and had moved all his stuff into S's little flat in time for New Year. At midnight they were drinking port on Westminster Bridge, childishly flicking Vs at Big Ben - V-ing out the old year, warm in each other's arms.

By February, Accelerator had taken off, and Stevie was on Top of the Pops. Jacob stood in front of the TV, shrieking with laughter - it was a thrill beyond anything he'd experienced before - just to see Stevie - Stevie, for fuck's sake - doing it, bouncing around the stage like a fucking idiot, staring down the camera lens, singing some song about nothing.

Winter loosened its grip, and Jacob found that he was drinking less. He started going to the gym now and then. He was sort of starting to enjoy his job. And he could go a few days at a time without agonising over what Reilly had done to him. The wound was hardening, becoming a scar.

S was doing really well - she was shooting bands and actors for Time Out, getting her stuff out there. There was talk of her work being included in an exhibition.

They bought a house in the spring, a battered old renovator outside Sevenoaks. They started to repair it, slowly making it liveable. Jacob found a satisfaction from this process that shocked him - the simple pleasure of tearing something old down and crafting a replacement, making something better than it was before. Better than before he came along.

They did the kitchen first, ripping out the old units, steaming off the wallpaper, tearing up the tiles. They kept going, raising the carpets in the lounge and bedrooms, exposing the old floorboards to the air, letting the wood breathe for the first time in decades.

They attacked the bathroom, now on a roll, Jacob pushing the old toilet and sink out through the window, letting them drop into the skip below.

By mid-summer, the house was in some kind of shape, unrecognisable from the shell they'd moved into. A new kitchen, bathroom - painted, repaired, cosy. It was theirs. And Jacob revelled in this newfound DIY lifestyle, in how fundamentally conventional it was. It felt like a rebellion of some kind.

One July evening, Jacob found himself at the bottom of the garden, smoking a cigarette, watching S as she tried to get the barbecue going, swearing sweetly to herself as each successive match went out. Jacob smiled. Life was good. He was a lucky man.

Unaware she was being watched, S had ten or so attempts and then in frustration, chucked the box of matches at the barbecue, gave it a kick. She heard Jacob's laughter and turned around, shot him a smile. She ran down the garden and jumped at him, planting a firm kiss on his mouth. Jacob toppled and then fell, S coming with him to the ground. They lay laughing on the grass.

Inside the house, up in the loft above them, sat a cardboard box, now forgotten and half crushed under a pile of old curtains, lampshades and other junk. In the box were eight hundred CDs, the unsold copies of Serpico - *Life and How to Live It*, the greatest album ever made.

Acknowledgements

Many people have assisted me in ways large and small in completing this novel. Some took the time to read, some offered advice and others practical help. Some did all of these things. Thank you:

Jamie for Then Jericho fact-checking and various other things, Rob - a prince among men, Lucy, Jonny Good Vibes, Tony Tiger, Mum, Hat, Laura, Dad, Tess Mc, Adam G, Kate and Jase for your generosity and constant encouragement, Bolton Matt, Yvonne, Ginger Julie, Steve Humby for computer whispering, Peter Culross, Adam Kirkman (fellow sufferer and leader of the Stalinist comma purge), Gary Crew, Nairne (you big twat), Pip, Marie, Will, Kerry, 'Stephen Reay,' and Sarah for having the patience of a Saint Bernard.

Life and How to Live it is a song by the god-like R.E.M. and appears on their album *Fables of the Reconstruction*. The chapter titles in this book are also song titles that I happen to like and kind of fitted. These songs are by (in chapter order): Six by Seven, The Afghan Whigs, dEUS, Radiohead, Tricky, Madder Rose, Pavement, Radiohead, PJ Harvey, Nirvana, Elbow, Wilco, Wilco, Primal Scream, Madder Rose, Guided by Voices, Radiohead, Lambchop, The Flaming Lips, Madder Rose, R.E.M., Manic Street Preachers, Subcircus, The Afghan Whigs, Radiohead, Pavement, Pavement, The Flaming Lips, Madder Rose, dEUS, Elbow and Radiohead.

And finally, sincere thanks to you for spending your hard-earned money on this book and for reading it.

Daniel Mayhew,
January 2007.

www.danielmayhew.com